A BLIND EYE

D0809582

Also by Jane Gorman

The Adam Kaminski Mystery Series

A Blind Eye
A Thin Veil
All That Glitters

A BLIND EYE

*Book 1 in the Adam Kaminski
Mystery Series*

Jane Gorman

Blue Eagle Press

This is a work of fiction. Names, characters, places and incidents are the product of the author's imagination and used fictitiously. Any resemblance to actual events or persons, living or dead, is entirely coincidental.

To my mother.

CHAPTER ONE

ŁUKASZ KAMINSKI collapsed against the rough stone wall as a wave of pain passed through him. He curled into himself, his lean body pressed against the hard stone, no longer caring why or how he got here.

A few minutes or a few hours later, he couldn't be sure, he opened his eyes and forced himself to move. He moaned, the shock of cold air painful against his face and hands. He sat up, leaned forward, and retched. The sound of his spasms filled the narrow street, echoing off the yellow stone buildings.

With a final cough, he rolled away from the steaming mess on the ground and stood, wiping his face with the back of his sleeve. Leaning against the wall, he shivered and hunched his shoulders, tucking his bare hands under his armpits. A freezing mist shrouded the cobblestones around him. Tiny particles of ice covered every surface, catching the dim yellow light escaping from old-fashioned *gazowy* lamps that sprouted at uneven intervals. A man and a woman hurried toward him, huddled together into one dark, moving mass. Their heads touched as they leaned into each other, their already low voices muffled even more by scarves and high collars.

"Która godzina jest?" He heard a female voice complaining. *"Szybciej, szybciej."*

The couple glanced at him as they drew closer then

1

looked away, their faces registering their disgust at the stink of the vomit. Łukasz opened his mouth to speak, but turned his eyes down when he saw their expressions. The clicking of their boots on the cobblestones faded as they turned the bend in the road. He stood for a minute, considering his options, and limped in the same direction.

Walking reduced some of the pain in his legs and back, but his sides felt bruised, and after only a few steps he paused to catch his breath. He shoved his hands in his pockets, then stiffened as his fingers wrapped around the phone. Basia's phone, dead beyond repair since its immersion in the frozen river. Completely dead.

Grief flooded through him, threatening to overwhelm him. In an effort to maintain control, he focused on trying to remember what had happened to him. He remembered leaving his apartment, following yet another lead from the investigation that now dominated his life. But whoever had attacked him had succeeded in erasing the memory of what that lead was and where it had taken him. He let the phone drop in his pocket, wrapped his arms around his injured body, and kept moving forward.

His path dead-ended at a large town square. A handful of couples and some groups of youth still lingered in the area despite the cold. Nearest him, outdoor cafes were dark and shuttered, tables packed away for the night, shops deserted by their keepers. Across the expanse of the cobblestone and brick paved square, Warsaw's Royal Castle loomed out of the darkness. Lights placed low on the ground shone up at its facade, setting fire to the red brick and yellow stone of its walls. He walked toward the castle, hoping for solace and warmth in its lights.

A group of young men, the oldest no more than seventeen, turned to watch him. One of the boys, his head shaved almost bald, his skinny form draped in a worn black leather jacket and thin metal chains, stood.

"*A co to jest?* Hey, mister, you lost?" he asked.

"Lost your mind, maybe," came from another.

Closing in on him, they continued to taunt him. "Lazy-ass drunkard... loser... old-timer."

One of them tossed an empty beer bottle behind him as he spoke and it shattered against the street, shards of glass sliding over the frozen surface.

Łukasz flinched at the noise and tried to turn away, but the gang surrounded him, pushing him back and forth between them. Already weakened, he kept his eyes down, hands by his sides, refusing to engage them. Waiting until they lost interest and moved on to find their next target.

When the sound of their hobnailed jackboots had faded, he looked toward the castle and the two uniformed policemen who stood there. They seemed not to have noticed the drunk gang of young men. Or hadn't cared enough to walk over. He stumbled in their direction.

His first attempt to speak failed, producing only a dry, croaking sound. The officers looked over as he was coughing to clear his throat.

"Move along now," one officer said as he moved toward him, his hand reaching for the nightstick that slapped against his leg. "It's almost morning and you can't stay out here."

His older partner spoke more gently. "There's a shelter just down the street, grandpa. You can get a warm bed there, maybe even some breakfast."

"No..." Łukasz finally found his voice. It sounded harsh and scratched. "No, I need your help. Something has happened."

A look of concern crossed the face of the older officer. "What happened?"

"I'm... I'm not sure." He bowed his head as he spoke, an unintentional gesture of defeat.

The officer came closer, though still keeping an arm's length between them. He wrinkled his nose and looked

3

him up and down. "Who are you? Why are you here?"

"That's just it, officer, I can't remember." He closed his eyes, struggling to pull a memory from the haze of his mind. He failed. "I don't know what happened or how I got here."

The older officer looked at Łukasz's hands and face. "He looks like he's been in a fight. Is that blood?" The officer peered into Łukasz's eyes. "Are you in pain? Were you beaten?"

"Yes." He nodded, placing his hand on his side. "Yes, I'm hurt."

The younger officer growled slightly under his breath, but it was clear now they would have to do something.

"Don't worry," his partner said, one side of his mouth turning up into a grin. "Once we get him to the hospital, I'll handle the paperwork. You'll still make it home to breakfast with Eva before she has to head out to work."

Łukasz's shoulders sagged as he turned to follow the officers to their patrol vehicle. Surely at a hospital he could find someone to help him remember. Streaks of pink and orange chased away the night's darkness as the officers bent to help him into their car, a glint of early morning sun reflecting off the metal wing of a plane. Though he was closer to finding out what had happened to him, he knew he still didn't have the one answer he needed. No matter what had happened to him, one thing wouldn't change. The only thing he cared about. Basia would still be dead.

DETECTIVE ADAM KAMINSKI tucked his book into the pocket in front of him and leaned forward in his seat, trying to catch a glimpse of the sky outside the window to his left. The woman in the window seat had left the shade up throughout the flight, and as they flew toward the morning sun, the light crept into the cabin. He liked the view of sky and clouds from a plane window. It was peaceful, calm. With no view of the ground, he could respect the height without fear. He sat back in his seat.

His captain had been right. In some ways, it hadn't been hard for Adam to accept a last-minute assignment to join the Philadelphia delegation to Poland. No wife or girlfriend to work things out with. His parents were thrilled. To them, this was a chance for him to see the land his grandfather had left, maybe even seek out lost relatives.

He'd been a little more honest with Julia.

"What am I gonna do on this delegation, Jules?" Adam watched her as she trimmed a matte, getting ready to frame another print. "I'm not the right person for this."

Julia finished her cut before laying down the knife and turning her head to look at him. "You're gonna do the same thing you always do, big brother. You're gonna get to know some people, you're gonna impress everyone, and you're gonna do the right thing." She smiled and shook her head before turning back to her work.

"If I were still a teacher, maybe I could see that. But a cop?" He shrugged and toyed with his mug, still half full of Earl Grey.

"The captain chose you, right? He must think you have something to offer."

"He probably thinks I speak Polish, or know things about Poland. Because of our name." Adam laughed and shook his head. "I guess he figures the assignment's pretty simple. Do good, make the department look good. That's all."

Adam's assignment mirrored one given a couple years earlier to a colleague who had the privilege of visiting Philadelphia's sister city in Italy. He'd done exactly as asked, so when a member of Philly's delegation to its sister city in Poland had backed out at the last minute, the mayor turned to the department to fill the gap. And who better to choose than someone named Kaminski?

"I'm just proud of you." Julia slid the matte she had been working on into a plastic sleeve and tucked the knife into a drawer in her table. "He clearly respects you, or he wouldn't have chosen you. No matter what your name." She walked over and perched on the sofa next to him.

Adam admired her confidence, not only in him but in herself. Her willingness to pursue a career as a photographer, against all the odds. At twenty-four, she was six years his junior, and he'd always believed it was his responsibility to look out for her.

"I'm sorry this means I won't be able to make it to your show next weekend." He gave her his best apologetic look, but it wasn't enough to soften the blow.

"What? You're kidding. When do you have to leave?"

"Day after tomorrow." Adam shrugged. "I told you, it's a last minute thing."

"But I wanted to take you out after opening night. To celebrate." The disappointment in her voice sounded real, which was sweet.

"I'm sorry, I really am. You know I wouldn't miss this for anything. I mean, if I had a choice." He tucked his arm over her shoulder, giving her a light hug. "Listen, if it means that much to you, I'll tell the captain I can't make it. Family comes first."

"No, don't be silly," she pushed him away and stood again, brushing her hair back off her face. "You have to go. It just sucks that it's so soon."

"It's just when it is, I'm sorry. The captain's hoping if we look good we might see an increase in our budget next year, so the timing's good, from his perspective."

"But this is so exciting. My pictures… hanging next to Ranjeet's and Hiroshi's. I could sell one. Hell, I could sell all of them." Julia threw her hands up and spun around in a circle that encompassed all the framed photographs stacked up in the small apartment that also served as her studio.

"I do know what this means to you. And I'm proud

of you. The timing isn't great for me either, I have a couple of cases I'm supposed to be testifying at. They're gonna have to get continued." He placed his mug of tea back on the worn wooden surface of her table and his glance fell on his watch as he did so. "Shit. Look, I gotta go. I gotta pack, wrap up a few things at work."

Julia's face softened, the freckled skin around her eyes crinkling as she smiled. "Take care of yourself, big brother. Say hi to Poland for me. And don't get into any trouble. That's my job, right?"

He smiled again to himself now, thinking about Julia. He was proud of her, he really was.

Leaning back in his seat, he shifted from side to side, struggling to get his large frame at least somewhat comfortable in the tiny space allotted to passengers sardined into economy class seats. He tried a few deep breaths, but the plane's stale, recycled air offered no respite.

He'd managed to sleep a little bit, on and off, during the main leg of the flight out of Philadelphia. Most of the passengers had disembarked in Berlin, leaving only a handful to continue the journey to Warsaw. He glanced around at the remaining passengers. Some were still trying to get a last few minutes of sleep. Others caught his eye and smiled back as if partners in a conspiracy. In a way, he supposed they were. Who but a mad conspirator would brave the Warsaw weather in late October?

Shifting in his seat once more, he raised his head to catch a glimpse of the other members on the delegation, then settled down lower to stare out the window. Even after they landed in Warsaw, they still had the journey to Toruń, Philadelphia's sister city.

The sun was fully up now, though the colors of the morning light still lingered in the shimmering clouds. As he watched, the clouds seemed to float upwards, higher into the sky, as the plane descended into Warsaw.

CHAPTER TWO

THE TRAIN from Warsaw approached Toruń from the south, offering its passengers a view of the brown brick walls of the historic city lit up by the orange October sun, the river a golden glow around the base of the old fortifications.

Adam turned his eyes away from the window as the train slowed. It was beautiful, sure, but he had no idea how he could turn this boondoggle into something good for the department.

He stowed his book in his shoulder bag and reached for his suitcase in the overhead rack, but shifted his weight to grab for the bag next to his when he felt the silk of Angela Tarallo's suit against his hand. She had stepped close to him, her brown eyes scanning the rack.

"Thanks." She smiled as he pulled her suitcase down.

"No problem, let me get that for you."

One eyebrow arched above the black frame of her glasses as Angela assessed Adam. "Thanks again. And here I thought chivalry was dead."

"Not with legs like those, pretty lady." The comment came from Ray Pagano, standing in the narrow hallway outside their train compartment. "Now hurry up, you two, Chris said the train's not stopping here for long."

Angela wiped the smile from her face. She turned to Adam and he thought he might have heard the word "jackass" floating on her breath, but couldn't be sure.

Ray swaggered away and Adam followed him off the train, pushing Angela's bag ahead of him and dragging his own behind him.

Chris Burns, member of the Philadelphia International Council and head of their delegation, walked ahead, leading the rest of the team toward the main station. Passengers crowded the platform, weaving past one another toward the trains that waited or the station ahead. Adam watched Angela as she kept pace with Chris, walking with confidence even as she scanned the station, absorbing the sights and sounds. Her long dark hair swayed against her shoulders as she walked and he had to admit, Ray was right about her legs. This trip might have even more to offer than he'd expected. Then his attention shifted as a different woman on the platform caught his eye.

She stood alone, oblivious to the crowds moving around her. And to the men whose eyes lingered on her as they passed. Her gaze moved from the clock high on the wall to the train schedule below it and she shifted her weight as she waited, her long woolen coat failing to conceal the generous curves that added a seductive promise to the classic beauty of her features. When she turned toward the group approaching her, a smile lit up her face. Adam tripped over the suitcase he was pushing.

She stepped forward and extended her free hand in greeting as Chris neared. Angela stopped, looking over her shoulder at Adam then turning back to the woman in front of them.

"Chris Burns, yes?" the woman asked.

"Yes, that's me. I'm the head of the delegation from Philadelphia." Chris nodded as he spoke and shook her hand.

"Good. Good afternoon. I am Sylvia Stanko, your liaison here in Poland. Welcome to Toruń."

She smiled at each of the team in turn, her eye lingering on Adam, who had come up to join the rest of the group as she introduced herself. Adam couldn't help but smile in return, then brushed his hand across his face to hide his dimples, which he thought were inappropriate for a man of his age.

"And I think I know who each of you are. I have been reviewing your details. Angela Tarallo, with the Philadelphia Commerce Department?" Sylvia asked.

Angela nodded and shook Sylvia's hand.

"And you must be Ray Pagano." She smiled at Ray, who winked back as he shook her hand. "I'm glad that Philadelphia was able to include a local business owner on this trip."

"It's always a pleasure to meet such a beautiful woman." Ray held her hand longer than necessary.

Sylvia simply smiled, then turned to Adam. "I believe you will be Jared White, no?" She smiled engagingly at Adam, but Jared jumped in.

"Nope, that would be me." He thrust his hand out and greeted Sylvia with enthusiasm. "Jared White, at your service."

"I am sorry." Sylvia seemed unsure of herself for the first time since Adam had noticed her. "You look very much alike."

Adam wasn't surprised. If Sylvia had only a physical description to go by, instead of a photograph, their similar size, hazel eyes and chestnut hair would make him and Jared hard to distinguish. Though he was pretty sure his ears didn't stick out like that.

"That's okay." Jared's broad smile showed all of his teeth. "Not a problem at all. It's a pleasure to be here. I'm really looking forward to this visit and to learning more about your fascinating country. I'm sure I'll learn a lot I can take back to my students in Philly."

"Adam Kaminski." Adam spoke at last. "Pleasure to meet you."

Sylvia shook his hand with a smile. "Then we are all here. Wonderful. I will take you to your hotel. We will take a scenic route, I think. A chance for you to see this beautiful town for the first time."

She started walking as she spoke, and the rest of the team followed. Passing quickly through the station, Adam and his colleagues were soon seated in the small van that had been arranged for them, Sylvia sitting up front next to the driver.

The luggage barely fit into the storage area in the rear of the van. Every time they hit a bump in the road, Adam felt the back of his chair pushed forward by the shifting bulk of it.

Captivated by the history around them, Adam hardly noticed the discomfort. Narrow winding streets carried them through the medieval town. Many of the buildings were of brown brick, topped with distinctive orange roofs. Closer in toward the historic market square in the old town, the architecture became even more vibrant and joyful, with building fronts painted in yellow, orange and green.

As they drove through the centuries-old city, Sylvia narrated their journey, pointing out twelfth- and thirteenth-century buildings, the home of Copernicus, a castle built by Teutonic Knights. Jared and Angela listened attentively, their eyes seeking out the details Sylvia described. Ray seemed less captivated, his head drooping, eyes closing. Whenever the van hit a bump, his head would jerk up, his eyes fly open.

Adam watched the cobblestoned streets around them, pedestrians and motorists going about a typical twenty-first-century day in a thirteenth-century town. He couldn't help but wonder what his life would be like if his grandfather hadn't left Poland. If he had been raised in this country. Maybe this trip wasn't such a bad thing after all. He could try to look up his cousins, find out what had become of the Polish side of his family. It could be nice to take his mind off crime for a while.

Angela turned from the seat in front of him, adjusting her glasses as she shifted. "Beautiful, huh?"

"It is." He nodded. "Makes me think about my family. They came from Poland."

"Oh, yeah? Not me, this trip is purely professional for me, a way to learn a few things and build up my resume." She gave Adam a flirtatious look. "But I could be inspired by this place, I think."

Adam laughed. "I thought you were keeping this trip purely professional? Focusing on your career?"

"Hey, nothing wrong with networking." Angela grinned and winked at Adam, then sat back in her seat.

Adam smiled, forgetting his dimples as he turned his attention back to Sylvia's melodic voice and her commentary about Toruń.

The van pulled up in front of a large stone mansion. "Ah, we are here, your hotel," Sylvia said as she opened her door.

The others stepped out of the cramped van, stretching their legs.

"We have booked rooms in the Hotel Bulwar for your stay here. It is an excellent hotel," Sylvia explained.

"Of course, what a perfect idea," Chris smiled. "Does this street look familiar to anybody?"

Ray, Angela, Jared and Adam all looked around, but nothing struck them as familiar, and they said so.

"This is Philadelphia Boulevard," Chris announced triumphantly. "Named so after we first became sister cities in 1976."

The others made unintelligible sounds that could have been amazement, sarcasm, or complete disinterest. Adam followed the group into the hotel, his mind dancing around the idea of seeking out his lost cousins.

CHAPTER THREE

ŁUKASZ KAMINSKI sat behind his simple wooden desk, his hands resting, fingers splayed, on the scuffed surface. He took a deep breath, shutting his eyes and shutting out the familiar sounds of the newsroom outside his door.

It *was* all familiar, and the thought comforted him. He heard the distinctive tread of young Marcin, dragging his feet as always. With each ring of the phone, he knew another lead was coming in, another story being followed up by one of his eager colleagues. Even Michał, who walked so silently, left his own trail. Łukasz caught the odor of *Mocne*, the familiar brand of tobacco that lingered in Michał's coat and sweater as he passed by his open door.

With a crack that resounded into the hallway, Łukasz slapped his hands onto the surface of his desk, venting his frustration as he opened his eyes. He could remember so much. Why could he not remember everything?

Dissociative amnesia, the doctor had said. It would clear with time. Had he suffered an injury, the doctor had asked. Or perhaps suffered an emotionally traumatic experience? Yes, and yes, Łukasz now knew. He should have been at home, healing. But the fastest way for him to heal was to figure out what happened.

He turned his attention back to the box of files on the floor to his right. Half the folders that had been resting comfortably in the file box were now strewn about the floor around his desk. He didn't care. These were the files he'd already reviewed and discarded as useless. They gave him no clue as to what lead he had been following when he was attacked. What dangerous secret he'd unearthed.

"Ahem…"

Łukasz sat up from the file box at the sound of the gentle cough from his doorway. "Michał."

The other man smiled at Łukasz. The sad kind of smile reserved for the sick or the bereft.

Łukasz consciously avoided looking at the framed picture on his desk. It didn't help. He knew every shadow and line in the photograph anyway. He blinked.

"Łukasz, I'm so sorry. We all are." Michał gestured vaguely at the newsroom behind him. "She was a beautiful girl. Please, if there is anything I can do. Anything at all…" Michał let the words hang in the air, where they blended with his smoky aura.

"I know, Michał, thank you." Łukasz's response was gruff, but he meant it. He knew how much his colleagues wanted to help. He looked at last at the picture of Basia, smiling up at him from a bench in the shade on the Warsaw University campus. Perhaps he wasn't alone, after all.

Looking up, Łukasz opened his mouth to utter the words that would call on his friends for help when another familiar figure loomed in the doorway, blocking out the rest of the newsroom.

"Łukasz, Łukasz." His editor spoke loudly, as if wanting everyone to hear. He rested a well-manicured hand against the door, the other deep in the pocket of his silk trousers. "You poor, poor man. You should not be here today. What can we do to help you? What can any of us do?"

The words were kind, but the eyes behind them cold, calculating. Or so Łukasz told himself.

He turned back to the box of files on the floor. "Nothing, sir. Thank you. I'm just getting back to work. Trying to forget. There's nothing anyone can do to help now."

With a nod, Łukasz's editor left the doorway. Michał lingered a few seconds longer. When Łukasz failed to look up, he, too, walked away.

Alone again, Łukasz picked up the next file in the box. Another half-written story about corruption in the government. A government official taking bribes in return for helping a private company navigate Poland's complicated tax system to its advantage. Łukasz placed this file on one of the two piles on his desk.

A few minutes later, three more files added to the mess growing on the floor around him, Łukasz paused with a folder in his hand. Another file about the previous regime. Why had he been researching the Soviet era? What could he hope to find from such dated information? With a shrug, he added it to the second, smaller pile on his desk. Then turned back to the box.

It didn't take long to work through all the folders in the box. These were all that remained of his notes. A box left behind accidentally, now his only tie to the leads he had been following before he was attacked. Everything he had taken home with him — the most important notes he wanted to spend more time on — had been stolen from his apartment while he lay recovering in the hospital.

If only he could remember more. Who had he been talking to? Who had attacked him? Why had he been left for dead in that alley?

The attack had left him without any memories of most of a day. But it hadn't blunted his memory of the thing that mattered most. The death of his daughter, Basia. The determination by the police that it had been a suicide. Łukasz's own determination to prove it wasn't.

The police refused to take the attack on him seriously, insisting he had just been in a drunken fight. What nonsense. A drunken fight that left him without memory and his apartment ransacked? Only days after his daughter died?

It didn't matter what they said. He wasn't letting them off the hook that easy. They were the only people he could trust at this point. Assuming he could even trust them. He would continue to haunt the station closest to where Basia was killed, reminding them every day that he wouldn't let the case drop. And at least now he had a lead — if he found the person who attacked him, it would bring him that much closer to finding the truth about what happened to Basia.

Muttering under his breath, he kicked at a piece of paper lying on the floor near him and it took off, floating three or four feet before settling again on top of another piece just like it.

Breathing deeply, he closed his eyes again. His memory would come back. He just needed to be patient. To wait. And to keep searching.

CHAPTER FOUR

EYES STILL CLOSED, Adam reached for the bedside lamp. His arm hit the wall. Hard.

He opened his eyes but lay still, confused for a moment, not recognizing the bed or the room. As his mind cleared the swamp of sleep, it all came flooding back — the flight, the train ride, their first afternoon of meetings followed by a formal dinner.

A pale orange light crept around the edges of the thin curtains that hung over the window. A stronger light would have come right through them, but the sun was still warming up, not yet ready for its big entrance.

Adam reached for his watch on the night table, carefully this time so as not to hit the wall again. Six thirty. In the morning. He groaned and rolled over in the bed, pulling the warm goose down duvet up over his naked shoulders, covering the eagle tattoo. Shouldn't he be jet-lagged? Sleeping until ten or so?

But Adam had always been an early riser. The first rays of the sun were all the alarm clock he usually needed. Plus the group was meeting for breakfast at eight to start another busy day of tours and meetings. With a final groan, he rolled out of bed and into a hot shower.

Clean and bundled up against the chilly October day that awaited him, dressed in his standard uniform of khaki pants and button-down shirt, Adam needed one more thing before this day could really begin. A good cup of coffee. With an hour to kill before breakfast, Adam stepped out into the newborn day.

Philadelphia Boulevard twisted and turned as it followed the path of the river. Adam turned right, walking briskly toward the ruins of the Teutonic castle. The frozen air burned his nose and he felt his chest constrict against the cold, but he tucked his hands deeper into his pockets, his head lower into his collar, and kept walking.

A light mist was gradually burning away from the surface of the river to his right as he walked, and he could see its last tendrils creeping up over the banks then fading into nothingness. A few stores stood opposite the river and women in smocks and babushkas worked in the doorways of these, sweeping up and preparing for the day ahead.

The aroma of fresh baked bread carried across the boulevard. Adam turned to see a shopkeeper busy laying out baskets of tomatoes, fresh bread, dill, and the ubiquitous root vegetables any household could store safely through the winter.

An orange-gold light lit the walls of the ruins as he stepped into a small cafe looking out over the castle. The owner stood behind the bar, sweeping out a back room. He nodded as Adam took a seat at the counter that ran along a window, facing the water. From here, he could see the morning sun glinting off the river as the mist finally cleared, the castle ruins standing tall and golden in the early light.

He ordered an espresso and when it arrived he sat for a few minutes simply enjoying the bitter aroma before he swallowed it and signaled for another. A Warsaw Weekly lay farther along the counter, and Adam reached over to grab it just as a blast of cold air blew in with another customer to the cafe.

Published on Saturdays, the Warsaw Weekly was an English-language newspaper for the large expatriate and

18

English-speaking community in Warsaw. And in the rest of Poland, too, apparently. It was a few days old already, but Adam browsed through it, reading about gallery openings, theatrical productions, and general gossip that would be of interest to anglophones in Warsaw.

The story came toward the end, a short piece tucked away at the bottom of a page. Up to that point, he had simply been skimming, mostly reading headlines and only glancing over the articles. This one caught his full attention.

The subject matter was grim. A young woman had drowned, killed herself, by jumping from the *Most Łazienkowski*, the Łazienkowski Bridge that crossed the Wisła River at the end of *Aleje Armii Ludowej*, a main avenue that crossed the heart of Warsaw. A student at Warsaw University, she had just started interning on the staff of a member of the Polish legislature, the *Sejm*.

It wasn't the subject matter alone that caught Adam's attention. It was the name of the young woman. Basia Kaminski. She smiled up at him from a photo attached to the article, a beautiful young woman bundled against the Polish winter in a heavy coat and high laced boots. Her hair was dark but something about her smile, the joy in her eyes, brought Julia to mind.

Kaminski must be a common name in Poland, Adam told himself. Purely a coincidence. It nevertheless sent a chill down his spine, and he focused his attention on the story the article had to tell.

As he read, he turned his trained eye to the details included in the article, though not a lot of information was available. Perhaps there simply weren't that many details to tell. Adam wasn't even really sure why this story made it into the English-language newspaper, unless the editors thought their readers might have seen the sad event. Or seen the aftermath.

The young woman had jumped in the early hours of the morning, before there was any traffic on the bridge. No witnesses had come forward. Her body had been found in the river by a local man walking his dog along the banks. More exactly, her body had been found by the dog.

Adam read the few details the paper had to offer, then placed the paper down next to him and leaned back in his seat. He shuddered at the thought of dying by falling from a height. It made his healthy respect for heights seem reasonable. Cautious, even.

He shouldn't be reading this, shouldn't be focusing on this. He was here to strengthen the relationship between Philadelphia and Poland, helping the department's budget in the process. Not to solve crimes. Crimes that weren't even really crimes, as the police had determined it had been a suicide.

The door opened again, and another blast of cold air rushed across him. He breathed in deeply and caught the reedy scent of the river over the strong aroma of coffee that pervaded the cafe. Looking out at the water making its turbulent way to the Baltic Sea, the same river that ran through Warsaw, Adam thought about the young woman, Basia Kaminski, and what she had been through.

He could picture it. The dog walker braving a chill morning, much like this one, to walk his dog down by the water. The river would have been shedding its mist, just as it had for Adam today. The body would have floated near the banks, perhaps getting caught in the long grasses that lined the water. The dog, sniffing for small animals or ducks or the scent of another dog had caught a whiff of something unexpected. Something recognizable but unusual.

He would have barked and his owner would have come running. Calling to it to stop barking first, perhaps, but then coming to see what was creating such excitement in his animal.

The man would have seen her at that point. Facedown in the water, most likely. Corpses usually were, in Adam's experience. The dead man's float. Her shoulder-length brown hair would be fanned out around her head, stretching off into the water, waving with the rhythm of the tide.

She had been wearing a winter coat, the article stated, which made sense. It was a cold time of year, and even someone contemplating suicide would instinctively have bundled up against the freezing temperatures of the night. Someone contemplating jumping into the even more frigid water that ran below the bridge.

It wasn't a tall bridge. Someone could jump off it and survive, the journalist had been good enough to explain.

If the goal was death, that was easily accomplished by jumping toward the moving tide in the middle of the river. If the impact of hitting the water didn't kill you, it, along with the pain of the bitter cold, would likely render you unconscious. Long enough, at least, for the tide to slam your body into the rocks that cropped up just downstream from the bridge. If she hadn't been dead yet, she would most likely have drowned at that point.

The graceful image in Adam's mind changed, against his will, her corpse battered and bruised by the time she reached the shore. Her hair tangled around her neck and armpits. Her warm winter clothes torn and pulled from her body.

Adam shivered.

Something about the image still wasn't right, though. He paid for his coffee and headed back out into the cold, back up the river to the hotel to start his real work for the day.

A detail from the article was niggling at the back of his mind and wouldn't let go. Was it the peaceful image he had conjured of the dead woman, one he knew couldn't be accurate?

No, that wasn't it. He looked out over the water as he moved his Italian leather loafers carefully along the still icy bricks of the pavement. In a few hours these bricks would be dried by the sun and the winter wind, but for now they were still slippery from the frozen morning mist.

Her feet — that was it. When she had been found, Basia had no shoes. The police assumed they had come loose in the water, the article had explained.

Adam frowned. One shoe could be lost, perhaps. But two? And winter boots at that?

It struck him as odd. As unlikely. And in a murder investigation, you had to focus on those things that were unlikely or odd to find your first clue. To start down the path that would lead, hopefully, to the truth. To a killer.

His face grew warm as his anger mounted at the thought of another young life wasted. At the idea that someone might have killed a young woman just starting out. He closed his eyes and took a few deep breaths, his standard practice when trying to get his anger under control. This time, it worked.

He blew on his hands and tucked them safely back into his pockets. This wasn't a murder investigation, he reminded himself, this was a suicide. A suicide in Warsaw that had nothing to do with him. Her name was simply a coincidence.

Yet someone, somewhere, was mourning her, Adam thought as he jogged up the stairs to the hotel lobby, trying but failing to get the image of the dead girl out of his mind. Her death had left a void in someone's life, and that pain would take a long time to heal.

CHAPTER FIVE

THE DOOR swung wide. Łukasz looked in through the open doorway. The apartment was empty. Hollow. It was just one step away, but to step inside her home was somehow to accept the emptiness. Admit the loss. He stayed where he was, looking in.

He could see straight through the apartment to the window looking out over the *Praga Południe* district of Warsaw. The view showed more of the same, gray apartment buildings that lined the streets in this part of the city. Tall, square, thick, undistinguished.

A kitchenette ran along part of the wall to the right. To the left, a small table pushed against the other wall left just enough room for a person to pass through. A low bookcase had been placed strategically at the far end of the kitchen to create a break between the eating and living spaces. At the other side of the long, narrow room, a sofa, chairs and coffee table created a cozy seating area. Łukasz knew that the sofa pulled out into a bed.

A small apartment, perhaps, but enough for one young woman living alone. Her ability to cover her costs of living was a point of pride for Łukasz. His daughter had always been independent. He had raised her that way — to work hard and to aim high.

He lifted his chin and smiled as the pride surged through him once more, then his face crumpled and his head dropped as he was swamped by the grief that now dominated everything, all the time. There was no escaping it.

He stepped into the room.

Basia had been dead for almost a week now but the scent of her in the apartment was so strong Łukasz felt as if she were standing next to him. He closed his eyes and inhaled. His hand reached out, but there was no one there. He stood, imagining, for a few minutes more.

It would almost have been better had these memories been taken from him as well. He could have stayed in that alley, in the dark and the cold, without remembering the loss or the pain.

Parts of his mind were still blocked to him, black holes where no memory floated, no ideas emerged. Had there been something else? Someone else? Someone he wanted to remember — or someone he wanted to forget?

Shaking his head in frustration, he opened his eyes.

Someone had attacked him, beaten him and left him for dead. It must have been the same people who killed Basia and it could only have been because he'd found something. Something that brought him too close to the truth to be safe. But what? Hours spent searching the one box of files left from his research had produced nothing definitive, just ideas. Wisps of ideas, really.

Four steps took him through the kitchen into the living room. A plant drooped on a shelf near the window, its leaves withered and dry, but Łukasz turned his attention to the shelf below it. Books filled that shelf and another like it farther along the wall. Books on structures of government, economic policy, analyses of voting practices and European Union policies.

He ran his eye over the spines of the books neatly shelved, then turned to the few still lying on the coffee table. A report from the World Bank, Jacek Kuron's book about student involvement in the Solidarity movement, a pile of old newspapers.

Basia had loved Polish politics, had lived for it. When she received the offer from Minister Novosad to join his staff in the Polish legislature she had almost cried with joy. And Łukasz had rejoiced with her. She had taken him out to eat. Nowhere fancy, it was true, but it was her turn to treat him, she had explained, now she was a working woman. After all her father had done for her.

Łukasz picked up the World Bank report and flipped through it. Charts and summaries comparing governments of various Central and Eastern European states. Comparing the structures of government and levels of corruption. Łukasz was familiar with the book by Kuron, every journalist was. His firsthand account of what it had been like as a student at Warsaw University, recognizing the Poland that could be and fighting to make it a reality. This is what Basia had been reading when she was killed.

There was no sign that anyone else had been in her apartment. No books knocked off a shelf, no wrinkles in the rug that covered the floor, no furniture out of place. Not like his apartment when he'd returned from the hospital.

Yet someone had killed her. Łukasz knew that. Basia was too alive, too full of hope for the future to have killed herself. Whoever had done this had covered his tracks well, but there was a clue somewhere, he just needed to find it.

He would keep digging and he would keep pushing the police to reopen the investigation. He didn't care if that meant he had to set up a tent in front of the police station. He would spend every day there if he had to. He wouldn't give up.

CHAPTER SIX

CHRIS LEANED toward Sylvia, their heads almost touching as they both bent over the schedule, sharing notes from the meetings they'd had so far in Toruń, planning ahead for their time in Warsaw. Adam's lips pulled into a tight line and he turned his back on the scene within their train compartment.

Snow fell in large, soft flakes that melted away as they landed, leaving only a thin coating on the fields visible beyond the train windows. When Chris had snagged the seat next to Sylvia, Adam had instead opted for a window seat. Now he leaned his head against the wall on his right as he watched the countryside pass by. It would be over three hours before they reached Warsaw. His copy of *The Mauritius Command* was in his bag, but he wanted to see as much of Poland as he could while they were passing through it.

Farms and small towns gradually replaced the sprawl of the city. Yellow and brown fields, harvested of all crops and carpeted lightly in snow, spread out before him, some still spotted with the giant wheels of hay the farmers had rolled at the end of the summer.

The train rolled past picturesque chalets that looked like they belonged on a Swiss mountain. These were mixed among small brick farmhouses with clothes hung out to dry in the chill air, the men of the household still hard at work in the fields, even at this time of year.

He heard Ray, Chris and Sylvia talking about their schedule in Warsaw, heard Jared announce he was making a trip up to the dining cabin, but he sat still and quiet, watching the countryside pass by, taking it all in.

His family in Philadelphia followed the Polish newspapers closely. There was always a *Gazeta Wyborcza* or *Nowy Dziennik* lying on his parents' coffee table in their narrow row house in the Port Richmond area of the city. His parents' neighbors would gather in the evenings to read the news and discuss the latest turn of events. He would listen to their stories, try to follow the language as best he could. Sometimes his father would talk of the family left behind in Poland.

They had all been so proud and excited when Adam told them of his assignment. Adam had kept his concerns to himself. The economic difficulties wracking Europe had also touched Poland. A series of political transitions within only a few years hadn't helped, either.

It was a lot of change for the country and the people. Wherever there was change, there was turmoil. Adam had been around long enough to know that. Political change meant people who had been leaders no longer were. And men forced out of positions of power rarely left easily.

Without warning, the picture he had conjured of the dead young woman, floating in the Wisła River, came to his mind. The image was so real, he could almost smell the reeds along the river, hear the barking of the dog. He glanced around the compartment, listening, wondering what made him think of her. A young life taken.

Suicide, he whispered to himself, suicide, not murder. He shook his head, forcing his attention to stay on the view outside the window. He was inventing problems because of his uncertainty about his role on this delegation. Even after their first few days of meetings, he still wasn't sure how he could add any value or accomplish anything for the department.

He was looking for murder because it was something

he could tackle. Plus, an investigation would drown out the sounds of his own ghosts. It always did.

The train passed through Kutno, the tracks turning south to take them along the banks of the Wisła River to Warsaw. Adam was still wondering how he could complete his assignment and satisfy the captain when Jared stepped back into the compartment. Staggering through the narrow space, he plopped down on the seat facing Adam, balancing a tiny paper cup of pungent black coffee on his knee.

Seeing Adam glancing at the coffee, Jared said, "There was beer on offer, but I figured I'd be better off with coffee. Gotta get my head ready for our meetings later today." He paused and took a sip from the cup, then screwed up his face. "Man, this is strong stuff. Maybe I would have been better off with the beer."

When Adam didn't respond, Jared grinned. "So people are mixing us up already. We'll be getting that a lot on this trip, I suspect. Big guys, same hair, same eyes. Angela said she even thought some of our expressions are the same."

Adam nodded. "Yeah, she said that to me, too. We're both from Philly, I guess that's part of it. I used to be a teacher, too. Maybe we both come across as pedantic."

"Hey! Speak for yourself." Jared flapped a hand in the air as he spoke, then held his coffee cup more securely as the train took a bend in the tracks at speed.

After a few minutes, Jared spoke again. "So you were a teacher, huh? Did you work in Philly?"

"Yeah, that's right. History. I worked in Northwest Philly. Williams High."

Jared whistled. "Tough area, I can see why you left. Not very satisfying, I guess, huh?"

Annoyance flitted across Adam's face but Jared was blowing into his coffee cup, his expression one of simple innocence. Noticing Angela looking his way, Adam forced a smile.

"It was satisfying. When I was able to teach. I had

28

some great students, and I miss them." His attention was caught by a glimpse of sunlight on the river, and he continued softly, as if speaking to himself, "Some I miss a lot, and so do their parents."

He jerked his leg as he felt a light touch and turned to find Angela sitting next to him. "I worked for the School District for a few years before joining the Commerce Department. I know how tough some of those schools are." She leaned her head forward, looking at Adam carefully, and the sunlight flashed across the lenses of her glasses.

He didn't hold her glance, instead looking out the window.

Angela frowned, glanced at Jared. "You must have similar stories. You teach in Philly too, right?"

"I do," Jared agreed. "I'm at the Charleston Art and Technology School. Center city. We're in the middle of the lesson on Chaucer, one of my favorites." Jared's eyes lit up and he laughed as he spoke. "When I explain to the kids what some of these words mean. Ha! They're all —"

"It's good you could get away, then," Angela interrupted him before he could get too deep into his story.

"Right, well." Jared's head bobbed up and down. "This was such a unique opportunity, you know? How could the principal say no? He's covering my classes himself, in fact, while I'm away."

"You're lucky." Adam's voice was low, his mind still on other things. "Your kids aren't afraid to come to school. Afraid of who they'll meet on the way in, afraid of who's waiting for them once they get there."

"If you liked teaching, then why'd you become a cop?" Jared asked, his head tipped to one side.

Adam shrugged. "Because keeping our kids safe — keeping them alive — has to be the first step. You can't teach a dead kid."

He glanced around and saw that all eyes in the

compartment were on him. He shifted in his seat as the train bumped over the tracks. "So, Chris, what happens once we get to Warsaw?"

"Right... well..." Chris pulled a folder out of his shoulder bag and opened it on his lap. Passing out maps of the town, Chris started filling them in on the meetings scheduled for that day and the next. Adam listened with interest, though he couldn't help glancing out the window one more time when the first glimpse of Warsaw came into view.

CHAPTER SEVEN

THE SEDAN was dark. Dark splatters of dirt covered dark paint, and it sat in a pool of darkness that grew between spurts of light. Tinted windows hid the dark interior. The narrow Warsaw street seemed to lie in perpetual night, the afternoon sun trying desperately to crawl through gaps between concrete buildings.

The visitor slid into the car, pulling the door toward him without closing it. He glanced at the man in the driver's seat, then jerked the door closed. The interior light clicked off again.

The passenger handed the driver an envelope. "Seems like our roles are reversed now, eh? How time changes things. Now you work for me." When the man in the driver's seat didn't take it, the passenger placed it on the console between the seats.

The driver sat silently, his hands loose on the steering wheel, his eyes and posture alert, as if he could take off at any moment. The engine of the car still ran, keeping the interior uncomfortably warm. It was close, but better than the chill outside.

"This is for your work," the passenger explained, nudging the envelope that still sat on the console between them. "There may be more, I may need you again."

The driver looked forward, as if the car were moving through Warsaw traffic instead of sitting still in the cramped alley.

"You failed, you know," the passenger continued after a pause.

"Failed?" The driver finally spoke, turning his gaze on the passenger, dark eyes looking out from under gray, cropped hair.

The passenger shrugged and looked away before speaking again, his fingers tapping on the door handle. "The journalist is still alive."

The driver frowned and nodded, turning his unforgiving gaze back to the street.

"He went to the police already, pushing them to investigate."

"Hmm…" the driver grunted as his brows lowered, his eyes grew even darker.

"You can't kill him now, though," the passenger added. "It would only add credence to his story. Let him flail about. He can't remember what happened. Nobody believes him."

The driver nodded, as if considering his options, still frowning.

The passenger leaned toward him. "I'll let you know if your instructions change. If I need more from you."

The driver dipped his head once, then smiled. He turned his dark eyes toward the passenger and smiled again. "I'm sure you will, old friend."

The passenger shivered and slid back out of the car.

CHAPTER EIGHT

SOMEWHERE NEARBY a clock chimed the hour, four o'clock, as Adam and his colleagues left Warsaw Central Station to find the van that was waiting to take them to their hotel. At this hour, the sun sat low in the sky. Buildings were tinged with orange and gold in the weak autumn light. Even in the heart of the city, the scent of burning wood from countless fires carried over the odor of the diesel-fueled buses.

They piled into the waiting van, automatically taking the same seats they had chosen in the similar vehicle in Toruń. From the back of the van, Adam watched Sylvia as she once again gave the group a quick overview of the city they were now in. Her eyes lit up as she described Warsaw, its long history and its recent changes, talking excitedly as they wound through the streets.

After only a few days in Poland, the group was happy to arrive at the Newport Hotel, which catered to British and American tourists and businessmen. They were each welcomed in impeccable English and given their room keys along with a quick overview of the amenities the hotel had to offer.

"We have a little time before we will meet our hosts here in Warsaw for dinner," Sylvia announced as Chris made the final arrangements with the front desk and had their luggage sent up to their rooms. "You may use this time as you wish, and I will be back here at the hotel at eight o'clock to take you to the restaurant for dinner."

"If I'm not mistaken, we're right next to Warsaw University here, aren't we?" Jared asked no one in particular.

Sylvia smiled and nodded.

"That's where I'm headed," Jared continued, "check out the local college, see what campus life looks like in Poland." With those words, he headed toward the front door.

"Wait up, I'll walk with you," Chris called as he signed a final document then turned to follow Jared.

"Not me. I just heard all about a sauna, pool and gym in the basement." Ray stretched his neck from side to side and the rest of the group heard the cracking sound it made. Adam frowned at the sound and turned away. With a last shrug of his shoulders, Ray asked, "Anyone else for a couple hours poolside?"

"How about you?" Angela asked, looking up at Adam, "Can I tempt you to join me in a sauna and poolside lounge chair for an hour or so?"

"That does sound tempting." Even as he spoke, he glanced at Sylvia's retreating back.

"Then why not, what else do you have to do?" Angela's smile was warm. Comfortable.

"I would like the chance to talk with you…" His eyes shifted almost against his will toward Sylvia. "But not right now, maybe another time."

He jogged across the hotel lobby to catch up with Sylvia, who turned as Adam called her. "Yes? Can I help you find something?"

"I'm hoping you can point me in the direction of the nearest police station."

"Is something wrong?" Sylvia's brow furrowed. "Has something happened?"

"No… no." Adam shook his head. No point in sharing his thoughts with Sylvia, his curiosity about a suspicious death. "No, nothing like that. I just thought I might have a chance to stop in and introduce myself, say hello. Get to know my Polish counterparts. That sort of thing."

"Ah." Sylvia nodded. "Of course, I should have realized. I'm sorry." She glanced at her watch. "I do have to stop by my office before we all meet for dinner. Between my work and my classes I've missed a lot over the past few days... but I think there's time for me to take you to the police station on the way."

Adam followed Sylvia as she led him down *Aleje Krakowskie Przedmiescie*, the avenue that ran in front of their hotel, to a nearby tram stop. Pale stone and marble buildings lined the street. Elegant arched windows looked out from below decorative cornices, muted greens and grays showing as highlights against the light facades of the carefully renovated buildings.

Casually dressed students pushed past women in fur coats and men in business suits on the crowded sidewalk. As they stepped to the side to avoid a group of students, Adam put his hand on her back. He felt a tingle run through his fingers as he touched her, but if she felt it, too, she gave no indication.

"So what do you think about our time here?" He smiled.

She looked up at him without a word, so he kept babbling. "I'm just asking for your take on things, what you think about our activities here. That's all."

"I see." She didn't smile back. "I think your work here is very important, Mr. Kaminski. I believe we must strengthen our ties with the United States if Poland is to grow and thrive."

"Is that why you agreed to serve as our guide?"

"It is." Sylvia nodded. "Plus this is one more way for me to learn about America — your language, your culture."

"Your English is perfect already, I don't know how much you can improve on that."

He hoped she'd appreciate the compliment, but her face remained grave. "I take every opportunity I can to strengthen my knowledge and skills, Mr. Kaminski. You know that I work for the Warsaw government, of course. But I am also a student, at the *Szkoła Głowa Handlowa*, the Warsaw School of Economics."

"Studying Polish economics?"

"No." The smile she gave him made Adam feel like a student himself, one who'd just asked an obvious question. "I am taking an international MBA program in English. This way, I learn international business and improve my English skills, and have a chance to meet other students from all over the world."

"That's ambitious."

She shrugged. "I take every opportunity I can to develop my career. To be successful." Her pale blue eyes stared out at the street as she spoke, giving the impression she was speaking to herself rather than to Adam.

He waited, but she added nothing more. He finally broke the silence. "I only just got added to this team at the last minute, you know. Three days ago I had no idea I'd be here."

"You are glad that you are here, no?"

"No... I mean, yes. I'm sorry, I'm not saying things right." Adam shrugged and smiled, raising his hand to his cheek. He gestured at the street around them. "I love history. Being in a place like this makes it all so real. It's almost like seeing history firsthand, if you know what I mean."

Sylvia smiled at him. "I am glad to hear that you are a fan of history. For that is something we have quite a lot of here in Poland."

Adam laughed. "Someone who can make history jokes, I like that." He glanced at Sylvia, then looked back down at his hands. "It is serious, though, isn't it?"

"History?" Sylvia asked, her brow furrowing.

"Sure," Adam shrugged. "You know what they say, those who don't know history are doomed to repeat it."

Sylvia's smile faded and Adam noticed small lines

forming around her eyes, as if she were about to squeeze her eyes shut but changed her mind.

"I'm sorry, I didn't mean to upset you." Adam put his hand out toward her, then pulled it back, unsure.

"No, no." Sylvia waved away his concern and his hand. "I'm fine. It's just here we have what you in America might call a love-hate relationship with history." She shook her head but her smile didn't return.

Adam was about to ask her what she meant when the next tram came, already overflowing with people. Sylvia and Adam stepped into the back of the car, gripping overhead leather straps for balance as the tram lurched through the city streets.

"There, *Ulica Miodowa*." Sylvia pointed out a tree-lined street to Adam as they crossed over it. "That is where I live, just off the Old Town Square, a building called *Wojska Polskiego*, named for the church next door."

Adam nodded and ducked his head to watch as the yellow stone buildings that lined the cobblestoned street passed out of view. "It's a beautiful area."

"It is. The apartment belonged to my grandmother, who left it to my mother, who passed it on to me. My neighbors all knew my mother when she was young, so it feels like I am always surrounded by family."

She smiled, and Adam's attention was diverted from the beauty of the neighborhood to the beauty of her smile, the faint scent of lavender that surrounded her.

The tram pushed forward, turning along Warsaw's crooked streets.

CHAPTER NINE

TEN MINUTES LATER, Adam and Sylvia ascended a short flight of marble steps up to the yellow stone building on *Ulica Wilcza* that housed Warsaw's central police station.

"*Nie! To nie prawda!*" A man's angry shout greeted them as they entered the cramped space. The man slammed his fist down on the gray countertop as he shouted at the uniformed officer standing behind it.

Adam and Sylvia stopped short in the entranceway.

"What's going on?" he whispered in her ear.

She put a hand up to touch his shoulder. "I don't know, something happened to that tall man and they seem not to believe him." She kept her attention on the scene as she spoke.

"What are they saying?" Adam asked again.

"It does not concern us." Sylvia shook her head as she spoke.

Adam watched the interaction without understanding a word.

The man confronting the officers was tall and well dressed, though his elegant clothes were well worn. He rubbed his hand across his forehead as he talked and when he did, Adam could see that he favored his right side, as if he had been recently injured. After the outburst Adam and Sylvia had walked in on, he had not yelled again. But his voice held a tension and anger that did not need translation.

The response of the two officers behind the desk made Adam question their training. In a similar situation at home, the uniformed officers would take steps to calm and reassure an angry member of the public, either to elicit accurate information or just to get him out of their hair. These officers smirked up at the tall man, rolling their eyes in response to his statements. One leaned heavily against the cracked countertop and rolled a rubber stamp around between his fingers as he spoke.

A glint of metal from around the collar of the shorter officer caught Adam's eye, and he jerked his head to the left as he recognized the pendant the officer pulled out from behind his shirt. As the officer fingered the small gold medal of Saint Casimir, the patron saint of Poland, Adam stiffened. His hand reached out for Sylvia's shoulder, looking for something real. A human touch to keep his mind here, in the present.

He could see the other Saint Casimir medal as if that Philly cop were standing in front of him. Smell the scent of the lilies. That cop had thought the kids deserved it. Adam could tell by the way he swaggered toward the grave. The way he glanced at the parents out of the corner of his eye. Black kids, center city Philadelphia, of course they deserved it.

But Adam knew better. And he knew that cop, and others like him, were the reason too many kids were being hurt in the city. With no one to defend them. No one to look out for them.

Adam felt himself falling. Knew he was at risk of losing himself in the memory. The shame. The anger.

Finally, a third uniformed officer approached from a back room and said a few sharp words to the two behind the counter. He turned to the tall man. "*Nie możemy pomóc, Panie Kamiński.*"

The words were enough to pull Adam back to the present. Back to the station where the tall man had stopped speaking and was now nodding. Adam tore his eyes away from the medal, trying to forget the past and focus on the present. "What did that officer just say?"

Sylvia shook her head and frowned but didn't answer.

The newly arrived policeman reached under the counter. Producing a sheaf of papers, he pulled off the top sheet and handed it to the officers at the counter. These two shared a look. Adam wasn't sure of its meaning. Was it derision? Concern? The officer who had been leaning on the counter slammed the rubber stamp down on the paper, leaving a blurry red mark. He then handed this stamped sheet to the tall man. The man glared at him as he took it, along with a clipboard and pen, and turned toward a chair against the far wall.

As he turned, his shoulder brushed roughly against Adam's. The man looked toward Adam and nodded, only slightly. His green eyes seemed to glow in his face, though it was probably the contrast with their redness that gave this impression. Adam nodded in return, and the man continued toward the chair, where he sat and started filling in the form.

Sylvia turned to Adam. "I think that is over now. I shall introduce you."

She moved forward as she spoke and Adam followed her up to the counter. The third officer, who seemed to be in charge, still stood there and Sylvia addressed her words to him.

Adam focused his attention on this officer as well, avoiding eye contact with the shorter officer who reminded him far too much of his Philly counterpart. His interaction with his Polish colleagues, however, was limited by the language barrier. None of the officers present spoke much English, just a few words between them, so Sylvia served as an interpreter for the brief conversation.

Adam was greeted warmly by these officers, but the awkwardness of their responses to his basic questions made it clear to him, even without understanding their words, they were at a loss for how they could work with him in any meaningful way.

After five minutes of this, the lead officer suggested that perhaps Adam could come back another day.

"He says there may be someone on duty another time who can speak in English," Sylvia translated for him, "to show you around the station and explain the processes they use here."

Adam nodded, almost grateful this meeting was coming to a close. As they shook hands to take their leave, the tall man returned to the counter with his form completed. He glanced toward Adam and Sylvia, then spoke harshly to the men behind the counter.

They simply accepted his paper without speaking, tucking it into a folder on the countertop already overflowing with similar forms.

"Bah." The man waved his hand disdainfully toward the officers as he turned back to the door.

"What was that all about?" Adam asked the officers, hoping Sylvia would translate. When she stayed silent, Adam looked toward the officers, raising his eyebrows and his shoulders in what he hoped was the universal sign for a question, pointing toward the departing man.

The lead officer responded, his disbelief painted plainly on his face. "He says he was attacked," Sylvia translated the response. "But he does not remember where or by whom. The officer says they do not believe he was attacked, they think maybe he got drunk and got in a fight but has forgotten."

She turned to look up at Adam. "It has nothing to do with us, we should not be involved."

"Okay, I understand." Adam shrugged and expressed his thanks once again to the officers, promising to return another day to try his luck.

As he held the door for Sylvia, Adam saw the tall man outside, standing on the sidewalk with his hand to his face as if deep in thought. Adam felt the eyes of the Polish police officers burning a hole through his back as the door lumbered closed behind him, but he couldn't help himself. Descending the steps, Adam walked toward the man.

"Good afternoon. Do you speak English?"

The man looked at him without responding for so long Adam was sure he hadn't understood. Just as Adam was about to wave Sylvia over to help with translating, the man spoke. "I do, of course. How can I help you?"

He spoke with a strong accent, but his voice was low and melodic and he clearly knew English well. Adam reconsidered what he was going to say. "I couldn't help overhear you in the police station just now. I understand you have some problems."

"You speak Polish?" the man asked, sounding surprised.

"Only a little, not much. I understand all the same. I'm sorry the police aren't able to help you."

"There is much going on in Warsaw for them to be concerned with. An attack I cannot even remember… I can understand their disbelief." The man shrugged and looked up and down the street, heavy with cars, buses and trams. "I will manage."

He looked back at Adam and smiled. "Thank you, all the same, for your concern. Łukasz Kaminski." He held out his hand as he introduced himself and Adam caught a whiff of simple soap and sandalwood.

"Kaminski?" Adam asked, then added under his breath, "Like Basia."

"What was that?" The man's face darkened, his shoulders stiff. "What did you say?"

"Nothing, sorry," Adam shook his head, smiled. "My name is Kaminski, Adam Kaminski."

"Kaminski? From the United States, I gather from your accent?"

"Yes, that's correct. Philadelphia."

"Aha." Łukasz's eyes lit up. "I think we might be related."

"I'm sure it's a common enough name, at least here in Poland. It probably means nothing." Adam forced thoughts of the bloated corpse away.

"No, no, I think it might." Łukasz nodded as he spoke. "Are you the son — or more likely the grandson — of Witold Kaminski, whose family moved to Philadelphia from Poznan in 1940?"

"I am." Now Adam was smiling. "How did you know?"

"My grandfather was Jan Kaminski, cousin to Witold." Łukasz laughed and slapped Adam on the shoulder. "So you are my... what would that be?"

"Second cousin, maybe?" Adam ventured.

"Yes, when I was younger I heard stories about this cousin who moved to America, but I think not so much recently. The family that got out." Łukasz's brow furrowed as he looked at Adam. "The ones who didn't have to endure the war. What a pleasant surprise this is."

A movement at his side reminded Adam he was not alone. "I'm sorry, I'm being so rude. Łukasz Kaminski, may I introduce Sylvia Stanko, my Polish colleague."

"*Pani Stanko, bardzo mi miło,*" Łukasz took her hand in his and held it as if to kiss it rather than shake it. Sylvia smiled at him and retrieved her hand.

"Sylvia, we've just discovered we have distant relations in common," Adam explained. "What an amazing chance to run into each other like this. Though in unfortunate circumstances, I think, at least for you." He looked questioningly at Łukasz.

Before Łukasz could respond, Sylvia jumped in. "I am very pleased to meet you as well, *Pan* Kaminski, a great pleasure." She turned her attention to Adam. "I am sorry, but I must make it to my office before we all meet for dinner this evening. Adam, I'm sorry to tear you away. Can I show you the way back to your hotel?"

"That's not necessary Sylvia, I'm sure I can find it on my own."

Sylvia glanced briefly at Łukasz before turning back to Adam. "If you are sure. I am sorry to leave you. I hope you do not find yourself in any trouble."

"Absolutely not, no problem at all." Adam paused and took her hand. "And Sylvia, thank you for your help."

She smiled and gave a small wave as she walked back down the street toward the tram stop.

"Beautiful lady, no?" Łukasz asked Adam, a glint in his eye.

Adam dragged his eyes away from Sylvia's retreating form and turned his attention back to Łukasz. "Yes, she is. But I'd like to hear more about you... if you're interested, that is. I don't want to impose."

"Ah yes, it would be interesting to find out more about this American branch of the family." He glanced at his watch, then back up at the door to the station, which remained closed. "But not today, I fear. I have other obligations I must see to."

"Of course, I understand." Adam gave a casual wave of his hand. "It really was a pleasure meeting you, Łukasz, I hope I have the chance to see you again. If you find you have the time, I am staying at the Newport Hotel. You can always reach me there."

The two men shook hands again and Łukasz strode down the street, away from the direction taken moments before by Sylvia. Adam watched him go, then turned toward the tram stop. As he turned, he saw the door to the police station closing. No one had gone in or out while he was standing there. Someone must have opened the door to look out.

Adam frowned as he glanced back up the street at Łukasz's receding back, wondering what kind of trouble Łukasz was in.

CHAPTER TEN

"PLEASE HAVE your passports ready," Sylvia announced to the group. "The security team will check your identification and run any bags you are carrying through the scanners." She indicated a pair of conveyor belts at the far end of the room, bumping and grating as they carried visitors' personal belongings past the scrutiny of the guards.

After a morning spent visiting a local school and history museum, the team from Philadelphia planned to spend Thursday afternoon at the *Sejm*, home to one house of Poland's legislature. Security was tight, as they had expected, but they had been assured by Sylvia that the building was open to the public and there would be no problems getting in. While they were there for scheduled meetings with specific legislators, they hoped to find some time at the end of the afternoon to observe a committee meeting from the public balcony.

The *Sejm* inhabited a plot on *Ulica Wiejska*, a quiet street in a diplomatic neighborhood near the center of Warsaw. The classically designed and well-kept building was tucked away from the street, creating an enclave of peace and harmony.

The main visitor entrance was just as grand as the rest of the white marble building. Plush red carpets left only small squares of wooden parquet floors exposed while thick golden curtains hung before large windows.

Guards in the drab olive uniforms of the Polish military stood at every entrance or interacted with each guest trying to gain access to the building. Small monitors revealed the contents of visitors' bags as they passed through the scanners, and guests were asked to stand, crucifixion-style, while a metal detecting wand scanned their person.

Adam smiled at a guard as he held out his passport for inspection, but the man did not smile back.

As Adam waited behind Angela while her bag ran through the scanners, he heard a familiar voice. Turning to look over his shoulder, Adam saw Łukasz engaged in a conversation with two guards near another scanner.

Łukasz leaned against one of the conveyor belts, which had been immobilized. His satchel sat upright on the surface, its top flap flung open to expose its contents. Small items that had been safely ensconced in their proper places now lay scattered along the belt.

Łukasz's attention, and that of the two uniformed guards leaning toward him from the other side of the conveyor belt, was focused on the object one of the guards now held in his hand.

As the guard waved it in his hand as he spoke, Łukasz reached over and pushed a button on the side of the device. He spoke rapidly to the guard in a tense voice, only stopping when he pushed another button. Łukasz's recorded voice floated back across the room.

Adam smiled again and moved to take his turn through the inspection, thinking that would be the end of it. When he turned after passing through the inspection, Łukasz was still engaged with the two guards. Other visitors who had lined up behind him had all moved over to the line Adam and his colleagues had used, like shoppers in a grocery store trying to choose the fastest queue.

Adam paused as he passed through the doorway leading to the halls of the building, resting his hand against the door jamb and allowing the others to pass by him. Łukasz was now leaning forward over the conveyor belt, his head falling down between his shoulders. He seemed to be listening to what one of the guards was telling him as he nodded periodically.

"*No... no...*" Łukasz nodded as he addressed his words to the belt below him. "*Tak... wiem...*" Adam knew enough Polish to understand that Łukasz was acquiescing to whatever the guard was saying.

The guard continued his monologue in a brisk, authoritative voice. Łukasz simply nodded and mumbled his affirmative responses.

It seemed like this exchange could go on forever. The guard holding Łukasz's bag gave no indication he was ready to return it to its owner. Łukasz wasn't going to be let in.

Adam took a step toward the scene. Not that he could do much. But he could at least try to intervene. There was no good reason why Łukasz should be kept out of the building.

He held back when a fourth man appeared. His wire-rimmed glasses caught the light as he approached the trio and spoke quietly into the ear of one of the guards.

The stranger was young, wore a suit rather than a uniform, and ran his hand over his short brown hair as he spoke. But the guards nodded as they listened to him. The uniformed guard glanced at Łukasz with dislike clearly painted across his features, then handed his satchel back.

Łukasz took the bag. Without saying another word, he gathered the other items that had been set aside on the conveyor belt.

Adam examined the young man who had made such an immediate impact. Despite his confident dress and style, the man conveyed a sense of nervousness. Perhaps it was the way he kept smoothing his hair, or the way his eyes flitted about while he spoke, never settling for long on any one object or person. Or perhaps it was simply a reflection of his youth and something he would grow out of.

"Adam, are you joining us?" Adam's thoughts were interrupted by Sylvia's call. She and the rest of the team were already moving up the long hallway toward the stairs that would take them up to the private offices on the second floor.

"Of course, sorry." Adam glanced back into the entrance area.

Łukasz had restored all of his items to his satchel and was turning toward the door where Adam stood. Adam ducked through the doorway to follow Sylvia before Łukasz could see him, forcing himself to focus on the people he was about to meet.

CHAPTER ELEVEN

A SMALLER OFFICE would not have been able to hold Minister Kuhl. Given the energy and speed with which Kuhl moved about the room, Adam was sure he would have broken down the walls of any tighter space. Or perhaps he already had, and this room was the result. For it was the size of two offices, at least.

A large conference table filled one part of the room. Farther from the windows, silk-upholstered armchairs gathered around a coffee table that Adam was sure was a true antique. Kuhl's red cherry desk covered the back wall, and from the leather chair behind it, he gazed out at his domain like a tensed leopard ready to pounce.

Minister Kuhl, Sylvia had explained to them, was one of the four hundred and sixty ministers who were elected to represent Poland in the *Sejm* every four years. Each minister was elected from a region of the country based on a system of proportional representation.

Minister Kuhl was a member of *Prawo i Sprawiedliwość*, PiS, the second most powerful party in the legislature, a party formed by a number of the leaders of the Solidarity movement. As a leading figure within the party, he was offered the prime post of Chair of the Committee for Environmental Protection.

"This was a good position for me," Kuhl explained to the group seated before him. "Yes, it makes sense. We have much farmland in Poland — most in all of Europe

— and this is very sensitive. We are facing much pressure from the European Union right now on how we manage our farmlands. And our subsidies. They want certain changes from us, but we shall see." He nodded, giving the appearance of a bobblehead doll rather than the sage look he was probably going for.

"So you are responsible for deciding how the farmland is managed?" Ray asked.

"Yes... yes... with the committee, of course." Kuhl could sit still no longer. He jumped up and started pacing between the conference table and the seating area as he answered their questions. The team followed his movements with their heads, giving a fair imitation of a crowd at a tennis match.

"I understand that before you entered politics, sir, you were a truck driver. What prepared you for this position?" Angela leaned forward as she asked, her eyes on Kuhl.

Adam glanced at Angela, surprised she knew so much about Kuhl's background. Clearly, she had done her homework before joining this delegation.

Kuhl did not seem surprised by the question. "Oh yes, yes. I was prepared, this was not a problem. This was a very good position for me. I was a truck driver, as you say. Before the change in regimes. Ah, what a change, I can tell you!" He smiled broadly at the group, then resumed his pacing.

Adam and Angela exchanged glances, but didn't smile.

Kuhl smiled enough for all of them, waving his arms as he spoke. "What a dream. A dream come true. Imagine this. We — we, the people of Poland — we brought down that communist regime. Those socialists. Yes. We did this. And it is much better now."

He paused and looked back at the group. "It is so important that you are here, of course. We did not do this alone. Oh no" — he resumed his pacing — "we had such great support from the United States. From the great Ronald Reagan —" Here, Kuhl spread his arms wide as if thanking the heavens for Reagan. "And the President George Bush. Yes, these were great men. Great men." His smiled broadened as he spoke, as if laughing at a joke only he could hear.

Tired of watching Kuhl move back and forth, Adam turned to look around the office. Framed paintings and photographs dotted the walls. The oil paintings were all modern in style and didn't catch Adam's interest. The photographs did.

The artistic shots captured images from around the country. A farm laborer paused in the field, caught on film leaning against his hoe. A truck driver, maybe Kuhl as a young man, stepping up into the cab of an 18-wheeler. A woman in a drab blue suit smiling into the camera in front of a gray-looking department store. The people of Poland that Kuhl was so proud of, Adam assumed. The people he now represented.

Adam looked back at the man with a little more respect. At least he seemed to be exactly who he said he was: a truck driver who was so excited about the change in politics that he stepped up and took on the responsibility of leadership. Yet Adam couldn't help but smile again as the man almost knocked one of his paintings off the wall as he gestured with exuberance.

"And who else will you meet with while you are here?" Kuhl was asking Sylvia.

"We have a meeting arranged with Minister Kapral next," Sylvia answered, checking the schedule in her datebook.

"Good, good." Kuhl nodded vigorously, resuming his seat behind his massive desk. "Good, Kapral is a good man. A good leader. He will be very helpful for you." Kuhl looked over the group assembled before him as he spoke. "You must listen to him. He has some powerful ideas for Poland and her future. Me, people like me, we are part of Poland's past. A good part" — he held up a finger — "an important part, no doubt. But Kapral, he looks only to the future. To what may be. To what else may be," Kuhl corrected himself.

"And then we will see a committee meeting…" Sylvia continued.

Kuhl nodded energetically.

"Oh, and before that we will meet with Minister Novosad."

Kuhl's head stopped and he sat still. Adam realized that was the first time he had been still since the group had entered his office. Kuhl frowned. "Novosad… hmm… You must meet with him?"

Sylvia looked up at Kuhl with surprise. "Well, he was kind enough to make time for us." She frowned. "And of course we are interested in meeting with as many ministers as we can while we are here. We have only the one afternoon for these visits. The group will also meet with representatives from schools, from local businesses, from museums…" Sylvia's words trailed off and she shrugged, still looking questioningly at Kuhl.

"Yes, yes, of course." His head resumed its bobbing. "Yes, I'm sorry. My reaction was bad. Very bad." He waved both his hands over his desk and looked down. "But, you see," he added, looking up again, "he was part of *Sojusz Lewicy Demokratycznej*, SLD, you know, before he joined his current party. SLD is the post-communist party. They prefer many of the old ways, they do not support the economic changes we have been making to move closer to the rest of Europe."

"He switched parties?" Adam asked, interested.

"Oh yes, yes. And quite a drastic shift, you see. From one extreme to another. He didn't even join PiS, my party. No, he went straight to *Platforma Obywatelska*, the Civic Platform."

"Doesn't your party work closely with them?" Adam pressed.

"Of course, yes. But they are very Western, very European in their approach. Maybe too much so. This is still Poland, you see. We may have changed our government, but we have not changed our people. We are still Poles, we must not forget that."

"So why are you not happy with Novosad?" Ray asked.

"Oh… well… Perhaps I should not have said anything. He has changed, I'm sure, I'm sure. People can change, no?"

"No." Angela and Ray spoke in unison, then smiled at each other.

"No?" Kuhl shrugged. "No, perhaps not. Perhaps that is why I spoke. He is Russian, too, you know?" Kuhl added, jumping up once again. Adam figured the man had a ten minute time limit on sitting still.

"He's in the Polish government, surely he must be a Polish citizen?" Jared asked.

"Well, of course, yes," Kuhl waved away the concern. "Yes, he is Polish. He was born in Białystok. But his family is from Russia, just the previous generation. Is he Polish?" Kuhl stopped and looked closely at the group. "Or is he still a Russian at heart?"

CHAPTER TWELVE

FOLLOWING THE REST of his team down the plush hallway, Adam watched as Sylvia spoke excitedly to Chris, Ray, Jared and Angela. The graceful motion of her hands, the glint in her eyes, all spoke to her love for her country. Or perhaps her love for politics. Her enthusiasm was contagious and the others were nodding and occasionally laughing at Sylvia's remarks.

As they approached the stairs to Minister Kapral's office, a man stopped the group. His silk suit tagged him as someone of importance in the building, but something about him, maybe the bend of his shoulders or the way his eyes narrowed when he saw the group approaching, gave Adam the impression more of a bureaucrat than a politician. Adam thought he saw a trace of Mongolian ancestry in the man's features, but it vanished as his smile widened, transforming his face.

"Ah, Sylvia, what perfect timing." He spoke to Sylvia, and them all, in English. "I have a quick request for you, if I may pull you away for a moment?" He smiled around at the group gathered on the small landing.

"Of course, Mr. Malak," Chris answered for the group. "I had been hoping a meeting with you was also on our schedule."

Chris turned to the rest of the group. "Mr. Tomek Malak is the Director of Government Affairs for the city of Warsaw. He is responsible for serving as a liaison between the city government and the national legislature, since they must work so closely together." He paused and smiled at Sylvia. "And he is also the person generous enough to let us take Sylvia away from him this week to show us around."

"Aha, your boss, huh, Sylvia?" Ray asked, pumping Sylvia on the back.

She coughed and stepped forward slightly. "Yes, that's right. Tomek, I am glad we ran into you. Perhaps we can take a moment of your time before we meet with Minister Kapral?"

That was all the group understood of what she said, as this statement was followed by a quick exchange between the two in Polish.

"Yes, yes." Sylvia nodded as she finished her brief conversation with her boss. "Tomek and I have some very short business to take care of," she finally said to the group. "Can you all please follow me?"

With these words, Sylvia led the way up the narrow stairs that provided private access to the smaller offices on the higher floors. Malak waited until they had each passed him, then followed them up the stairs, his shadow following them last of all as he passed under the bare bulbs dangling from the ceiling.

Sylvia took the group up two flights to a small office on the third floor. A utilitarian wooden desk stood near the window, filing cabinets lined one wall. News clippings and posters plastered the opposite wall, some in frames, others simply stuck to the wall with tape. This was clearly a well-used working space, but it was clean and organized and even held a slight odor of disinfectant.

As Sylvia and Malak leaned over his desk, conducting their business in Polish, Adam walked slowly along the wall, reviewing the materials posted there. Most he couldn't read, but some were in English, and in others he could pick out enough words to get a feel for the message they communicated.

Sylvia kept up her conversation with Malak, speaking far too quickly for Adam to follow, as Malak handed her a sheaf of papers. She walked them over to the far corner and Adam heard the familiar grind of a small shredder. He kept his attention on the news cuttings in front of him.

One section of the wall in particular seemed to focus on recognitions Malak had achieved in his work for the city. Clippings showed images of Malak standing with smiling crowds of people, shaking hands, cutting ribbons and even, in one, placing his hand on the head of a crying baby.

Angela came up next to Adam and joined him in examining these posts, adjusting her glasses as she stepped closer. "He seems like a well-liked politician," she commented, nodding her head toward an English-language article that summarized Malak's success in encouraging new, Western businesses to open up in Warsaw. Another posted next to it praised Malak's role in creating a scholarship to send students abroad.

"He does." Adam nodded and looked down at Angela. He couldn't read the expression on her face. "It looks like his interests are broad and generous." Adam gestured toward the clippings on the walls. "Helping businesses... helping students..."

Angela glanced up at him sideways, a smile playing at her lips. "That's important to you, isn't it?" she asked under her breath.

"What?"

She gestured at a photo of a student receiving an award. "His support for students. For young people."

Adam shrugged. "I guess. Isn't it for everyone?"

Angela frowned and put her head on one side, stepping closer to peer at the image. Lines appeared on her forehead, then disappeared just as quickly. "We all have our own priorities." She looked back at Adam. "And our own guilt to manage."

Adam was still considering how to respond to this

when Chris approached them.

"You haven't heard of Mr. Malak?" he asked them. "He's pretty well known for all the things he's done for Warsaw. He's even been covered in the New York Times because of his pro-Western stance and creative ideas for encouraging economic growth."

Adam admitted, with more than a little shame, that he had not heard of him before today. "I'm impressed that you know so much about him," he added.

"It's my job, Adam," Chris smiled at him. "Don't feel bad you're not familiar with him. This is what I do. We follow the news in every country we work with as sister cities." Chris shrugged. "I love this kind of stuff. Particularly the good stories, and Malak's is definitely a success story."

"Oh?" Angela smiled to encourage Chris.

"The citizens love him. It's not just that he brings in new business now, he has a respectable history within the Solidarity movement. He was young at the time, it's true, but he was always one of the good guys, supporting freedom, supporting justice. In fact, everyone believes his party has tapped him to be their next candidate for president. He hasn't run for office before, only served as a political appointee, but everything I've heard is that he's already agreed and is planning his strategy."

"Ahem." Malak's cough brought Chris up short.

Chris started turning an entertaining shade of red, but Malak spoke almost immediately. "I appreciate the kind words, I really do. And I am proud of my history and of my accomplishments. My position is not political, I am appointed by the mayor, but I believe I serve at the will of the people. If I ever find that the people of Warsaw no longer support my vision or my methods, it will be time for me to move on to the next stage of my life." He paused and smiled at the group. "Until then, who knows what the future holds?"

"Your accomplishments are very impressive, Mr. Malak," Jared chimed in.

"Thank you, sir. As I said, I am proud of what I have done. And I believe there is still more I can do for the city of Warsaw." He walked over to one of the clippings Adam had not been able to read and tapped it as he spoke. "Minister Kapral, now there is a man who has the interests of the nation in the front of his mind."

Malak turned back to the group. "I don't want to keep you from your meeting with him, but I must ask Sylvia to do one quick task for me. Why don't I accompany you to his office? I always enjoy a conversation with Kapral."

Angela tilted her head to the side as she spoke to Malak. "He's a strong leader in the government, isn't he?"

When Malak nodded, Angela continued, "And you're considering a run for president. So that makes him your competition, doesn't it?" She smiled to take the edge off the words, but her eyes were sharp.

Malak simply smiled. "Not at all, not at all. In fact, Nelek Kapral and I make a good team. We share many ideas, but we also differ in certain fundamental ways. In this way, we complement each other. We will both achieve more if we work together."

Angela looked skeptical, but said nothing more.

"Minister Kapral will achieve great things, oh, yes, I'm sure of it." Malak nodded as he spoke, glancing back at the news cutting taped to the wall. "He has some original ideas and the strength of will to carry them through. Mark my words, he will lead this country into the future."

"IT WAS NOT necessary for you to join me, *Pan* Kaminski. This errand will not take long."

"I know." Adam shrugged. "To be honest, it seemed more interesting to visit a local printer than to sit through another meeting with another politician."

Sylvia's smile grew wide and she raised an eyebrow at him.

"Sorry. I'm sorry, I keep putting my foot in my mouth. I know, this is your job. I'm sure you love it."

She shrugged. "I do, yes. I look forward to the future as well, where I might go."

"I guess I do, too. I'm not sure how far I can get. I have a feeling my past will always catch up with me."

He followed her as she turned down a narrow cobblestoned alley, a street heavy with the echoed footfalls of generations of Poles. Small storefronts lined the path, shops selling paper goods or offering copy services. Modern stores that seemed out of place in this picturesque setting.

Sylvia looked at Adam and slowed her pace. "In America, you feel that the past 'catches up with you,' as you say?"

Adam nodded and slowed to match her stride.

"Yes, we have a similar experience here. That's too bad. I wouldn't mind going to a place where there is no history. Where everyone lives only in today."

"Now why would you say that?" Adam asked with a frown. "Surely Poles must derive great value from your nation's long history?"

"Of course, of course, I didn't speak correctly." Sylvia waved her hands as if to wave away the words she had spoken. "It's just *lustracja*, that's all."

"Ah, lustration. I get it." He did. He'd read about the law, which had been updated again five years ago. Anyone who worked in politics was required to submit statements in which they declared any cooperation they had with the communist-era secret police. The law applied to all politicians, as many people who worked in politics now were also part of the previous regime. Sometimes by choice, sometimes not.

"*Lustracja*," Sylvia repeated. "These are good people. They were good at their jobs under the previous regime, and they are still good. But they were communists, and that must come out." She ran a hand through her hair as she spoke, her eyes focused on the pavement ahead of them. "Now the law is being challenged in courts, and who knows... the uncertainty of what may happen is sometimes worse than what the law requires."

"And would this law apply to you, too?"

Sylvia frowned and considered the question. "I work for the city of Warsaw, not the national government, but the law still applies." She glanced at Adam, then looked back at the cobblestones below their feet. "I submitted a form, as did others."

Adam's curiosity was piqued, but he kept his questions about Sylvia's past to himself. If she, or anyone, had collaborated with the previous regime and admitted it in her lustration form, she would be free from any repercussions. On the other hand, if there were any doubt about a politician's denial of collaboration, his statement would be evaluated by the Institute of National Remembrance and the Lustration Court. After reviewing the evidence, the court would decide if the lustration statement was accurate or not. Anyone who lied about his involvement with the secret police would lose his job and be banned from holding another government position for at least ten years.

They had reached the printer's, and Adam pulled the door open for Sylvia as he spoke, placing his hand lightly on the small of her back to guide her through the door. "Surely this law is a good thing, right? You want to know who these people are who are running your country?"

"Sure." Sylvia nodded, looking back at him. "But sometimes the past is best left in the past. Sometimes we just need to move forward. Some people — some important and powerful people — are not happy with the way this is going." She glanced at the shopkeeper coming toward them. "And we will all suffer the consequences."

CHAPTER THIRTEEN

THE MAN smiled at each of them as he spoke, his teeth as straight and white as if he were auditioning for a toothpaste commercial. The meeting had started without them and Adam glanced around at the rest of the team as he slid into a chair, to see if they were as unimpressed as he was.

They were gathered in another large office. Minister Kapral sat behind his oak desk, his hands clasped in front of him on the gleaming wood surface. Only a pile of folders stacked neatly in his inbox gave any clue that he used this office for work. Angela, Jared and Ray were seated around the conference table with Chris but Adam and Sylvia grabbed chairs near the windows, so as not to cause any further disruption as they joined the group. The gray Warsaw sky hung heavy above them and Adam could see dark clouds on the horizon. More snow was on the way.

As far as Adam could tell, the rest of his team was hanging on Kapral's every word. His English was perfect, with a slight British accent, and they peppered him with questions about how the Polish legislature worked and what his particular interests were.

"Well, of course it is slightly different from your American system. And many of us would like to veer more in the direction you have shown works so well," Kapral was saying in response to a question from Angela.

Adam thought it was a somewhat aggressive question, challenging the high number of political parties active in Poland. A valid inquiry, but not an easy one to answer.

Kapral addressed her with diplomacy and grace. "But there are still many different voices that must be heard in Poland. We were kept quiet for so long, you understand. Now is our opportunity to make some noise."

He pumped his arm as he spoke, like the master of a parade, and smiled engagingly.

"But eventually," Kapral continued, "soon, I hope, we will settle into two, three or four major parties. Then we will be more in line with the US or the UK. I am confident of that."

Watching Kapral's eyes, Adam thought he recognized the same raw ambition he'd seen before on the streets of Philadelphia. He shuddered, but he knew the drill. He tried to put on what he thought was his most engaging smile. Kapral glanced at him with a questioning look and he reverted to a normal expression.

"I can tell you have high expectations of Poland's future. Does that include the next generation? Do you know much about who Poland's future political leaders will be?" Jared asked the next question.

Adam saw Angela glance at him out of the corner of his eye, but he avoided making eye contact.

"Ah, of course. Our future is bright because of these young people." Kapral smiled once again. "Many of us here in the *Sejm* encourage young people to be interested in politics. We meet with them at their schools, we help them find work here in our offices. It is important we support these young men and women today, so they can lead us tomorrow."

He inclined his head toward Sylvia. "And we encourage our staff always to look for ways of improving themselves, better educating themselves. For we are all students, in a way, are we not?"

"Do you have many young people on your staff?"

Adam asked, as an image of Basia Kaminski floating in the Wisła came unbidden to mind.

"I have a few, yes…"

"How do you select…" Angela and Kapral spoke at the same time, then both paused and laughed.

"I'm sorry," Angela said, "please, go ahead."

"No, *Pani*, please, I am interested to hear your question." Kapral invited her to continue.

"I was just going to ask how you select your staff. It must be very competitive, I'm sure. Does each office hire its own, or does the *Sejm* as a whole offer internships?"

Adam had been watching Angela as she asked her question and only turned to look at Kapral as she finished, so he almost missed the flicker of annoyance that crossed Kapral's face. It came and went in the blink of an eye, replaced by Kapral's easy smile once again. But Adam had seen it, he was sure.

"That is an individual decision, *Pani* Tarallo. I cannot speak for the *Sejm* in answering that question. We all have reasons for the choices we make."

Angela frowned and looked as if she were about to say more when a light tap on the door interrupted them.

Without waiting for a response, a young man entered the office. Adam tensed when he recognized him as the man who had intervened in the scene with Łukasz earlier. The man nodded to the group, but didn't speak to them. Instead, he leaned over Kapral, saying something in rapid Polish.

Kapral leaned back, tipping away from the young man but still listening intently to what he was saying. The rest of the group looked on in interest without understanding anything.

Finally, the young man stood and stepped away from the desk. Adam was expecting some sort of explanation, as Sylvia had graciously translated every interaction for them in their other meetings. Instead, Kapral simply nodded subtly at Malak.

Sylvia leaned toward the young man, as if to speak, but their eyes met and she stayed silent.

Adam felt the slight toward Sylvia as if he had been slapped. His face grew warm and his grip tightened on the arms of his chair.

Malak immediately stood. "Ladies and gentlemen, you must excuse me. My apologies, I have much work to do today and I do not want to take up any more of your time with Minister Kapral or with visiting the *Sejm*."

He walked around the room and shook hands with each of them as he spoke. Adam rose as Malak approached him but Malak simply patted him on the shoulder as he passed. Adam sat back in his chair. The young man, who had not been introduced, nodded and followed.

"What the hell just happened?" Adam kept his voice low as he leaned toward Angela. "Who was that asshole?"

"Calm down, cowboy." Angela grinned but her eyes were questioning. "What's got you so worked up?"

Adam's brows knit together over his eyes as a dark shadow formed across his face. "I just don't like getting the blow off like that, that's all."

"Uh-huh," Angela leaned away from Adam, as if feeling the heat of his emotions. "You mean to you? Or to our good friend, Sylvia?" With that comment, Angela turned in her chair, leaving Adam staring at her back.

The change in atmosphere hastened the end of the meeting.

Sylvia stood. "I think we have taken enough of the minister's time today." She turned to Kapral. "Minister Kapral, thank you so much for answering our questions and speaking to us about the Polish political system. I am sure we have all learned much in this meeting."

CHAPTER FOURTEEN

AT FIRST, Adam thought the committee must be on a break. From the public balcony, the room seemed as if it were in silence, the musty air heavy and still. A cough from below drew Adam's attention down. He shifted forward just an inch or so to glance down, then slid back quickly into the safety of his seat. Almost all the carved wooden chairs on the floor below were taken.

"Sorry about earlier." Adam leaned to his right to whisper in Angela's ear. "I guess I overreacted a bit."

"A bit?" Angela kept her attention focused on the people below them.

Adam shrugged, looking anywhere but down. "Yeah, anyway, sorry."

He opened his mouth to say more when one of the ministers stood and strode to the lectern. The rapping of his gavel on the wooden surface filled the room, and those seated before him closed the document they had been reading and looked up expectantly.

A member of the legislature was invited to step forward to make remarks and Adam's attention wandered as he listened to the steady stream of Polish. He leaned back toward Angela.

"I guess I just let my anger get the best of me sometimes, you know?" He glanced at her then looked away. "It's kind of embarrassing."

This time she looked at him when she responded. "As

long as you don't act on it."

He grinned and shook his head.

"That was pretty intense, though. Seriously," she added, emphasizing her point.

"I know." He shrugged. "I've heard that before. But I don't act on it. I mean, not rashly, anyway. I always stay in control."

Angela nodded, her glasses slipping down her nose. "You were pretty quiet during our meeting with Minister Novosad. You didn't say a word." She turned to face Adam, examining him. "Not great for a cop, though, is it?"

Adam grinned again and tipped his head to the side. "Maybe that's why I didn't always want to be a cop."

"Yeah? What did you want to be when you were growing up? A teacher?"

Adam laughed, and Sylvia looked over at them. Jared shushed loudly.

"Sorry," Adam responded in a stage whisper, then lowered his voice again as he turned to Angela. "Ready for this? A forest ranger."

"A forest ranger?" This time Angela laughed. "That's what you wanted to be?"

"Sure, why not?" Adam smiled and shrugged, not covering up his dimples. "Who doesn't want to be a ranger?"

"Well, me, for one." Angela raised her eyebrows. "Did you join the Forest Service?"

Adam shook his head slowly and sighed. "Nah, I didn't get that far. Just the Boy Scouts."

"And there it is, of course you were a Boy Scout..." Angela nodded as she looked up at the ceiling. "I bet you were an Eagle Scout, weren't you?"

Adam shrugged. "What's wrong with that? And yes, as a matter of fact, I was."

"Uh-huh." Angela smiled as she shook her head. "That explains it."

"Explains what?"

"Your approach to this trip, to your job. You want to do the right thing, you know? It's just…" Her smile faded and her brows lowered as she shook her head, "I'm sorry, I don't want to psychoanalyze you or anything."

"No, go on." He said the words easily, but felt his muscles tense in anticipation of what she might say.

"You always want to do the right thing, but sometimes it's not so easy to know what the right thing is, is it?"

"Shh." Ray stepped forward, between Angela and Adam. "Sylvia, what are they saying now?"

Before Sylvia could respond, a shout drew their attention to an area farther along the public balcony.

Łukasz Kaminski stood, his back to a wooden chair lying awkwardly on its side, the victim of whatever struggle Łukasz was engaged in with the uniformed guard facing him.

As Adam watched, the guard lunged, grabbing at Łukasz. Łukasz took a step back, seamlessly avoiding the tipped chair. The guard fell forward, calling out as his knee struck the heavy wood.

Adam tried not to grin. This wasn't a funny situation. "What's going on, can you tell?"

He looked at Sylvia, but she said nothing, just watched the scene unfold. The presentation from the committee floor continued, though two or three faces turned up to see what was causing the commotion.

Łukasz spoke to the guard. From where he sat, Adam heard nothing more than an angry hiss, though he wouldn't have understood the words even if he were closer.

As he spoke, Łukasz swung his satchel over his shoulder and turned his back on the guard, moving toward the door at the back of the balcony. But the guard had regained his balance. He was heading for Łukasz and the look in his eye made it clear he wasn't giving up.

Two quick strides brought the guard up behind Łukasz's back. He pushed hard and Łukasz stumbled toward the door. Just as he reached it, a second guard came through, catching Łukasz before he fell, then swinging him out into the hall. The entire confrontation had taken less than a minute.

Sylvia coughed gently, bringing the group's attention back to her. "Perhaps it is time we leave now, too."

Angela looked at her like she was crazy. "What? What's going on over there? Aren't you curious to know?"

"It is not our business. We should not be involved," Sylvia responded. "Come, let us leave now. We have a little bit of time before our next engagement, we can enjoy one of the cafes around the Old Town Square."

Sylvia directed the group out to the waiting van, explaining she needed to run back upstairs for a minute to let her boss know they were leaving. Following Sylvia's directions, Ray and Jared left the room.

Angela looked at Adam, but he simply shrugged and raised his eyebrows. "I don't know any more than you do. But I admit I'm curious."

ADAM JUMPED as a hand fell on his shoulder. He turned but his retort was cut off by the sound of Łukasz's voice.

"Cousin, there you are."

Łukasz leaned into him, and over his shoulder Adam could see two burly guards moving in their direction.

"They want me to leave, cousin, but I told them I was waiting for someone. A stretch of the truth, perhaps, yet here you are, so perhaps I was telling the truth after all."

Łukasz turned as he spoke, guiding Adam away from the building.

"What's going on, Łukasz? Why do you need me?" Adam stopped walking and pointed toward the van waiting to whisk him off to the group's next appointment. Chris had paused in the act of stepping into the van, turning to stare at Adam. "I have people I'm supposed to see."

Łukasz glanced in the direction Adam had pointed, then turned to watch the guards who had stopped approaching but were still eyeing him cautiously.

"You must walk with me, Cousin Adam. We must walk away from this place, look casual."

Adam paused for only a second. He saw Angela leaning out of the van and waving toward him. He thought about the meetings lined up for that afternoon. More politicians. More community groups. And less and less that he could contribute.

With a nod, he waved back at Angela and called out to her, "It's okay, go ahead without me. I'll meet up with you all later. I'm going to catch up a little bit with my cousin here."

Łukasz turned, smiled and waved at Angela, then turned back to Adam with a grim face.

"We walk now."

The two men walked down the drive away from the grand marble facade of the building, the guards watching them closely. They walked slowly, chatting about the weather and good places to visit in Warsaw.

Only once did Adam glance back. The guards had stepped back toward the building; one lit a cigarette. At Adam's look, they both took a step toward them.

"He's with me," Adam called out, putting his arm across Łukasz's shoulder and shaking his head. The guards stopped where they were, but did not step back.

As Adam turned away, his eye was caught by the movement of a curtain on the third floor of the building. The window was still now, but Adam was sure someone had dropped the curtain back into place when he or she stepped back from the window.

Stepped back from watching him and Łukasz leave.

Was Sylvia concerned about him and keeping an eye on him? Or was someone else watching?

CHAPTER FIFTEEN

HE LET the curtain drop back into place, hiding the view of the journalist and the police officer leaving the grounds together. Nothing to worry about yet, he tried to convince himself.

Yet.

There was no point in taking chances, though.

Stepping back to his desk to pick up the phone, he shivered, though his office was warm and comfortable. He paused with the phone in his hand. How had it come to this?

But he knew the answer. He could picture the very moment when he had realized he was no longer in control of the situation. Or of his life.

When he thought of it, he could still hear the peal of the church bells. To this day, the bells still scared him.

He had joined a group of fellow university students heading out to the five o'clock mass, so many years ago. He blended in with the noisy cluster scurrying across the grounds of Warsaw University toward the seventeenth-century cathedral that beckoned just beyond the campus border.

This had become a regular routine for him. As they passed through the arch that marked the main entrance to the campus, he let himself fall behind. Slowing his pace until he no longer walked within view of the group, he made a sharp right turn.

The rest of the students rushed forward to hopes of salvation. He headed in the opposite direction, almost jogging as he moved deeper into the darkening alley. He kept his eyes peeled for witnesses, turning occasionally to look behind him.

No one followed. He picked up his pace.

A few minutes' walk past gray stone buildings brought him to a small storefront. Like other buildings he had passed, its walls were plastered with Soviet propaganda. They were simply a facade. Torn remnants of Solidarity signs still remained, words visible under the propaganda. The bulk of the rebellious signs had been torn down by the police, but at this point in the movement, even martial law hadn't stopped the signs from reappearing.

Grimy windows exposed little of the building's interior, though the smell of cooked cabbage permeated the air around it. The door of the establishment opened to release a customer. Waiting only for the cloud of smoke that escaped with the patron to subside, the student stepped inside.

Wading through air thick with smoke and dill-scented steam, he crossed the room and slid into a vacant seat. Wilenek looked up from his tea.

Dark eyes stared out from below cropped hair. A faint scar knitted the skin across one cheek and a crooked nose hinted at a violent past. Wilenek's eyes seemed ageless, though the student knew the man was only a few years older than him.

Wilenek's expression was as still as ever, giving nothing away, but he knew enough to be nervous. He shifted in his chair. Wilenek nodded and grunted out a few words.

Though brief, Wilenek's words scared him into speaking, opening the floodgates of his memory, his observations. Wilenek lit a cigarette as he nodded, listening to the torrent of words. After twenty minutes of talking, Wilenek put up a hand. At the signal, he stopped talking.

In a fluid movement, Wilenek stood. Crossing the table on his way to the food counter, Wilenek patted him on the shoulder. It could have been the gesture of an older brother. The student cringed and ducked his head. Wilenek grunted again as he walked on. The man was short and stocky, but he was youthful and moved with the stealth and grace of a lion. Or a hunter.

On his return, Wilenek dropped an envelope onto the table as he put down his tray laden with soup, bread and kielbasa.

The student glanced up, then swept the envelope off the table and tucked it into his coat pocket. Keeping his hand on his pocket, he asked the question that had been burning within him for days. "What will you do with this information?"

The other man barely glanced up from his soup. "That's none of your concern." Wilenek's accent was thick, Russian.

The student leaned forward, prepared to stand, but held his chair. "I've heard the rumors. People getting hurt because of this. Jakub was taken during the night, and no one's heard from him. I didn't bargain for that."

Now the other man looked directly at him, and he shifted back in his seat. Wilenek spoke slowly, enunciating each word.

"That's none of your concern."

He had made his decision then. The side of angels or the side of devils.

He feared Wilenek — feared the man, feared what he stood for, who he worked with. He knew that lining up on the side of Wilenek and his kind would be a choice he could never back away from.

But he feared even more what would happen to him if he walked away from this connection. Away from the secret police. Away from the financial support they were guaranteeing him. Away from the thrill of power he felt when he shared a confidence, shared secret knowledge.

The thought of what would happen to his life if he

gave it up, slinked back into anonymity, scared him almost as much as the man sitting across from him. If he had to choose between protecting his own life and helping others, so be it. It wasn't really a choice at all.

He would do whatever he had to do to protect himself and his interests.

He said no more to Wilenek, simply nodded. Grabbing his satchel, he stumbled out of the dining room, back into the now fully dark street. Turning to his left, he headed toward the campus where the evening mass was drawing to a close.

Up on the crowded main street, he'd tucked his head into his collar and blended into the crowd of students streaming through the cold night, the sound of church bells reminding him of what waited for him once this life had ended.

CHAPTER SIXTEEN

PEDESTRIANS BUNDLED against the chill of the evening brushed past them, moving quickly to reach the warmth of their next destination. Businessmen and students rushed home after a long day's work. Women, some still in their business suits, stopped in at narrow markets lined with shelves of canned goods, boxed juices and root vegetables to pick up a last few items for the evening's meal.

At this time of the afternoon, the sun was too low in the sky to provide sufficient light, and street lamps lit the wide sidewalks of the *Aleje*.

Adam and Łukasz picked up their pace as they walked and talked, blending into the moving crowd. Only a few blocks away from the *Sejm*, they walked north up *Aleje Ujazdowksie*, passing quickly out of the diplomatic quarter toward the elegant shops on *Ulica Nowy Świat* and the historic Old Town Square.

As they walked, they talked of nothing more significant than the stores they were passing, how the weather had been recently, and stories Adam and Łukasz remembered about their grandfathers' time together in Poland. Adam pulled a few funny tales from his memory, stories he'd overheard his father telling his friends.

Łukasz smiled at the memories, though his own stories carried a hint of sadness, even regret, that Adam couldn't understand.

Adam waited patiently, knowing Łukasz would talk to him when he was ready. It wasn't until they had been walking for over twenty minutes that Łukasz's voice deepened and his words slowed.

"It was no accident, Adam." He glanced in Adam's direction.

Adam nodded, but kept his eyes on the facade of the National Museum across the street to their right. Its walls seemed to glow golden behind the high fence that surrounded it, giant carved statues of Soviet-era heroes standing guard from niches in the walls.

"When you were attacked, you mean?" he finally responded.

"Yes. I am sure of it."

"Does that mean you remember more now?"

Łukasz inhaled sharply. "No!"

He paused, and when he spoke again his voice was once again low and calm. "I still cannot remember the attack. I was attacked, of that I am sure. And I know why."

The two men paused their conversation as they crossed the busy *Aleje Jerozolimskie*, sidestepping cars whose drivers preferred not to follow the suggestions of the traffic lights. Large, boxy Mercedes hogged the roads. Tiny Fiats swerved by, looking as if they could bounce off the pedestrians without causing any harm.

The orange stones used to construct the grand buildings that lined the street carried over into the fabric of the sidewalk, merging everything into a blur of orange below brown wool and fur-wrapped people.

"I was working on a story, you see," Łukasz continued, but Adam could tell he was struggling with the words. "About my daughter. She was killed."

Adam turned his attention from the street and looked at Łukasz. "I'm so sorry. What happened?"

"I do not know for sure. But I am sure she was killed." Łukasz turned his face away from Adam as he spoke. "They say it was suicide. It wasn't. It couldn't have been. Basia would not have killed herself. I know this."

Adam nodded, remembering the image of the body floating in the river. The loss of a young life to the currents of the Wisła river. "I'm so sorry, Łukasz. I read about her death in the papers. I wasn't sure until now she was your daughter. That's a terrible thing to go through. But what does it have to do with the story you're writing?"

Łukasz looked at Adam in surprise. "I intend to find out who killed her and expose him. To write the truth the police refuse to see."

"Łukasz," Adam cautioned, "you should let the police do their job. I've had some experience with journalists trying to get involved in police work, and it never turns out well."

"Hah." Łukasz looked cynical. "Yes, the police. Your colleagues, I understand. You must understand that the police here are doing nothing. They do not care to investigate."

Adam took a deep breath, brushed his hand across his eyes, attempting to keep control of his memory. It didn't work.

Handfuls of dirt landed on a coffin in Adam's mind, his view of the Warsaw street blocked by the image of a woman kneeling on the ground, her face twisted in grief. He was overcome again by his own feeling of helplessness as he watched, knowing he had been responsible for providing protection. For keeping those children safe. And that he had failed.

"I don't believe that." The denial sounded weak, even to him. He took another breath, inhaling the smell of diesel fumes, the scent of perfume as a woman crossed his path. He felt his hands relax, his clenched fists opening.

Too engrossed in his own grief, Łukasz hadn't noticed Adam's silence. He put his hand out and patted

Łukasz's shoulder, the contact bringing him fully back to the present. "They wouldn't simply ignore it."

"They are. In fact, they believe they must." Łukasz paused before continuing, his internal struggle deepening the lines already encircling his eyes and mouth. "It was made to look like suicide, as I said. It was done very well. The police, they believe what they see. They have no reason to investigate further. But I know... I know."

"Why do you think she was killed?"

"My little Basia." Łukasz smiled at his memories. "She was so young, so full of life. She had just started a new position — in her last year of university — and she had such dreams for it. Dreams she would share with me. She wanted to be president of Poland one day! But she was happy starting where she was. She was very lucky to get a position as staff for Minister Novosad. Well, not lucky perhaps, she earned that position. She worked very hard for it."

"She worked at the *Sejm*, in Minister Novosad's office? I met with him just this afternoon with my group." Adam pictured the grave, composed gentleman they had met earlier. "Do you think something at her job is what got her killed?"

Łukasz shrugged. "I think it's possible. But I do not know. I know that I had been pursuing that line of inquiry when I was attacked. I just can't remember exactly what I was working on, what I had found. And all of my notes, they were destroyed that same night."

"What do you mean? At your office?" Adam tucked his hands into his pockets as the fading light encouraged the cold night air.

"No, from my home. Someone broke into my apartment that night. They took my computer, even my backup drives. I reported the theft to the police, but what can they do? They took a report. And my notes... they were all gone."

"Do you always keep your notes at home, and does

anyone else know where you keep them?" Adam asked, the policeman in him coming through.

"No, you see, this was different," Łukasz explained, stepping around a group of students gathering on the sidewalk. "I typically keep my notes in the office of the newspaper where I work. It is safer there, at least I thought so. But as I was working on this story, gathering information from the archives, from informants, from my contacts involved in the government, my editor... well, I didn't trust him."

"Why not?" Adam pressed, "What did he do, exactly?"

"It seems so innocuous, you may not believe me."

"Try me, you'd be surprised what I believe."

"He assigned me other stories. High-profile stories, stories that would sell and do well for me. He even offered me a promotion, to assistant editor."

"Uh huh... I can see why that doesn't build a good case for accusing him of stopping you."

"No. But I was sure of it. He had never offered me these things before. And he knew very well what I was working on. He was trying to stop me from writing this story. I am sure. So I started taking my work home with me. I was afraid to leave any of my notes in the offices where he would have access to them. That night, they were stolen."

The men stopped in front of a store window just as the first flakes of snow started to fall. Elegant leather bags, belts and purses were laid out in the window, brightly lit from inside. A woman in a long fur coat passed them as she entered the store and Adam could hear the clerk greet her by name as the door closed.

"So what about your story? You must have been close to the truth. Somebody was willing to break into your apartment, to physically attack you, to prevent you from writing it. What did you find out?"

"Not as much as I think my attackers believe," Łukasz said sadly, rubbing his hand across his forehead.

"I was tracing a trail of corruption within the legislature. That's as much as I can remember. I know I started by investigating the people who worked most closely with Basia, then spread out further. Following the network. Following the power... and the money."

They were still examining the fine leather goods in the window when the fur-robed woman left the store, once again brushing past them, this time carrying a large paper bag.

"It was the money that finally told me something, I remember that. The money." Łukasz paused. "But what? And who? And why was my sweet Basia killed?" Łukasz's voice cracked and he paused.

"Maybe she found something," Adam suggested. "Maybe she planned to expose the criminal. To go to the police."

"Yes, Basia would do that," Łukasz agreed. "If she found any evidence of corruption, I am sure."

Adam shivered as a few flakes of snow found their way under his collar. Łukasz glanced at him then turned to continue their walk. Warm lights glimmered on the sidewalk ahead of them, and when a heavy wooden door to their left opened, Adam caught the rich, sweet scent of beetroot and dill, along with the more familiar smell of grilled steak. A handsome couple stepped out of the restaurant. Glancing in, Adam saw that thick velvet curtains were pulled closed beyond the door, ensuring the winter's chill wouldn't enter the restaurant along with the customers.

Only a few yards farther along the sidewalk, a glass-fronted store bore the sign of a *Bar Mleczny*, or milk bar. Łukasz smiled sadly.

"Basia took me out to eat here, to the *Baru Mlecznego*," he explained. "When she first got her job. She couldn't afford the fancy restaurants in this area, but the *Bar Mleczny* was always affordable. Anyone who needs it can always get a warm meal of traditional Polish food here."

Adam glanced in as they passed. The place was mostly

empty. A few plastic tables were occupied by elderly gentlemen, widowers perhaps seeking a warm meal they didn't have to cook themselves. A pair of students lined up at the bar ordering their food, served to them on plastic trays they could carry to a nearby table.

Milk bars were a holdover from the previous era and they were slowly disappearing. Supported through government subsidies, these bars managed to serve kielbasa, sauerkraut, barszcz at minimal prices. The same foods being served in the expensive restaurant up the street, Adam was sure, but at a fraction of the cost. And without the decor and service.

The location of this milk bar seemed odd, tucked away between five-star restaurants and high-end stores. Perhaps this was where they were most needed, by those who could least afford the cost of living in this neighborhood. Pensioners, students, and young men and women just starting out on their careers. Like Basia.

Adam turned his attention back to his companion. "I hope you understand, Łukasz, there are great risks involved in what you're doing. I know you need to find out who killed Basia. But exposing the corrupt and the criminal means putting yourself in danger. Someone who has killed once is more likely to kill again. Hell, he already left you for dead once."

"That was his mistake, then, not to finish the job. I must find whoever killed my daughter. I have no choice. I am alone now, you understand." Łukasz looked at Adam as he explained. "Basia's mother, my wife, died a few years ago. Natural causes, I assure you." Łukasz spoke over Adam's condolences. "But she is gone. Now Basia is gone." He paused, shaking his head. "I must find the man responsible."

"If it's corruption that you're following, tell me, how common is that in your system? I'm sorry," Adam explained as Łukasz raised his eyebrows, "I don't mean anything by that. You know how politics are. In the States, there are politicians who are willing to sell their vote and that isn't even considered corruption anymore. There are others who are caught with thousands of dollars in their freezers... What is Poland like right now?"

"Ah yes, there is corruption, no question. There are men and women who see capitalism as an opportunity to make some easy money. There are leaders who have held on from the previous regime and who will do anything to keep their power, including bending some rules. There are some who have ties to Russia and the mafia there. They are involved not just in corruption, but in violent criminal activity. Yes, it is all around us."

Adam thought about this, then asked, "And what about lustration? I've heard a little bit about it. Has that caused problems? Would that lead anyone to murder?"

"Only the honest man," Łukasz chuckled. "For those who are honest, lustration means admitting your past, admitting your mistakes perhaps. But once it is admitted, there is no punishment. So nothing to kill for. For those who are dishonest, well, they can lie about their past. They can cover it up so easily. Records from the previous regime are not easy to access. They are considered classified. So if someone has lied, chances are he or she will face no penalty for that. So no reason to kill, you see."

"You never know what will drive a person to murder. Sometimes the cause is big, maybe even just. Saving a loved one, for example. Or seeking revenge." Adam looked at Łukasz out of the corner of his eye. "I've known people who killed for fifty dollars. Or less." He laughed gently under his breath, more a sharp exhale than anything else. "People never fail to surprise me."

Łukasz glanced at his watch, then turned to Adam. "It is getting late and we have been talking for some time. Your group will be missing you. You have been most kind, walking with me and listening to my story. And now I have a further favor to ask of you."

"Of course," Adam responded quickly, "what do you need?"

"I need your help. You are a policeman, no?"

"I have no authority here in Poland. Here I'm just a civilian, like you."

"Of course, I understand this. But the police are not able — or not willing — to help me. Someone not connected with the police is exactly what I need. Someone with the ability to help me figure this out. To find out who killed my Basia."

Adam breathed in deeply, trying to figure out what his response should be. He was in Poland for a reason and he had responsibilities. He couldn't just abandon the Philadelphia International Council. Or forget Captain Farrow's demand that he make the PPD look good. On the other hand, Łukasz was family. And Adam had been raised always to put family first. Wouldn't his grandparents and their neighbors want him to stick with Łukasz, to help him find the truth?

Finally he nodded. "Maybe I can help. I'm not sure how much I can do, though," he cautioned. "I don't speak the language, I don't know the people."

"Ah, but you do know people, Adam, don't you? You are used to telling who is lying and who is telling the truth. And you search for the truth, just as I do."

Łukasz looked up and down the street. His eye fell on a small bar tucked down a narrow alley that ran between two large stores.

"We will meet here later, after you have had a chance to catch up with your group, attend whatever dinner event is planned for you."

"Okay," Adam agreed, "I can meet you later. Over there?" He gestured toward the bar that had caught Łukasz's attention.

"Yes, at *Pod Jaszczury*. Under the Dragon. Yes, we will meet here, in the dragon's lair, to discuss the beast itself."

CHAPTER SEVENTEEN

ADAM SPUN AROUND at the sound before he realized it was just a couple of university students calling to each other down the alley. He squared his shoulders and shook his head at his own nervousness.

After the lights and gaiety of the group's dinner that evening, the alley seemed particularly gloomy. Even more so given what he now knew about Łukasz. And Basia.

Orange light from lamps along *Ulica Nowy Świat* barely reached down this narrow path and the cobblestones flowed ahead of him like a dark and slippery river. But rowdy sounds from the bar just ahead on his right seeped out into the night as the door opened to admit a lone figure, presumably seeking warmth and comfort from the cold outside.

Adam followed the stranger into the small space, coming almost immediately into contact with the blackened oak bar that wrapped around one end of the place in a horseshoe curve. A few gray figures huddled around its counter in clumps but most of the noise came from the cluster of tables near the back of the room.

Students had gathered there, loudly sharing beer and conversation with the occasional spilled drink and accompanying laughter. The smell of beer that lingered in the air hinted at many nights of spilled drinks, not all of them completely cleaned away.

Adam turned back to what he assumed were the locals at the bar and soon spotted Łukasz at the far end.

"Interesting crowd here," Adam commented as a greeting. "Come here often?"

Łukasz looked around him and grunted. "It has changed over the years. There was a time when students were here to study, they had no money for entertainment. Or drink. But now" — Łukasz waved his hand in the direction of the tables where another peal of laughter had just broken out, combined with some angry shouting — "Now the students come to enjoy themselves. The university is very close, you know, just a few blocks away."

"Yeah, right next to our hotel. It's certainly convenient for me, meeting here." His eyes met those of the bartender and he said to Łukasz, "What do you recommend?"

Łukasz raised his glass toward the bartender and tapped the edge with two fingers. The bartender moved to his taps to pull two more of the same.

Settling onto his stool, Adam took a slow drink from his glass while looking more closely at the people around him. Including Łukasz.

The man's face was grim, even while he drank. He leaned heavily against the bar on his left arm, and after placing his glass down, he ran his right hand along his face, as if trying to wipe away the exhaustion and fear visible there.

The bitter tang of Adam's beer brought to mind the winterized wheat fields he'd seen from the train to and from Toruń and left him with a feeling of wanting something more, though he wasn't sure what. He never found beer satisfying, not the taste, not the way it left him feeling. He checked out the bottles behind the bar as he drank, hoping to see a good whiskey or two, but there was none.

Adam had considered his options carefully before

coming out this evening. He knew the first tool a policeman had to use was information, so he'd gathered what he could, from the person he trusted most. He'd called Pete.

"HEY, KAMINSKI. I wasn't expecting to hear from you. How are things in Poland?" Pete's words came quickly, as they always did, not slowed at all by the thousands of miles between them. Adam could hear the sounds of the precinct in the background, Pete still at his desk.

"Polish," Adam responded. "Kind of what you'd expect, but a little different."

"Yeah, okay. Thanks for the description, it's like I'm there," his partner responded with sarcasm. Again, as he usually did.

Adam smiled, glad to hear Pete's familiar voice. His smile faded when Pete continued, "Hey, Julia called me yesterday."

"Why's my little sister calling you? Is there something going on between you I should know about?"

"Calm down, Kaminski, don't get your panties in a twist. She needed a little help, that's all. I guess with you out of the country she turned to the next best thing."

"Hmph." Adam tried to stifle his laugh. "She turned to you because she knew she'd get another lecture from our dad if she asked my parents for more money. She's got a show coming up, she told me before I left. And with the wedding shoots she picks up sometimes, I thought she'd be okay." He tried to ignore the guilt he felt for not leaving some money with Julia before he left. "Is she okay, though?"

"She is now, buddy —"

"Shit, Pete, you shouldn't have." Adam cut him off mid-sentence.

"Don't worry about it, partner. I just loaned her a few bucks, that's all. She says she's got a job coming up this weekend, she just needed some help to get through the next few days. It's nothing."

"I'll pay you back as soon as I'm home. I promise." Adam tried to put the thought of his sister hitting his colleagues up for money out of his mind. "How's everything else? Is Luis cooling his heels waiting for me?"

"He is. The judge granted the continuance." Adam could hear the grin in Pete's voice as he filled Adam in on the status of a recent arrest, one of the many responsibilities waiting for him back at home. "You're doing a good thing there, Adam, don't worry. You'll get your chance to testify when you get home. But you're paying for a long-distance call to check up on that slime? Things must be more boring over there than you expected. I thought you said Polish women were known for their beauty. Why aren't you out there sweeping one off her feet?"

"Maybe later. I called because I have a question for you. I need you to look someone up for me. Łukasz Kaminski."

"Woocash?" Pete sounded out the name. "What is that, some kind of lottery?"

"It's a name." Adam spelled it out for Pete. "Take a quick look and tell me what comes up when you run it."

"Okay." Adam could hear Pete typing in the background, entering Łukasz's name and nationality into the system, seeing what popped out. "What else can you give me besides his name?"

"He lives in Warsaw, he's a journalist." Adam paused, "And he may be the grandson of Jan Kaminski."

A few minutes going through the newspapers provided by the hotel had verified to Adam's satisfaction that Łukasz Kaminski was a successful journalist. But was he who he claimed to be?

"Are you using police resources, using me, to draw your family tree, Kaminski?"

Pete asked the question lightly, but Adam knew him well enough to know he was serious. Pete was a good man, a great partner. And part of his greatness came from the fact he took his job seriously. He wouldn't steal a pen that had been paid for by the people's tax money. Let alone use the police database to track down a long-lost cousin.

"It's not personal, Pete. Well, it is, in a way, I guess. He asked me for help. Looking into a death. A suspicious death."

"That would be Basia, his daughter?" Pete's fingers had stopped typing, and Adam figured he was reading now.

"Is that right? Is Basia his daughter? And Jan his grandfather?"

"Jan Kaminski, cousin to Witold, who is grandfather to our beloved Adam. Kaminski, he is your cousin. What's going on over there?"

"He told me about Basia, Pete," Adam explained. "He's crushed and he wants me to help find out what really happened to her."

"Not to be crass, but it looks from this like what really happened to her was she jumped into a freezing river in the middle of Warsaw and drowned. Gruesome, but not criminal. What else do you hope to find?"

"I'm not sure." Adam considered the question, winding the phone cord absentmindedly in his hand. "Łukasz is convinced she was murdered. I guess I could just talk to him, maybe find out a bit more about Basia."

"He started his career with crime reporting..." Pete's voice faded out as he read silently to himself for a few seconds. "He may be seeing crime where there isn't any, falling back on things he knows. Trying to find a reason. Trying to find someone to blame."

"Even if I can just help him accept her death, that would be better, wouldn't it? I can't let him go on pursuing this obsession. At least not alone."

"He's tilting at windmills, Kaminski. Don't get caught up with him." Pete's warning was gentle but firm. "I know you, and you always want to help people. The captain keeps going on about how he expects you to do something great over there. You know, impress our city leaders enough they're willing to up our budget next year. Don't let him down." Pete paused, then added in a quiet voice, "And don't get involved in something without getting help. You're not the police right now, remember that. If you need something investigated, call the cops. We all need help sometimes."

"I will, Pete. Thanks. I'll just ask a few questions first, see what crops up. There are still a few more things I need to find out before I even know where to start."

Adam used the next few minutes to fill Pete in on the other members of the team from Philly, as well as some of the Polish personalities they had already encountered.

"I want to start by finding out as much as I can about the people who worked with Basia," he concluded. "It's as good a place to start as any. So any details you can find will be a great help."

"I'll see what I can come up with on this end. Though if I were you, I'd be asking more questions about those lovely Polish ladies."

Adam laughed and thanked his partner before hanging up the phone. So Łukasz's story checked out. At least that was a start. But there was a lot more he didn't know and Łukasz was the only person who could fill him in.

ADAM PUT his empty glass back on the bar, gestured to the bartender for another round, and turned to Łukasz. "So what else is there? What didn't you tell me earlier today? And how do you think I can help?"

Two hours later, Adam had a lot more information about politics in Poland, the tragedy of the recent past and its many victims, and the differences that divided Polish society between those eager to move quickly into capitalism and those reluctant to change. Between those who wanted to go back and expose the past and those who simply wanted to put it behind them and move on.

The Solidarity labor movement had brought the end of the communist regime. Solidarity took great pride in its role not only in creating the new government in Poland — some members of the labor union were still active in the Law and Justice or PiS political party — but also in aiding the dissolution of communist regimes throughout the former communist bloc.

Since the fall of the communist regime, Poles had looked in a variety of directions for answers to the question of how best to build their government. Some had followed the charismatic and well-schooled leadership of the Freedom Union and later the Civic Platform. Advocating for full and immediate capitalism, their leadership was enhanced by the support of a strong youth movement, the Young Democrats.

Against these forward-looking parties, Łukasz described the *Soyusz Lewicy Demokratycznej*, SLD. The post-communist party. Leaders within this party were good people, Łukasz explained; they simply believed that too abrupt a change would hurt Poland.

Basia had been a Young Democrat and an ardent supporter of the Civic Platform. She accepted her position with Novosad because he had had a change of heart, switching his allegiance from SLD. She saw hope in his personal transformation, she had explained to her father, hope for the future of all Poland.

"How could someone so hopeful ever commit suicide?" Łukasz asked, downing the rest of his beer. "Nonsense. Just nonsense."

"This is all helpful, Łukasz. I know none of this speaks directly to who might have killed Basia. But sometimes the truth is hidden in the smallest of details. The more I know about Basia's background, and the people she spent time with, the better I'll be able to help," Adam explained. "If there's anything else you can remember, no matter how small a detail it may seem to you, please tell me."

"I wish I could remember more, I really do," Łukasz said for the third time that night. "It was all in my notes, I know, but they are gone. Who knows where. And whatever was in my head" — Łukasz beat gently on his head with a balled fist — "whatever was there is hidden from me now. I simply cannot remember."

"All right, then let's work it out. If you can't remember who you suspected, maybe you can remember where you found your information. We can follow your footsteps, put it together all over again."

"Yes." Łukasz looked over at Adam hopefully. "Yes, we can do that. I know where I went. At least, I think I do. I started as always with the newspaper archives. When the subject is corruption, you'd be amazed how much the same people crop up again and again, whether now or in the previous regime."

"Great. Anything else?"

"Another place I often do my research is in the national archives. They still have most of the official documentation from the previous regime. Well, at least those files that haven't yet been transferred to the Institute of National Remembrance. But I need a letter from my editor to access them. And I can't go back to him now to ask for that. Why would he support me if he is the one trying to stop me?"

"If you can't get access, can I? As a Polish-American, can I apply to review the documents to see what I can find out about my own family?"

Łukasz moved his head slowly from side to side, his hands open to the ceiling above. "Well... I doubt it would be that easy. You would have to apply through the embassy. After weeks, maybe months, you might be given permission only to view those documents connected to your direct relatives. I do not think that will meet our needs."

"No, I guess not." Adam looked into his empty glass and ordered just one more for the road. "There must be a way. I can reach out to my contacts in the force back home, too. Or at the Philadelphia International Council. We are here to help forge a stronger relationship between the US and Poland, after all. That might be worth some special privileges. Who knows?"

"It's certainly worth trying. And I will start with the newspaper archives. I have easy access to those. I will retrace my own footsteps, as you say." Łukasz put a hand on Adam's shoulder. "Thank you, cousin. Thank you for your faith in me, for believing me and for helping me."

Adam thought with guilt of his phone call before he came out to meet Łukasz, then put it out of his mind. He was here to help, that's what family did.

"I may be able to offer you some help, too. If you're interested." Łukasz raised an interrogative eyebrow as he added the last few words.

"About what?"

Łukasz frowned and looked down. "You mentioned seeking records about your family. Where you come from. How your family ended up in America. Would you really like to know more about that?"

Adam shrugged. "I figured my grandfather left the country looking for his fortune. Didn't exactly find it." He laughed to himself. "But no harm in trying, right?"

"Hmm, yes. I suppose you could say that." He took a sip of his beer. "But he was only ten years old when he left. You haven't wondered how his father — your great-grandfather — managed to leave in the middle of a war, when Poland was occupied by the Germans and the Soviets?"

Adam's surprise showed on his face. "I've only heard that it was a difficult time. A difficult journey. Why, what do you know?"

Łukasz pushed himself off the bar and stood behind his stool. "Not many facts, just rumors. But I can see what I can find out for you. Now it is time, I think, to head home. Can you find your way back to your hotel on your own?"

"No problem. I'll just finish this, I'll be fine."

Łukasz nodded and made his way out the door. Adam turned his beer glass in his hand, watching the shafts of amber light reflected onto the bar. He had heard so many stories about his grandfather. When Adam had asked about him, he'd always been told about his bravery. His willingness to take risks. He'd died when Adam was still young, so perhaps he'd only gotten the version of the stories fit for young ears.

He shook his head. For now, he had to focus on the problem at hand. There had to be a way to use his connections here in Poland and in Philly to gain access to those records without alerting Łukasz's editor they were revisiting them. He didn't know how things worked over here, but he knew exactly how to get the information he needed when he was back in Philly. How much different could Warsaw be?

With a determined nod to himself, Adam replaced his still half-full glass on the bar and headed for the door. A trio of men at the bar stood just as Adam was walking in their direction, blocking the narrow path to the exit.

Adam waited patiently while they buttoned their coats and donned hats, talking slowly to each other all the while. One older gentleman struggled with the buttons on his coat, his arthritic fingers unable to gain traction on the tiny plastic objects. His younger friend finally leaned over to help, fitting one button after another. Adam waited, smiling politely as the group acknowledged him and apologized for the delay.

Finally able to pass by, Adam pushed through the door into the dark alley. He turned to his left, intending to head out to the main street to make his way back to the hotel. It was a little longer than cutting down through the alley, but Adam didn't want to risk getting lost.

The sounds of the scuffle were unmistakable to Adam's ears and he turned to face it. In the darkness that engulfed the narrow space, Adam could just make out Łukasz's long gray coat, bent double like a folded sack. He heard the groan, and saw the large man in front of Łukasz raise his arm again.

"Hey!" he called out even as he ran headlong toward the larger of the two.

The guy took Adam's full weight in the gut. They went down together with a thud, but Adam was back up on his feet first, ready to confront the second thug.

Pausing with his hands at the ready, Adam assessed his situation. The guy he now faced was smaller than him and Adam was sure he could take him. But the guy's colleague was slowly lifting himself off the ground, and once he was up, Adam didn't like his chances against both of them. One glance at Łukasz made it clear the older man was in no condition to join the fight.

Thinking fast, Adam swept his right leg out and the big guy fell heavily one more time. Keeping an eye on the little guy, Adam put his knee into the back of the big guy, expertly twisting his arms painfully behind his back. He wasn't going anywhere.

"Łukasz," he said, still keeping his eyes on the little guy, who had let go of Łukasz, "I saw some cops up on the street just ahead, go and call out to them."

The little guy glanced up the alley toward the street, then took off into the darkness the other way. That just left the one.

"Sorry, buddy," Adam grabbed the back of his hair and slammed his face hard into the cobblestones. It was this or keep fighting, and Adam figured this was better for both of them. The guy would have a headache when he woke up, but at least he'd wake up.

"Come on." He grabbed Łukasz's arm and turned toward the main street and the lights that were still lit there.

The two men stumbled out onto the street, startling a group of students passing by. Realizing how strange they must look, Adam dropped Łukasz's arm and straightened himself out. "Where to, Łukasz? Where's home and where's safe?"

"I live in Mokotów," Łukasz replied, wincing as he brushed down his coat and wiped his face. "It is a few tram rides from here. I can catch a bus at this corner, then change at the train station."

"No way." Adam shook his head. "I can't let you make that trip on your own. You're a hunted man, cousin. I don't know who is after you, but he clearly hasn't given up yet."

He looked up and down the street. Even though it was late, students still roamed in small groups, some drunk and singing, others moving quickly from one bar to the next.

"You'll stay at my hotel. I don't think they know who I am yet, you'll be safe there. Here —" Adam reached into his pocket and pulled out a key. "The key to my room."

"What about you, cousin? Won't you come with me?"

Adam pictured the tiny room with its twin bed. His choice was to sleep sitting in the armchair in the corner or lying in the half-tub. There wasn't even enough space to sleep on the floor at the foot of the bed. He had a better idea in mind.

He shook his head at Łukasz. "No. You'll be okay on your own."

"Where will you go?" Łukasz asked as he took the key from Adam.

"I have an idea, somewhere I can stay where I should be safe." Adam gave Łukasz a confident pat on the shoulder. But his expression dropped to a frown as he turned away, wondering if he was right about that.

Ulica Miodowa was a short walk from the bar along well-lit streets. Adam walked quickly, keeping a sharp eye on everyone around him, including the people behind him. The cold weather kept everyone tucked into their high collars and scarves, and everywhere Adam looked he could see only suspicious eyes peering out at him, the steam of breath on the air.

Adam found Sylvia's building without a problem. The church next to it stood out against the dark sky, its spires rising toward the heavens. The smaller building next to the church had a carved sign over the arched doorway, proclaiming its name. A plaque to the right of the doorway listed the names of the tenants, and Stanko was written clearly next to the third bell from the bottom.

Adam pushed the bell and waited for Sylvia to come out.

CHAPTER EIGHTEEN

WEAK MORNING light struggled to make its way through the white lace curtains, and a few brave birds called from the courtyard below. Adam sat up with a start before he remembered where he was and lay back onto the sheets.

It was Friday morning and he lay on a narrow sofa in Sylvia's apartment. He could hear her steady breathing through the frosted-glass French doors that led into the connecting bedroom.

Rolling himself off the sofa, Adam stretched the kinks out of his neck and back as he made his way to the kitchen at the back of the apartment. An oven, sink and half-size refrigerator filled the space, with just enough room left for a table for two.

The night before, Sylvia had welcomed him as warmly as anyone could expect, showing up unannounced at someone's door after midnight. He hadn't provided her with too much detail about the events that had brought him to her apartment. He had simply explained his cousin had an emergency and needed to stay in his hotel room. Since it was too late to get a second room, he was hoping she would allow him to crash on her sofa.

In hindsight, he was a little surprised by how readily she had agreed. She had invited him in, offered him a warm drink. They sat comfortably on the small sofa, holding the steaming cups and taking small sips until the cinnamon-laced tea cooled off enough to drink properly.

"So, are you enjoying your time here in Poland? Are you glad you got this assignment?" Sylvia asked with pursed lips as she blew on her tea, her eyes looking at him over the mug.

"I am. It's a beautiful country, plus I got to meet my cousin, which is good." He nodded. "I think I'm going to learn a lot on this trip."

"Learning about your family, your history... that's nice." Sylvia paused, considering her tea. "I have a large family, you know."

"Are you close?"

"No."

Taken aback by Sylvia's abrupt response, Adam sat silent for a minute. "I'm sorry."

"No, it is fine. My parents are very good people. I have cousins who were my friends when I was small."

"Where does your family live?"

"In the north. A small village. A very small village." One side of Sylvia's mouth raised in a quasi-smile.

"Do you not stay in touch?"

Sylvia shrugged. "We talk, we do. I see them sometimes on holidays. But they have no interest in coming here, visiting Warsaw. It is the big city, you see, and they are happier where they are."

"There's nothing wrong with liking a simple life."

"No?" Sylvia looked up at him. "No, I suppose not. Or perhaps they simply don't know any better."

"You don't mean that." Adam smiled. "I'm sure they love hearing about your life when you do talk to them."

She shrugged again. "Perhaps. The parts they understand. My job... no, this they don't understand. But I will travel farther, I'm sure."

"Oh, yeah? You got the travel bug?"

Sylvia's smile widened. "Yes, the travel bug, as you call it. I have only been to Germany and England so far. Thanks to the Young Democrats. But I will travel. I will see more of the world."

"I have no doubt you will." Adam put his mug down on the glass-topped table next to the sofa. "Now, me, I'm very close with my family. Still live in the same town, talk to them every week."

"You are a good son."

"I don't mean you're not a good daughter..."

"No, I know." Sylvia raised a hand to clear the air. "Of course not. I just mean, they must be happy to have you near them."

"They are. And I like being able to drop in and see them now and then. I get to hear stories about my grandfather." Adam's eyes clouded as he thought of what Łukasz had said about his grandfather, wondering what more there was for him to learn.

Sylvia watched him closely, but said nothing.

Adam shook his head and smiled. "And then there's my sister. Julia."

"You are close?"

"You could say that. She certainly relies on me. But, man, she's crazy sometimes."

Sylvia smiled, her eyes on his face. "Why do you say that?"

He shrugged. "It's just her way, I guess. She drives me crazy. But I do love her. Just don't tell her that."

Sylvia laughed and Adam's mind was torn from thoughts of his family to thoughts of the beautiful woman sitting in front of him.

A noise outside broke the moment. Sylvia stood, picking up his mug and carrying them both into the kitchen. When she returned, she pulled sheets and a blanket out of a closet in the hall. "You can sleep on the sofa, if it is comfortable enough for you."

"It will be perfect, thank you." Adam stood and took the pile of linens from her, smiling.

"Good night, Adam Kaminski. We will talk again in the morning, I think."

Adam shook his head now, forcing himself to wake up. To get the evening with Sylvia out of his mind. He stepped around the table to throw open the door that led to the narrow balcony overlooking the courtyard. Here, Sylvia had placed a cooler filled with perishable foods that wouldn't fit into the small fridge but could stay cool outside throughout the winter. The balcony, just wide enough for a person to stand on, looked out over an enclosed space formed by the backs of neighboring buildings. He didn't have to step far out onto the balcony to see the courtyard below, the yellow stone of the Polish Army Field Cathedral next door.

A thin layer of snow covered the pavement and patch of grass that grew in the sheltered space at the heart of these old buildings. A few black birds picked at what growth there was, calling to each other. Whether inviting other birds to join them or warning them to stay away, Adam didn't know.

He left the door open as he turned back to the kitchen to light the fire on the stove and get some water boiling for coffee. It wasn't until the scent of the coffee filled the room and he had had his first cup from the cafetiere that he felt alert enough to shut the door, blocking out the chill that had been keeping him awake.

He needed to check in with Łukasz first, to make sure he was still okay. Then he planned to launch his own investigation into what really happened to Basia Kaminski. Before that, he needed to finish last night's conversation with Sylvia.

CHAPTER NINETEEN

"GOOD MORNING." Adam handed Sylvia a cup of coffee as she emerged from her bedroom, wrapped in a pink robe. "I hope you managed to sleep."

"I had no problem, thank you. How about you, could you sleep on that tiny sofa?" she asked as she sniffed at the coffee before taking a sip. "So, now that we are awake, what are we to do? Or perhaps the question is, what are you to do. Today, I mean?"

"It's a fair question. To tell the truth, I'm not entirely sure. I need to look into a few things. And some of those things I'm hoping you can help me with."

With that, he shared with Sylvia the story Łukasz had told him the night before. She listened without interrupting, though her eyes occasionally betrayed her skepticism.

Adam wrapped up the story. "We know someone is still after him, because that someone attacked us last night as we left the bar. We managed to get away, but I didn't think it was safe for him to go back to his place, so I invited him to stay in my hotel. And I came here."

Sylvia was silent for a few moments longer, and Adam started to wonder what thoughts were hidden behind her pale blue eyes.

"Adam, you shouldn't be involved in this. You don't know our country, our way of doing things. This young woman... Basia... you do not know her. Any father would find it difficult to believe his daughter had killed herself. How do you know he is right, that she was murdered?"

"I know it sounds crazy, but I believe him."

"Why?" Sylvia persisted.

"Well, for one thing, he must be onto something, or why else would someone be trying to kill him?" Adam asked. "He's been attacked twice now. Once he was left for dead. And when they came back to finish the job he was just lucky I was there to stop them. He must be onto something, getting someone nervous."

Sylvia shrugged and looked away. "I think not, Adam. I'm sorry, I knew Basia Kaminski. You should not be surprised, she worked for Rafał Novosad. We are a small community, you know."

"Of course, I should have realized, I'm sorry. What can you tell me about her?"

"It was very sad, Adam, when she died. We all felt the loss. I can understand her father feels it most of all."

Sylvia looked directly at Adam as she spoke. He could still hear the birds calling faintly from the courtyard outside with plaintive cries.

She continued, "Basia was obviously struggling with her work. She was tense all the time. She was under a lot of pressure, and she finally gave up. I believe that is what happened."

"Łukasz doesn't believe that. He thinks she was killed."

Sylvia shrugged. "That is a hard thing to believe. Who would have killed her? And as I said, she was a troubled young woman. Suicide is horrible, but it is more likely."

"Think about it," Adam pressed. "What if her difficulties came from the fact that she knew something she shouldn't? Isn't it possible that something was bothering her and she didn't know who to talk to about it? Scaring her, even?"

She put her coffee down. "You are making up stories, Adam. You are a policeman, you see crimes when there are none. Secrets where there are none. These are all good people who I work with. They are not killers." She paused, and Adam could tell she was carefully considering her next words. "Is what you suggest possible, that she had a secret she couldn't share and that was why she was troubled? Yes, I suppose it is possible. But I do not think that is what happened. I think she found the job difficult, I think she struggled with it just as Laurienty does."

"Who's Laurienty?"

"You met him yesterday. Well, you saw him. He was very rude, interrupting our meeting with Minister Kapral without an explanation." Sylvia shook her head in amazement. "He has no skills, no diplomacy. He will not make it far in our government. I do not know why Kapral keeps him on his staff."

"I thought there was something odd about him. And about his relationship with Kapral."

"It is just Laurienty, I am sure." Sylvia smiled. "He puts people off right away. Always nervous, always late, always focusing on the wrong problem." She stood. "These are the problems we deal with, Adam, not murder."

"There is something dark here, Sylvia. I am sure of it. Something evil. And I need to root it out. Because if I don't, someone else will get hurt. I am sure of it," Adam repeated, almost to himself.

She shook her head. "No, I don't believe that. Corruption there is, I know, but to kill someone to hide it?" She shook her head again. "No, this is not possible. And how can you investigate this? You don't know our ways, you don't understand our culture."

"You're right, I don't understand. That's why I need your help. You do understand." Adam leaned forward and looked into her eyes over the metal kitchen table. "You must help me understand. Because one thing I've learned through my job over the years is the only way to catch a person is by understanding what he thinks."

Sylvia shut her eyes and shook her head. "No, I don't want to understand that. And I don't understand how you could want to, either."

Adam shrugged and tasted his coffee again. It was getting cold. "It's what I do, and I do it well." He paused, considering making another pot of coffee. He added, "Okay, I understand you don't want to get into the mindset of a criminal, I can respect that. I may still come to you with questions about your culture and your history, though, if that's okay?"

Sylvia smiled. "Of course that's all right, that's why you are here, no? And that's why I am here for you, to show you these things."

"And I have one more favor to ask of you, Sylvia. This might be a big one."

Sylvia looked at him expectantly.

"I need to get into the national archives." He pushed forward when he saw the expression on her face. "That's where the truth is hidden. I must go back through the files Łukasz looked at before, to figure out who he was homing in on, who felt threatened enough by his research."

Sylvia stood and walked back into the living room. Adam waited where he was, knowing she needed a moment to think.

Eventually, she came back into the room, standing in the doorway with one hand on the wall. "I may not be able to get you that access. You understand those archives hold some records of national importance? It is not simply a library. It includes... well, for example, many of the files on the lustration hearings, the reports filed about people's past activities and connections with the secret police. These are sensitive materials."

"But you'll try?" Adam pressed.

"No" — Sylvia shook her head and looked down into her coffee mug — "but I can tell you who might be able to help. If you are interested in the national archives, you are best served if you have the support of a member of the national legislature. One of the people you met yesterday, for example. You should ask one of them. Adam" — she looked over his shoulder as she spoke, at the snow now falling softly into the courtyard — "you must be careful. This is not your land, not your people. You don't know what you might find."

WITH SYLVIA'S warning still ringing in his ears, Adam walked quickly down *Ulica Miodowa* toward the university and his hotel. He kept his head tucked into his collar against the cold, matching the stance and stride of others around him getting an early start for work or school.

Gray stone buildings lined the sidewalks and Adam knew that each of these opened up to peaceful courtyards inside, just as Sylvia's building did. Quiet, private spaces hidden behind bland building faces.

There was more hidden in Warsaw than lying in plain sight, Adam was beginning to realize.

He had a half-formed plan in his mind of getting into his hotel room by telling the desk clerk he had lost his key, but fortunately he didn't need it. As he entered the lobby he saw Łukasz sitting in a comfortable chair, sipping a cup of coffee and reading that day's newspaper.

"Cousin." Adam took the seat next to Łukasz. "You look relaxed and well rested." The sounds of clinking dishes came from the restaurant behind the lobby and Adam thought he could just smell the thick ham, dill and fresh bread that would be laid out in the buffet.

"Only thanks to you, my friend. And how did you sleep? Did you find a comfortable bed?"

"Of sorts, yes." Adam smiled, and chose not to answer the question evident in Łukasz's eyes.

Both men turned their attention to the staircase as Angela stepped into the lobby. Clearly planning an early morning swim, she wore only a bathing suit with a towel wrapped around her waist. She tied her dark hair into a knot at the back of her head as she descended the stairs, and both men watched as she moved with the grace and confidence of an athlete.

She paused at the bottom of the stairs before turning the corner for the last flight down to the pool and saw Adam and Łukasz watching her. With a small smile playing on her lips, she made her way over to the two men.

"Good morning, Adam. And this must be the cousin you met up with yesterday. Angela Tarallo," she added, extending a hand to Łukasz.

Łukasz took her hand and lifted it slightly toward his lips, bowing his head. "Łukasz Kaminski. A pleasure to meet you, *Pani* Tarallo. A great pleasure. My cousin has been very rude and has not introduced me to this wonderful team from America he tells me about."

"I hope he will rectify that mistake. I also hope he will be spending a little more time with our group today?" She directed this last comment to Adam.

The sound of feet clattering down the stairs preceded Jared, who burst into the lobby. Seeing Angela, he grabbed at the railing, almost tripping over himself as he changed directions, heading toward her instead of continuing down the stairs.

"Angela, there you are." He panted as he spoke. "I thought I'd join you in that swim you mentioned."

Angela raised her eyebrows and smiled. "Great. Good. I just stopped to say hello to Adam. And his cousin, Łukasz."

Łukasz nodded at Jared, who smiled back. "Cousin! How wonderful for you. I'm so glad you've had the chance to meet up with your family, Adam. You must be spending a lot of time together. I guess that's why you've been skipping out on some of our meetings?"

"That's right. Sorry about that."

"No, that's cool. That's great. Hey, I'd love the chance to see Warsaw with a local. Maybe I can join you guys today? You know, just to hang out in a real home, do things real Poles do?"

Angela laughed. "Looks like I'm not the only one missing you, Adam. You're a wanted man."

"Ah... well... I actually have some things I'm going to need to do today. I'm sorry, but Łukasz and I do need some time together. Alone."

"Oh, that's too bad." Angela frowned. "I was hoping we would be able to spend some time together today. I didn't even see you come in last night. I was hoping for a nightcap."

Łukasz raised an eyebrow toward Adam, but Adam gave no indication of what he was thinking. "Perhaps later today, Angela. I would like that. You, too, Jared, maybe we'll catch up later."

With a quick smile, Angela turned and walked slowly back toward the staircase down to the pool below. Jared looked at Łukasz and Adam, then shrugged and trotted after her.

"And I better get myself dressed." Adam stood.

"How do you propose to start?" Łukasz asked, standing also.

"I've been thinking about that. I'm going to start with the people I have the most in common with — Americans and cops."

CHAPTER TWENTY

THE POLICE STATION was quieter today, no one standing yelling at the counter. Adam smiled to himself as he remembered Łukasz's barely controlled anger at the way the police had treated him.

Whistling softly under his breath, he leaned against the counter. The entrance area was empty. Through an open door beyond the front desk Adam could see a hallway, and every so often, a police officer would pass by the door.

He waited for over five minutes before a uniformed officer came to the desk.

"*Słucham?*"

"Yes, hi there," Adam answered with a smile. "Does anyone here speak English, by any chance?"

The officer said nothing, just turned and headed back the way he had come. Adam waited patiently, once again whistling under his breath.

Eventually his patience paid off. A second man came through the door to the counter, this one in plain clothes. "You speak English, I understand?" the man asked.

"Yes, perfect, thank you." Adam smiled and extended his hand, but the man did not take it.

"How can I help you, sir?"

"Adam Kaminski," Adam introduced himself. "I'm a police officer as well, from Philadelphia... in America," he added as he failed to see any recognition in the man's eyes. "I was in here the other day to introduce myself, and I was invited to return when there was someone here who spoke English."

"I see. And why are you here?" the other man asked without smiling or introducing himself.

"I'm in Warsaw as part of a delegation. We're visiting with some of your officials as we make plans for forming a sister cities relationship between Warsaw and Philadelphia."

The man was examining him with clear distrust, so Adam continued, "Yesterday we met with Minister Kapral, for example. Very nice guy, he told us a lot about Poland, your country and your history. So I'm just hoping you can fill me in a little bit on the more day-to-day stuff, the things that really matter. Things like law enforcement."

The man's eyes had softened slightly when Adam had mentioned Kapral, and now he nodded. "Of course, professional courtesy." He raised a flap on the counter and motioned for Adam to follow him through.

"Szczepański," he introduced himself as he walked.

Adam didn't try to repeat the name, simply nodded and smiled.

Szczepański led Adam back to a small lounge where a few other officers sat reading reports and drinking black coffee out of plastic cups. It was an all-too-familiar scene. Adam breathed in the stale smoke, the aroma of coffee so strong he could taste it, and felt immediately at home.

His comfort level dropped when he recognized a portrait of Saint Casimir on the wall. The far-too-familiar image of Casimir holding lilies, a pious expression gracing his saintly face. Adam shuddered, trying not to lump Szczepański in with that other cop from Philly, just because of the Saint Casimir connection.

It wasn't easy.

Gesturing for Adam to take a seat, Szczepański leaned against a worn wooden table and folded his arms. "So, *Pan* Kaminski, what can I tell you?"

His words were friendly, but Adam still heard caution in his voice.

"I have a few questions I'd like to ask you, to get a sense of how you do things here. To compare with our methods at home."

"Go ahead."

"Okay." Adam took a breath. "Let's start with statistics. What are your crime rates?"

From there, Adam proceeded to inquire about a variety of procedural, statistical and legal aspects of law enforcement in Poland, each drier and less interesting than the first.

After thirty minutes, Szczepański slouched in a chair at the table, his chin resting heavily against his hand.

"Is there anything else, *Pan* Kaminski, that you need to know about law enforcement in Warsaw?" he asked wearily.

"Well, there is just one more thing," Adam responded, choosing his words carefully. "I read an article in the English-language paper about a young woman who committed suicide. Basia Kaminski."

Szczepański looked at him expectantly, saying nothing, so Adam continued. "Her name caught my eye, as you can imagine."

He waited again, but Szczepański just nodded.

"So I was curious to see the file on that case. Just to see how you handle something like that, how an investigation is conducted over here."

Szczepański studied Adam for a moment, then stood and walked across the room. A rickety wooden desk was pushed up against the wall, perhaps leaning against the wall for support. A sleek computer balanced on its surface, precariously out of place, and Adam winced as Szczepański pushed the power button, actively willing the desk to stay upright. It shook, but it stood.

The computer came to life with a soft whirring. Szczepański leaned over it, hitting a few keys. Another noise farther along the wall drew Adam's attention to a laser printer, spitting out paper.

When the movement stopped, Szczepański brought a few sheets over to Adam.

"The report you ask about," he said, reading over it. "You think this may be useful for you?" he asked with a smile, handing it to Adam.

One glance told Adam it wouldn't be any use to him at all. While Adam could pick out a few words here and there, his grasp of the Polish language wasn't enough to gain anything meaningful from the report.

Adam smiled back at Szczepański. "I can't read that, of course. Maybe you can fill me in?"

Szczepański glanced over the sheet one more time. "It says here she jumped off the bridge. There are detailed reports about the scene, about the temperature of the water, about the current. All the things you would have in your reports in America, I am sure."

Adam nodded and reassured him it sounded like a very thorough report. "And what did you find about the body itself? Anything useful there?"

"The body? It was dead." Szczepański laughed, a cross between a bark and a cough, and Adam frowned.

"Yes, I know. But cause of death?"

Szczepański looked hard at Adam. "She jumped off a bridge, *Pan* Kaminski. The cause of death was drowning, as you would expect."

Adam shrugged, focusing on keeping his anger in check. "You never know. Jumpers sometimes die from wounds inflicted in the fall. Hitting her head, for example?"

"Yes, she hit her head." Szczepański pointed to the report. "She hit it on the rocks in the river, this says, when she fell. Then she drowned, that is quite clear."

"So she was alive when she went into the water. The injury on her head didn't kill her? And are you sure the injury on her head was made in the water, not before?"

"Why do you ask these questions, *Pan* Kaminski?" Szczepański had put the report down now and was glaring down at Adam, leaning against the wall next to the image of Saint Casimir, his arms folded across his chest. "What do you suggest, that we do not know how to handle our cases here? Because we are Polish?"

"Not at all," Adam tried to reassure him, now angry at himself for handling this so badly, trying not to look at the image of the saint. "On the contrary, I'm sure I could learn some things from your approach. Maybe questions you ask that we wouldn't think to ask, details you look at that are important. Did you talk to the woman's friends or family, for example?"

"Of course, this would be necessary. She was working very hard, it seems. Her job was quite difficult. Stressful. Her friends think that is why she died. It was too much for her."

Adam nodded, thinking. "Thank you so much for your time, *Pan* Szczepański." Adam knew he had butchered the name when he saw Szczepański flinch, but he continued. "I just have one more question. Did you test her blood? Was there anything in it, any drugs?"

"You think maybe she was drunk or on drugs when she killed herself. Yes, that would be normal, I know."

Adam had been thinking about very different kinds of drugs, but he didn't correct Szczepański, instead letting him continue.

"We did not test her blood, *Pan* Kaminski. Once it was clear she had killed herself, there was no reason to spend more time or money on this. Just to show she had one more weakness? One more thing for her family to regret? No, that was not necessary."

"And what about her shoes? Did you ever find her shoes? Doesn't it strike you as odd that she would walk out of her apartment in the middle of the night with no shoes on? A coat, yes, but no shoes?"

Szczepański's anger flared again. "This does not concern you, Mr. Kaminski. It cannot be of interest to you in your work here. It is time for me to return to work now, you must leave."

Szczepański walked toward the door, holding it open as he waited for Adam to follow.

"It may be very important." Adam took a gamble. "This may not have been suicide. It might be murder. I just need to find out who's involved, and I think I can do that if you let me review your files. With someone who can translate it for me."

"There was no crime, Mr. Kaminski, except suicide, a crime against the church," Szczepański said darkly. "And I repeat, it is none of your concern. Go back to America, conduct your police work there. Not here."

Adam walked toward the door. Before leaving he turned back to Szczepański. "She was just a kid — a student. We owe her the truth." When Szczepański's expression didn't change, Adam added, "If you can't help me, I will find other ways to get the information I need. I just wanted to come here first, since we are colleagues, of a sort."

"I am not your colleague, *Pan* Kaminski. I am not here to help you. If you need help, go to your fellow Americans, go to your embassy. Don't come here."

With that, Szczepański closed the door behind Adam.

CHAPTER TWENTY-ONE

THE LARGE CONCRETE, steel and glass structure loomed twenty yards back from the street, a fortress behind well-tended gardens. The landscaped entrance created a sense of gentility, though the security of the cubed citadel couldn't be in doubt. An iron fist in a velvet glove.

Adam's request on entering the US embassy to meet with Sam Newman had met with an immediate positive response. His team from Philadelphia had been hosted by embassy staff at dinner their first night in Warsaw. Adam had spent that evening sitting next to Sam, the Consular Officer for the embassy in Warsaw.

After passing through the security screening, Adam was invited up to Sam's office, a bright corner room on the second floor. It was comfortable and appointed like a typical American workspace, but the narrow windows that broke through the wall in spaced intervals reinforced the feeling of being within a fortress. Or a prison.

"Come in, come in," Sam welcomed him. "Please, have a seat."

Sam indicated the two office chairs arranged in front of his desk. When Adam chose one, Sam took the other himself, turning it to face Adam, creating a feeling of two friends chatting rather than an official visit.

"So, how are you enjoying your visit to Poland, Detective Kaminski?"

Adam chatted with Sam for a few minutes about his time in Poland. He shared some details about the various visits the team had made with businesses, schools, and politicians. Sam listened intently, taking it all in. He didn't write anything down, yet Adam was left with the feeling that he would be able to repeat their conversation almost verbatim if asked to later.

After ten minutes of small talk, Sam paused and looked expectantly at Adam. He waited for Adam to speak. Adam admired the man's interrogation skills. He could learn a thing or two from him.

Adam launched into his story. "One of my successes on this trip has been reconnecting with my family here. I met a cousin — one I hadn't met before."

Sam smiled, and Adam found it hard not to believe that he was genuinely pleased at Adam's good fortune. "How nice for you. I'm always happy to hear about people finding connections between our country and others. I always say, the best diplomacy begins in the home, in the family. The more international ties American families have, the more international security America has." He smiled again, encouraging Adam to continue.

"I'm interested in learning more. About my family, about recent events here. My grandfather's family left Poland during the war, in 1940. He has some stories he shared with me when I was a boy, but I'd love to read more about what's happened in Poland since then." Adam glanced around Sam's office as he spoke. "In fact, I would really like to get access to the national archives. I believe I could learn a lot that would interest me there."

Sam frowned for the first time during their conversation and seemed to consider Adam's comment. "That's some fairly in-depth research you're talking about. Not your typical American reading the family's old diaries."

Adam smiled. "I know. I was a historian before I became a cop. I guess I still have some of that historian inside me. I look forward to opportunities to go through old records, old books." He thought of his bookshelves at home, stacked high with books he'd spent years delving into, others he hadn't yet found time to read. "Hey, is that something you can help me with? Getting into the national archives, I mean."

"I'm sure you could learn some fascinating things in the archives about your family, yes," Sam said, then added as if an afterthought, "There are some very sensitive materials there as well, you may not know that. It has an impressive collection of historical documents, of course. But the archives are also used by the Polish government to house some political records that are classified as sensitive."

"I had heard that, yes. I hope it doesn't cause a problem for me."

"Well, it simply means that there is no free access to the archives, so it will affect your research. You must request the documents you want to review, you see. And when you submit your application to review those documents, you also set a date for your appointment to visit the archives and review them." Sam smiled at Adam and Adam once again felt that Sam was being sincere. "And of course you must review all these documents in place. They cannot be removed from the premises."

Adam smiled in return. "That all sounds very reasonable. I can work within those parameters."

Sam stood and walked over to his desk, where he opened a file drawer and flipped through the folders hanging there. Pausing in his search, he looked up at Adam with a start.

"Kaminski... this cousin you mention, he's not Łukasz Kaminski, is he, the journalist?" Sam leaned over his desk and picked up a copy of that day's *Nowy Początek*. "Łukasz Kaminski... I'm a big fan of his writing. His articles always seem to hit home for me."

Adam blinked, caught off guard by Sam's knowledge. "Yes, that's him," he admitted. "He's the grandson of my grandfather's brother."

Sam laughed lightly. "Ah yes, the tangled web of family relations. I never could wrap my mind around all the terms. In my family, we just call everyone cousin." Even as he spoke, Sam's face became serious. "I heard about his recent loss, though. I'm so sorry. His paper was thoughtful enough not to cover the story, of course, but competing papers did. His daughter committing suicide. Very sad... very sad."

Sam had not resumed his search of his files, and Adam watched his face closely. All Adam saw there was real concern for Łukasz's well-being and sadness at the loss of a promising young woman.

"What is he working on now, your cousin?" Sam finally asked. "I imagine he uses the national archives for his research?"

"Yes, he does. He also relies on his newspaper archives. Right now he's working on a story about political corruption. He tells me that in these types of stories, the same characters seem to keep cropping up."

"Ah yes, sadly, that's rampant here." Sam laughed without humor. "At least it's not as bad here in Poland as in some other former Soviet countries, though."

Adam and Sam examined each other for a few seconds, Sam with an expression of acquiescence to the political problems faced by Poland and other Eastern European countries. Adam hoped his expression was equally opaque, though he was sure Sam had had more practice at hiding his true feelings.

Someone passed by in the hall outside Sam's office, and Adam listened as the footsteps approached then faded away again without a pause. The air in this building was warm and dry, and Adam could feel a warm breeze blowing against his ankles from a hidden vent. This was the first building Adam had been to in Poland that didn't rely on steam radiators for heat. How American.

Sam coughed, as if somehow acknowledging the dry

air Adam had been pondering, and looked back down at his files.

"Poland is a great ally of the United States. And an important one, strategically. There are a lot of changes in this part of the world, Detective Kaminski, and it's important to us to have an ally we can count on." He looked up at Adam. "That's why you're here, you know, you and your team. To strengthen the bonds between our countries. I hope you are still working on that?"

Adam nodded. "As you said, family ties can help strengthen that bond. Make our relationship with Poland that much more secure."

"Of course, I did say that." Sam smiled and started running his fingers through his files once again as he spoke. "There are some members of the Polish government who believe we, the US, are their best friends. Their saviors, even. And then there are others who are not as enthralled with us."

Adam thought of some of the comments he had heard yesterday at the *Sejm*. "Yes, I see what you mean. Are we willing to use those who support our relationship, at any cost, regardless of who they are or what else they might be doing?"

Sam shrugged and raised his eyebrows. "Of course not. We must choose our friends carefully. Very carefully. Weighing the pros and cons, you know. Before we decide who we will work with and who we cannot. We must go into any political relationship with our eyes wide open."

"And do you believe you have all the information you need?" Adam asked directly.

"For now, yes." Sam smiled confidently at Adam. "We know who our friends are. We know who we can trust to support US interests — even if we can't trust them in other ways. As long as we know this, we can manage the relationship. And it's an important relationship. I can't stress this enough, Detective Kaminski. We can't support any activity that would jeopardize it, you understand."

"I understand what you're saying," Adam answered. "Can you help me get access to the archives?"

"I can, yes." Sam returned to his files. After a few seconds he stood. "I don't seem to have the right application forms here. I thought I did. Please excuse me for a minute while I dig them out, will you?" He smiled engagingly as he left Adam alone in his office.

What was going on here? Sam was friendly and open, but it was clear that he — or someone in the US embassy — didn't want Adam or Łukasz digging into Basia's murder. That didn't make any sense to Adam. Political relationships were important, sure, but would his government condone murder, just to preserve a strategic relationship? Adam laughed to himself when he realized the truth behind what he was thinking, then closed his eyes and sat back to wait for Sam's return.

The embassy was quiet. Maybe most staff took Fridays off. Even the sounds from the street outside didn't make it into this protected space. This American space. Adam hadn't heard anything else in the building beyond the lone footsteps earlier. Sam's tread as he returned sounded loudly in Adam's ears and he sat up in his chair as Sam entered the office.

"Here you go." He handed Adam a form. "Fill this out, specifying what documents you want to see. There's a general list there, on the third page. You can select from that using topic and date. You'll have to come back in January for your appointment, I'm afraid." Sam smiled apologetically. "I realize that might not be what you were hoping, but it was the earliest appointment I could schedule. I did try to see if we could find time while you're still here. They have cut staffing, I've been told. Part of the economic trouble. And that only leaves so many appointments available each week."

Adam stood and took the proffered forms. "That's not a problem. Thank you, Sam. I appreciate your help, I really do. This has been a beneficial meeting for me. I've learned a lot."

The two men smiled warmly at each other as they shook hands, then Sam escorted Adam back down and out into the Warsaw street.

The sun fought valiantly against the clouds that hung low in the sky. Adam turned his face toward it as he walked, trying to absorb any bit of sunshine he could. Any warmth that would have been provided by the sun was diminished by the cold wind blowing between the stone buildings. A bus belched black, acrid smoke as it went by, and Adam coughed and turned his attention back to the street before him.

Tucking his face down into his collar, Adam headed toward the *Sejm*. He had a little more time before he had to meet up with his group for lunch, and he intended to make the most of it.

CHAPTER TWENTY-TWO

SYLVIA'S WORKSPACE was even smaller than that of her boss, Malak. Standing in the middle of the room, Adam kept his arms close by his side to avoid knocking into the file cabinets that stood to his left or the simple desk that was directly in front of him.

"Adam, it's good to see you." Sylvia smiled as Adam ducked into the office, leaning forward to move out of the way as he shut the door behind himself. "I wasn't expecting you so soon. Do you not have visits planned with the group this morning?"

As she spoke, she tucked the book she had been reading into her shoulder bag.

"Yeah, I do." He smiled back at her, truly happy to see her again. "I'm going to meet up with them in a few minutes. I just wanted to stop by and see if you'd had any luck with that favor I asked you."

"Ah, that." Sylvia frowned. "Adam, it's only been a few hours. I haven't even thought about it yet. I did tell you that it's unlikely I'll be able to help you. You understand that, right?"

"Of course, of course." Adam nodded as he looked around the tiny office.

Snapshots and newspaper cuttings were pinned to the wall, just like in the office next door. And just like those, these, too, featured Tomek Malak in various poses of success. Except that in these, Sylvia also appeared, sometimes standing next to Malak, sometimes in the background.

He turned back to Sylvia and smiled. "Then, while I wait for your answer on that, maybe you can help me in a simpler way this morning?"

"Perhaps." Sylvia stood and walked out from behind her desk.

Suddenly the office seemed even smaller than it did before as Sylvia perched on the rickety desk immediately in front of Adam. Her knees rubbed against his legs and he knew he only had to lift his arm slightly to run his hands through her loose hair.

As if reading his thoughts, she put a hand up to push her hair back behind her ear and smiled up at him. "What can I do for you?"

"Right." Adam brought his attention back to the matter at hand. "I was hoping to meet again with *Pan* Malak, Minister Kapral and Minister Novosad. They were so helpful yesterday, I thought they might have some insight to share on this problem I'm trying to solve. And I'd also like to speak with Laurienty Szopinski." At Sylvia's look of confusion, he added, "There's something about him and his relationship with Kapral. You mentioned it yourself. I just want to dig a little bit there and see what I find."

"I still don't understand what you hope to accomplish." Sylvia shook her head. "You are digging, as you say, into a problem that doesn't exist."

Adam shut his eyes and nodded, taking a deep breath. "If you don't want to be involved, I understand. I won't push you."

Adam turned to put his hand on the doorknob, then paused. Waiting. Hoping Sylvia would change her mind.

She did.

Sylvia stood and walked back around her desk, her hand brushing against Adam's arm. He tried to step back to give her space, but there was nowhere else for him to go. She didn't seem to mind the closeness.

"Just give me a moment." She leaned over the desk, her hair falling down around her face as she grabbed the phone.

Adam recognized the now familiar scent of lavender and took a deep breath, losing himself for just a moment. With a shake of his head, he frowned and turned his back to her. He wouldn't get very far in this investigation if he could be distracted so easily.

After a few short conversations in Polish, Sylvia stood. "I have made some arrangements." She smiled, adding, "And I will be able to join you for the last meeting, so I can help in your discussion with Kapral."

Adam had his doubts as to the wisdom of that, but simply nodded as he opened the door. "Then let's see what I can find out."

CHAPTER TWENTY-THREE

THE FORCE with which Malak's fist hit the desk shook the surface. A pile of files that had been stacked neatly shifted and slid away from him.

"No." Malak's eyes narrowed and he shook his head roughly. "You ask too much. My job is to protect the people of Warsaw, not expose them to your base curiosity."

Startled by the strength of the man's response, Adam tried to repeat his request more gently.

"I'm not trying to pry, I promise you, *Pan* Malak," he explained, feeling like a fool for not expecting this sort of response. "I'm interested in learning more about my own family's history. I understand these files are very sensitive and I wouldn't dream of reviewing information that did not relate to my immediate relatives."

Malak's frown softened and he dipped his head. "I appreciate that, *Pan* Kaminski, and I apologize for my outburst. The way you phrased your request sounded as if you thought these records were simply an interesting novel that you could peruse. Of course that is not the case."

Malak shook a finger at Adam as he spoke. "You must be very careful how you talk to people about the past, *Pan* Kaminski. These are treacherous waters you are wading into. You may find some sharks waiting for you there. And you may also find that people are not

124

willing to jump in and help you."

"Have you seen these files, *Pan* Malak? Do the records hold information you want to keep secret?"

"Of course! I would prefer to destroy these records. I see no benefit in keeping them there. I am pleased the courts struck down parts of the lustration laws and I hope they eliminate them altogether. They do nothing more than keep alive the resentment that too many people still hold against the past. No." Malak closed his eyes and shook his head sadly. "No, the past is done. We cannot go back, we cannot change it. But we can move forward. We must move forward. It is the only way."

Malak opened his eyes and looked directly at Adam. "I have seen these files, *Pan* Kaminski. I have not studied them in great detail, you understand, but I have had reason to review them on several occasions. Your family is not from Warsaw, I believe. Not involved in politics?"

"No, that's right. My great-grandfather came from the Poznan area. He was a teacher as well, like I was."

"I do not recognize your name, *Pan* Kaminski. I do not believe your family has anything to fear from these records." Then he added more softly, "I do understand your concern, sir. I know how hard it is to have questions and doubts, to not know for sure about the people you care about. Yes." He stood and offered a hand to Adam. "I wish you luck in searching for your family here in Poland and getting to know them. This is an admirable and understandable quest. It is important to know where you come from, in order simply to understand yourself."

Adam saw he was being excused so he stood and shook Malak's proffered hand. "And you, sir, how do you propose to move forward?"

Malak smiled. "I will do my best to ensure that Warsaw and Poland leave the past behind. There are some evil men, to be sure, and perhaps some of them are still involved in the government. I do not know. I do know that our best hope for the future is to leave the past where it belongs. And" — he raised a hand to highlight his point — "to forge stronger bonds with the West. So in that regard, I wish you and your team the best of luck. I hope the result of your visit will be a stronger relationship between Warsaw and Philadelphia."

CHAPTER TWENTY-FOUR

ADAM FOLLOWED Sylvia to the cafeteria, where she found Laurienty Szopinski. The clink of dishes and glasses carried from the lunch counter at the far end of the room, where women in aprons and head scarves served up coffee and cakes for delegates on breaks between sessions.

Szopinski sat alone at a table along one wall, looking very young as he flipped through piles of files that surrounded him on the table, light glancing off his glasses as he moved his head back and forth across the pages.

"*Pan* Szopinski," Sylvia interrupted him and he looked up. "I would like to introduce you to *Pan* Kaminski, from America."

Adam put out his hand and Szopinski stood to shake it. "A pleasure. *Bardzo mi miło.*" The plate Szopinski had pushed to the side to make room for his paperwork was empty, but traces of poppyseed and the crumbs of a heavy babka suggested Szopinski had enjoyed a *drugie śniadanie* this morning, the midmorning snack referred to as a second breakfast.

"Nice to meet you, too," Adam responded, taking a seat across from Szopinski and glancing at the paperwork that surrounded the man. "I see you're busy right now, so I won't take up too much of your time."

Szopinski frowned but sat again and looked

expectantly at Sylvia, who still stood at the side of the table. "I will not stay with you, Adam. We only have a few minutes before we must leave for your next meeting. I will wait in my office."

Adam nodded and Sylvia turned to leave, waving a few hellos to staff sitting around the large room.

"*Pan* Kaminski, I'm afraid I, too, do not have much time." Szopinski indicated the folders in front of him. "I must review all of these files before the minister's afternoon session, to provide him with a summary. I am sorry that I did not have a chance to meet with you and your group while you were here yesterday."

"Yes, I'm sorry about that, too. I must admit I was quite curious to meet you. Tell me, what exactly is your role here?" Adam smiled at Szopinski and tried to look innocently interested.

"Well, I support the minister, of course." Szopinski's brow furrowed. "I am on his staff, you see. Not an elected position. Now tell me, how is this relevant to your work here?"

Adam shook his head. "I'm just curious, that's all. Does he have a large staff? How did you manage to gain this position?"

"You ask very personal questions, *Pan* Kaminski." Szopinski smiled even as his eyes showed his displeasure. "Since you ask, I have known Kapral for many years now. I met him while I was at the university. I was involved in *Młodzy Demokraci*, the Young Democrats. I'm sure you don't know what that is."

Szopinski grinned at Adam in satisfaction, but his grin faltered when Adam nodded, "Sure, I've heard of it. It's a chance for students to get involved in politics, here and in other countries."

Szopinski's eyes flitted about the room. "Yes, that is true. I was not so lucky, however. I remained in Warsaw."

Adam nodded his understanding. "And now you work full-time for Kapral?"

Szopinski lifted his chin and frowned. "Yes. So? It is a position of much responsibility that I take seriously," Szopinski added, frowning at the files in front of him. "And it takes much time, *Pan* Kaminski, as you see. So if there is nothing else?"

"Yes, I see that." Adam ignored the question. "Tell me, I've heard of another young student who was recently hired to work here; perhaps you know her. Basia Kaminski?"

Szopinski frowned and looked down at the table. He ran a hand over his hair, then adjusted his glasses on his nose. "Yes, I knew her, of course. She was also a member of the Young Democrats. It was very sad. Very sad." He looked up at Adam. "Why do you ask about her?"

"She was a distant relative of mine. The daughter of a cousin. I only just found out about her, and about her sudden death. I was hoping you could tell me more about what happened."

"Well..." Szopinski stretched out the word, "there is not much to say. She was a very bright young woman. Great promise. But this job" — he shrugged — "it is high pressure. Very difficult, in the public eye. It is easy to make a mistake. And easy to take the work too seriously."

"And do you think that's what she did? Take her work too seriously?" Adam asked.

"I believe that's what happened, yes." Szopinski nodded, still frowning. "I know that she took her own life, and I can only imagine that that was why. I can't explain it, *Pan* Kaminski, I can't give you the answers you are looking for."

"Let me ask you another question. My interest is not only about Basia. I also want to find out what happened to her father, my cousin, Łukasz Kaminski."

Szopinski's face showed no recognition of the name.

Adam continued, "He is a journalist, you see, here in Warsaw."

"And he is missing? You are looking for him?"

"No, nothing like that. He's here, he's safe. But he has been attacked. Two times now. And I want to find out why."

The loud clatter of a pile of dishes being dropped distracted Adam for a second and drowned out Szopinski's response, so he repeated it. "And how can I help you in this search?"

"I'm not sure," Adam responded. "You seem to be in the know here. In fact, I could have sworn you knew Łukasz. Just yesterday, you helped him gain entry into the building."

Szopinski looked at Adam in confusion, then his face cleared with understanding. "Ah yes, that reporter. Of course. I did help him get into the building. I had no idea he was Basia's father." Szopinski smiled. "I only knew he was a journalist. Our guards are very strict, sometimes. That does not help our cause. No, we value openness in our politics. We want the press here, to see what we are doing. I would have done the same for any journalist trying to gain entry, you see."

Szopinski paused, looking expectantly at Adam, probably hoping Adam was about to leave him to his work.

"I just have a few more questions."

"Of course." Szopinski's mouth turned down into a tight frown.

"I'm curious to get your opinion on the ministers you know and work with. Your boss, Minister Kapral. Basia's boss, Minister Novosad. I'd also be interested in hearing your thoughts on Tomek Malak."

"Psht." Szopinski made the sound under his breath as he looked back down at the files. "Kapral. He is a busy man, yes? A powerful man. But where is he now, when someone needs to do all the work?" He gestured to the piles of files.

"You don't like him?" Adam asked, cautiously.

Szopinski looked back up at Adam and shrugged. "He

has some good ideas. So I work for him. I expect the time will come when I will be in the position of power, not him."

"And the others? Do you feel the same way about them, too?"

Szopinski took a deep breath and smiled. He had been waiting for the opportunity to share his opinion, Adam could tell. Adam knew his type — convinced he was better, smarter than the people around him. This was a man who wanted nothing more than to be asked his opinion of others. "Novosad is a Russian. He will always be a Russian. Not a Pole." Szopinski's eyes narrowed as he grinned.

"I was told he is Polish."

"As a citizen? Yes, of course. But where is his family from? Where are his roots? Think about that. Whose best interest is he working for? Well, not for much longer, I can tell you."

"Novosad is at risk of losing his position?"

"Of course. He is not a true Pole. The people know this. He switches parties because he thinks it will help him get elected again. It will not. He will lose." Szopinski smirked with satisfaction at the thought of the older man's loss.

"And Malak?" Adam pushed, knowing Szopinski had more to say.

"Malak is a good man," Szopinski surprised Adam by saying. "Simple, perhaps. He means well. He simply is not in a position to get anything done. In the future, perhaps. Many of us believe he will be the next president of Poland. I would be happy to work with him on his campaign and once he is in office. His success will be good for many of us — including your friend Sylvia."

Adam waited to see if more information was forthcoming, but Szopinski's gaze had returned to the pile of paperwork in front of him. He looked back up at Adam. "I really must return to my work now, *Pan* Kaminski."

"You're right, of course." Adam stood. "I'm sorry to have bothered you. Thank you for your time and for answering my questions."

"Of course." Szopinski did not stand and did not offer Adam his hand again. "You do not have much time left in Poland, I believe. Does your group not leave tomorrow, on Saturday?"

Adam's eyebrows went up in surprise that Szopinski was so well informed about their visit. "That's right, we are scheduled to fly out on Saturday. This was just a short visit to Warsaw, I'm afraid."

"You will have to come back another time, *Pan* Kaminski. Goodbye."

Adam nodded, then walked out of the cafeteria. Behind him, Szopinski watched the closed door for a few minutes more before shaking his head and turning back to his papers.

CHAPTER TWENTY-FIVE

"WHERE HAVE you been?" Chris' voice came out as a hiss and a few people in front of them turned to stare.

"Sorry, I went to meet up with my cousin this morning," Adam whispered back, trying to keep his voice low enough so as not to interrupt the presentation.

At the front of the narrow room, a rector of Warsaw University droned on about the increased need for a university education in this day and age. To either side of them, the other members of the delegation stood and listened, while university donors and supporters stood along the bookshelf-lined walls.

"You shouldn't just take off like that, Mr. Kaminski." Chris wouldn't let the subject drop. "I am responsible for you while we are here, and I need to know where you are at all times."

Adam saw Angela glance in their direction and felt his face grow red. As if he were a child that needed to be reprimanded.

"I was with Sylvia this morning, Chris. Isn't she also responsible for our delegation?" He raised an eyebrow at Chris, then turned back to the presenter, who seemed to be wrapping things up.

Angela grinned and looked away.

"Well... well... I suppose that's okay." Chris stumbled over the words. "But you should've let me know."

"I know." Adam patted Chris on the shoulder as the speaker finished his presentation and the rest of the audience offered a light applause. "I will next time, I promise."

"Wait, what next time?"

But Adam was already stepping to the side to catch the attention of Minister Kapral, who stood against a tall oak bookshelf near a closed door. Sylvia saw Adam's movements and approached Kapral from the other side of the room.

Sylvia reached him first, leaning over and saying something into his ear. Kapral nodded as he glanced around the room, his eye landing on Adam. He raised his chin to Adam, as if in invitation, then turned and stepped through the doorway, leaving the door ajar behind him.

Approaching the open door, Adam glanced back to see Angela watching him once again. He grinned and winked at her, then entered the small office, pulling the door shut firmly behind him.

Kapral already sat in one of the chairs around an oval table that took up most of the cozy study room.

"Minister," he started as soon as he walked into the room, "I am sorry to pull you out of the presentation."

Kapral smiled his toothpaste commercial smile and stood to shake Adam's hand. "Not at all, it is a pleasure to see you and *Pani* Stanko again so soon." He indicated the chairs around the table, and they all sat. "I'm sorry I was not available to see you earlier this morning. I understand you were at the *Sejm* looking for me."

"Not a problem, sir." Adam paused before adding, "I spent the time chatting with Laurienty Szopinski. A very interesting young man."

This time Adam kept his eyes on Kapral as he spoke and once again he saw the flash of annoyance cross Kapral's face. Not just annoyance, he realized, anger. Deeply held anger.

"You should not talk to my staff without my

permission, *Pan* Kaminski." He turned to Sylvia. "*Pani* Stanko, you should know this."

"I am very sorry, Minister Kapral," Sylvia said with surprise. "You are correct, of course, I will not do that again."

Kapral paused a moment. Adam recognized the all-too-familiar signs of someone trying to get his anger under control. With a nod, he turned back to Adam. "Now, what can I do for you?"

"To be honest, I believe there is something I can do for you. I believe there is someone working here, in your government, who is a criminal. He — or she — has been involved in some sort of corruption and he killed a young woman to cover it up. Now that a journalist has found the truth, this person is trying to kill him to keep the secret."

Kapral stared at Adam in silence, his fingers tightening their grip on the arms of his chair.

Adam continued, "My cousin, the journalist, found proof, you see. He's not getting help from the police, so I offered to help him — to protect him and to catch the criminal responsible."

Kapral finally spoke. "This is quite a tale you have, *Pan* Kaminski. Something more out of fiction than real life, I think." He looked to Sylvia, but she simply shrugged and said nothing.

Adam responded, "It is true, I assure you."

"And what is this proof your cousin has?"

"I can't share that with you right now, minister, I'm sorry. As soon as I can, I will bring it to you."

Kapral nodded slowly, digesting the information. "There is corruption all around us. This is politics, after all. Whether it is individuals trying to make their own money in the new capitalist system, or those who were collaborators and now trying to work in the government. That is no surprise. We all know this. This is why we have the courts. Someone willing to hurt someone else to keep this secret... that is more than I have seen

135

before, *Pan* Kaminski. If you are certain this is true, how can I help you?"

Adam considered his words carefully. This was not a formal investigation, not on his part, anyway. But he didn't have the luxury of time. He was scheduled to leave Poland the next day. He knew the only way he was going to find anything was by pushing. Even if that meant making enemies.

"Tell me about your relationship with Laurienty Szopinski."

Kapral froze, his face a mask. For a full minute, no one spoke. Sylvia shuffled uncomfortably in her seat, but kept her silence. Adam sat as still as Kapral. He had played this game before.

Finally, Kapral spoke. "I repeat, how can I help you, *Pan* Kaminski? Aside from satisfying your prurient and inappropriate curiosity, that is."

Adam nodded. "Tell me what you know about your colleagues' past, then." After a beat, he added, "Minister."

"That is a very broad question, *Pan* Kaminski. Is there someone in particular you are interested in?"

"Everyone who worked with Basia Kaminski. Novosad. Szopinski. You." Adam raised his eyebrows as he spoke, but Kapral didn't bite.

"Basia worked with many, many people here, my friend." He smiled as if he and Adam really were close friends. "Including *Pani* Stanko, for example." He turned his engaging smile to Sylvia.

Sylvia smiled and dipped her head.

"She met with a variety of committees, many staff of many ministers. I couldn't possibly provide you with all of the background on all of these people," Kapral explained, staring at Adam. "I see what you are asking, though. This corruption you mentioned a moment ago. You believe this was in the past. Something long forgotten, perhaps."

Adam nodded but said nothing.

Kapral took a breath and glanced around the study room as he continued, "This is a difficult challenge for you, *Pan* Kaminski. You do not know our country and our history. How do you possibly hope to uncover something that has been hidden for... what... many years, perhaps?"

"Perhaps. I am not working on it alone. Łukasz Kaminski, my cousin, is a reporter with *Nowy Początek*."

"Ah... Yes, I know this paper. I know the editor slightly."

"Perhaps you can help me in this way. Łukasz needs his editor to write a letter providing him access to the national archives one more time. Including the files on lustration, if that's what he needs. He was able to do this before, so I'm sure he can do it again."

"And why does *Pan* Kaminski require this access again, if he already has the evidence?" Kapral asked, raising his eyebrows. "Is this a... what do you say in America, a fishing expedition?" Kapral's eyes met Adam's squarely, and he could tell Kapral was holding in a smile. Barely.

"There's more to this story, I'm sure of it. Just one more day in those records and we can have all the evidence we need."

"I shall help you, *Pan* Kaminski. There is no need to go through the editor. I can write such a letter of permission myself. I will provide it to your cousin through Sylvia."

"Thank you, sir." Adam didn't hide his surprise. "And thank you again for your time."

"Will this be the last time I see you, *Pan* Kaminski?" Kapral asked, standing.

"My team is scheduled to leave Poland tomorrow, sir, so this may well be our last meeting."

"I wish you success, *Pan* Kaminski." Kapral's smile was cold. Satisfied.

CHAPTER TWENTY-SIX

AS SOON AS Łukasz heard the elevator bell followed by the tread of unfamiliar footsteps, he swept the notes he had been writing into the top drawer of his desk. Tomek Malak had called earlier that morning to request this meeting. An unusual request, but not one Łukasz was likely to refuse.

The utilitarian clock on the wall clicked over to noon just as Malak stepped into the doorway, tapping politely on the open door. At least the man was prompt, Łukasz thought to himself as he waved Malak in.

"*Pan* Kaminski, thank you for agreeing to meet with me. May I offer my condolences on your loss. Basia was a beautiful young woman. I can only imagine how distressed you are."

He extended his hand as he spoke, and the two men exchanged a firm handshake.

"Thank you, sir." Łukasz was almost getting used to accepting these meaningless condolences, words of sorrow that meant nothing, in truth, to the speaker. Almost. "Please, have a seat."

"Ah…" Malak glanced uncomfortably at the open door. "May I?"

He moved to close the door as he spoke. Łukasz nodded his approval, wondering what could be so secret about this meeting. The sounds of the newsroom diminished to a low murmur that could still be heard within the office.

As both men sat on either side of Łukasz's scarred wooden desk, Łukasz said, "If you have information on a story you think I might be interested in, I would have been happy to come to your offices, sir. There was no reason for you to make the journey to this part of town."

"Yes, yes, I know." Malak waved away Łukasz's suggestion. "It is sometimes good for me to get out of the office, you know?" He smiled as he spoke, a friendly, genuine smile. "But that is not exactly what I wanted to speak with you about."

Malak paused, glancing around the room. At the crowded bookshelves that lined one wall, at the pile of papers pushed into one corner on the floor, finally at the framed photograph sitting on Łukasz's desk. He looked back at Łukasz. "I believe I know someone in your family. A cousin, perhaps?"

"Adam Kaminski, you mean? Yes. I only just met him myself. He's in Poland on some sort of diplomatic mission. Representing the city of Philadelphia." Łukasz looked at Malak with curiosity. "Is that why you are here? Because of Adam?"

"No, no." Malak once again waved away the suggestion. "No, I was simply mentioning it." Malak looked directly at Łukasz, staring almost. "*Pan* Kaminski, I have come to speak with you because I am considering running for the office of President of the Republic of Poland."

Łukasz's chair creaked as he leaned back, his fingers laced over his chest. "So, the rumors are true?"

Malak nodded. "Yes, they are true. My party, the Civic Platform, has invited me to run for office on their ticket, and I have accepted their invitation."

Łukasz sat for a minute, considering this information. "So the mild-mannered civil servant becomes a hot presidential candidate." He smiled. "Why do you come to me with this news? Surely there are other journalists you would rather have breaking this story?"

"It's not the story I came to talk with you about," Malak explained. "I'm here to ask for your help."

Łukasz leaned forward again, his interest piqued. "Help? How could I possibly help you?"

Malak, too, leaned forward as he spoke. He answered slowly, as if considering each word. "In a political campaign — in any political campaign, really, and particularly in one with such high stakes — information is king. You must realize that?"

"I've heard something like that, yes." Łukasz grinned, acknowledging his understatement.

"I need access to information. Real information. Not data that is corrupt by being biased. I need someone I can turn to who knows the political scene in Poland, but who is not part of that scene. An outsider with insider knowledge." He paused, examining Łukasz. "You fit that description, *Pan* Kaminski."

"I see." Łukasz's expression didn't change. He once again leaned back in his chair. The clocked ticked off the seconds as he thought about what Malak had asked.

Malak sat still, leaning in toward Łukasz's desk, waiting for Łukasz's response.

Neither man moved when a light tap on the door interrupted the silence. "Kaminski? Latest numbers," a voice announced from the other room, then a paper slid under the door.

It sat there in the middle of the floor, ignored.

"Everyone has skeletons in their closet, as they say, *Pan* Malak. Is that what you are thinking of?"

"Something like that." Malak smiled, letting out a breath. "I am hoping I can count on you, *Pan* Kaminski. Will you help me by sharing information? If there is something that would help me in my campaign. Or" — he paused and cocked his head to one side — "if there is some information out there that would hurt me."

Łukasz raised his eyebrows. "Are you thinking of anything in particular, *Pan* Malak? Is there information out there that, if revealed, could hurt your campaign?"

"Of course not. Why would you ask that?" Malak shook his head, frowning, as he stood up. He stepped toward the door, turning his back on Łukasz.

Łukasz wondered if his question had offended Malak so greatly he was walking out of the meeting, but at the door Malak simply rested his hand against the door jamb, as if testing to make sure it was fully closed. He turned back to Łukasz.

"There may be people — even within my own party — whom I cannot trust, *Pan* Kaminski," Malak said in a low voice. "I am turning to you for help because of your status as a journalist. As a neutral party, outside the political fray."

Malak's eyes moved about Łukasz's office as he spoke, as if expecting to find the very people he was worried about hidden somewhere behind a bookshelf or under a table.

"Who do you not trust, *Pan* Malak?" Łukasz kept his voice calm, conversational, but his mind was spinning. Was Malak aware of a secret? Perhaps the same secret that took Basia's life?

"What?" Malak turned back to Łukasz as if he had been slapped back to reality. "Who? No, no. Nothing like that. I just say there may be, because there always is, isn't there? Moles within each organization, willing to dole out secrets for the right price." Malak smiled, his mood once again shifting.

"Political secrets, you mean? Like campaign strategies?"

"Exactly." Malak snapped his fingers. "Like campaign secrets. And it could be anyone, you see. My colleagues, my friends. *Pani* Stanko, for example."

"Sylvia?" Łukasz couldn't keep the surprise out of his voice and he saw Malak's eyes widen ever so slightly.

"Sylvia, yes. You know her?"

"Only slightly." Łukasz shook his head. "I met her when I met my cousin. Just the other day."

"Ah, I see. Your cousin." Malak nodded. "Yes, Sylvia, for example."

"If you don't trust her, why are you keeping her so close to your campaign?" Łukasz asked, confused.

"Not that I really think she would sell me out, you understand." Malak held his hands out toward Łukasz as if trying to stop his thoughts from moving down that path. "Not at all. I'm just using her as an example. Someone I work closely with. Someone I trust."

Malak resumed his seat in front of Łukasz's desk. "It could be unintentional as well, you know. Perhaps something hidden in her past that could hurt my campaign. She is tied very closely to me. And if I win, I intend to keep her on my staff. But what if she has a secret that could hurt my chances of success? Or anyone else on my staff, not just Sylvia."

Łukasz knew what Malak was asking, and why. Malak was right. In a political campaign, secrets really could win elections or lose them. He also knew how he had to respond.

"I'm flattered you came to me with this request, *Pan* Malak. I can see it reflects your perception of my work. I regret to say I cannot offer you the help you are asking for. I am sorry."

"Your reputation is stellar, *Pan* Kaminski. You are an excellent investigative journalist."

"And I am not yet ready to give that up, *Pan* Malak. You must understand." Łukasz spoke firmly. "Offering you the help you seek would mean the end of this career."

"No, not at all." Malak frowned and shook his head. "I could hire you as a consultant. It would all be above board. Nothing illicit, I assure you. And it would only be temporary. Only until the election's over."

"It would be forever, I'm afraid." Łukasz shook his

head. "If I associated myself with you and your party, I would lose all appearance of objectivity. I could never get that back. I could never again publish as an objective investigative journalist."

Malak looked down at Łukasz's desk, his eyes tracing the pattern of the scars that ran across it. After a moment, he nodded. "I see. I have my answer."

He slapped his hands onto his legs as he stood, nodding and looking once more around Łukasz's office. Turning back to Łukasz, who had also stood, Malak extended his hand again.

"I appreciate you taking the time to meet with me, *Pan* Kaminski, and for considering my offer. It's still there, you know, if you change your mind." He smiled.

"Thank you, *Pan* Malak. But I will not be changing my mind."

Malak nodded once more, then turned and left the room.

The door bounced against the wall as Malak left it open, the clattering sounds of the newsroom once again swarming into the office.

Łukasz shook his head as he lowered himself back into his chair. Malak must have known he would turn down the request. He must have. Why would any self-respecting journalist agree to work for a political campaign, openly or otherwise?

There must have been more to that meeting. Something Malak wanted to ask and didn't, perhaps. Or information Malak was hoping to glean from Łukasz.

Łukasz thought back through their conversation, but he couldn't figure it out. What was Malak after?

CHAPTER TWENTY-SEVEN

ADAM KNEW he was in the right place when he saw the crowd gathering on the sidewalk in front of the square glass building. Sylvia had given him the address, but even so, finding the place had been tough. After two buses and a four-block walk, Adam was getting to know his way around Warsaw better than he'd ever expected.

It hadn't been easy sneaking away again. After the hard time Chris had given him that morning, he didn't want to admit he was playing hooky again. Instead, he'd told Chris he just needed to run back to the hotel for a few minutes and would meet up with the group at their next destination.

It was sort of true. He did plan to meet up with them again.

The ribbon cutting event at the new green postal facility served not only to show off the environmentally friendly work of the Warsaw government, but also to highlight the accomplishments of the small business that had created the updated electrical system.

Adam knew Malak had been involved in ensuring the business had the permits it needed to work, so he was surprised when Sylvia told him Novosad would be at the event. Perhaps Malak wasn't the sort of man who needed to get credit for his accomplishments.

Adam scanned the crowd of reporters, businessmen,

politicians and onlookers as the various speakers stepped up to the podium. After the final speaker, a group of leaders, including Minister Novosad, came forward to place their hands on the giant pair of scissors, "cutting" the ribbon that had been placed artfully in front of the main entrance to the building. The ribbon fell away to a smattering of applause.

Once all the photos had been taken and the crowd started to move into the building, Adam approached Novosad, the man deemed by so many to still be a Russian at heart. He was older than the other men Adam had met with that morning. But his eyes were shrewd and Adam didn't doubt this man had a few more years of politics still left in him. As long as Szopinski was wrong about his election chances.

"Minister, can I ask you a few questions?"

"Of course." Novosad seemed surprised by Adam's words. "Are you with an English-language newspaper?"

"Sorry, no." Adam understood the confusion now. "No, this isn't about this event. I'm Adam Kaminski. We met briefly yesterday. I'm with the delegation from Philadelphia."

"Ah, of course." The older man nodded, recognition dawning in his eyes. "I apologize, I didn't recognize you." He looked around as he asked, "And is the rest of the delegation here?"

"No, sir, it's just me today." Adam tried out his most engaging smile. "I was hoping to ask you a few questions about Basia Kaminski." When Novosad's confusion returned, Adam added, "She was the daughter of my cousin."

"I see, I see." Novosad looked around. A group still lingered outside the facility. One of the men looked in their direction, tentatively waving toward them. Novosad nodded for Adam to follow and turned to walk away.

They stopped just around the corner, out of sight of the others. Novosad glanced around one more time before turning his attention to Adam.

"How can I help you today?"

Adam started with a few easy questions. Feeling his way into the conversation by asking about Novosad's work in the *Sejm*.

When he turned to the topic of Basia's death, Novosad answered slowly, as if considering every word he said. And every word Adam said.

"It was suicide." Novosad nodded sadly. "Of that, I have no doubt. I understand that you are her... what, uncle?"

"Something like that."

"Yes, I see. I understand how difficult it is when a young person dies. Needlessly. Tragically. I do understand."

Listening to him, Adam knew Novosad spoke the truth; he did understand. "What was Basia working on while she worked for you?" he asked.

"Oh, this and that." Novosad's response was vague. "She had no specific portfolio, you see. She was relatively new to my staff. So she was helping others as the need arose."

Adam nodded as he listened. Novosad's thick gray hair surrounded a weathered face that had seen many changes over the years. The face of a man who had learned to adapt to change, not fight it. The best way to outlast your competitors.

"Politics is a fickle field. It is not a good field for those who might be easily overwhelmed."

"You yourself changed parties, I understand?" Adam asked. "Quite a change, too, as I've heard."

"It is true," Novosad admitted. "I shifted my political allegiance when my understanding of the world — and Poland's place in it — shifted. But I have never shifted my allegiance from Poland. I am now and have always been a patriot, *Pan* Kaminski. It is simply that I am able to learn from our past. To learn from our mistakes and to move forward."

Adam considered Novosad's words. The man had shifted his allegiance from the post-communist party, SLD, to the Civic Platform. This was an extreme change. A change in methods, a change in goals. A change in friends. A change that drastic could generate a lot of resentment, on either side. On the other hand, Novosad had a good explanation for his decision. There was nothing wrong in learning from the past, was there?

Adam put his thoughts into words, saying, "The past is one of the things I am interested in, minister. May I ask you about your past?"

"As I said, I have learned from my past. I have taken action to move forward, not backward."

"Many people say that you maintain strong connections with Russia. That you are more Russian than Polish, in fact."

Novosad smiled grimly. "Many people say many things, *Pan* Kaminski. I do not bother myself with what many people say, only what I know to be true. I move forward, not backward."

"My cousin believes — and I agree — that something in the past, something long since buried, came back to the surface recently. Perhaps Basia learned of that thing. And in the end that knowledge is what killed her."

"Perhaps, perhaps." Novosad shrugged. Then his expression sharpened and he looked carefully at Adam. "Do you speak metaphorically, young man, or literally? For I believe that the sins of our forefathers are great, and knowledge of those sins could lead a person to suicide. I tell you again, Basia committed suicide. No one did it for her. No ghost from the past, certainly."

"A ghost? No. Something real? Yes. I have requested access to the national archives, minister. I intend to follow the footsteps of my cousin, and perhaps of his daughter, to retrace their investigation until it leads me to the truth. The truth of what happened to Basia."

"You shouldn't do that, *Pan* Kaminski." Novosad

shook his head. "Don't go looking into the past. You do not know how strongly people feel about the past or about the changes that are coming."

CHAPTER TWENTY-EIGHT

THE *ALEJE EMILII PLATER* was familiar to Adam and his team. Their visit to Warsaw had started here, at the Central Train Station. The train station was an expanse of concrete and pavement, a low, flat structure of even lower architectural interest surrounded by openness and emptiness. It stood as a reminder of what had been.

Not the most noticeable reminder.

Just north of the train station and across *Emilii Plater* towered the Palace of Culture, Warsaw's most visible and most symbolic relic of the Soviet era. Its mud-brown stone walls reached to the sky in a futile effort to demonstrate the strength and power of the Soviet government. Giant carved statues of farmers and laborers, men and women, glared down pridefully from their perches along the wall.

It didn't take long to realize, however, that *Emilii Plater*, like Warsaw itself, had a split personality. The heart of the Warsaw business district started only a short walk from the train station. Shining glass and steel towers brazenly defied the former socialist order. Shocks of sunlight glinting off the surfaces reflected onto the sea of cranes below as Warszawians set to work busily building their city as a capitalist center.

Skyscrapers reaching toward the heavens cast shadows on the alleys below, blocking out low gray reminders of the previous regime. Blocked from light, but not from memory. For more was hidden than seen in Warsaw — the danger of any split personality.

The team's first meeting of the afternoon was within one of these steel towers. Members of the team all nodded appreciatively and smiled at the view shared with them by the president of one of the first independent banks to open in Warsaw after the Soviet era. A rotund man with a glistening bald head, the president smiled manically at each new vista as he walked them around the four corners of the floor his offices held on the fourteenth level of the skyscraper.

Adam expressed his appreciation of the view and the modern offices with the others, though he stayed a safe distance away from the windows. He couldn't get his mind off Łukasz and his troubles. After listening to the merits of the Polish banking system for thirty minutes, he realized he hadn't really heard a thing.

As the group passed from one office to the next, Adam grabbed Angela's arm and pulled her aside.

"Listen," he said quietly as the rest of the group continued on to the next level down. "I need to break away for a little while."

"Again?" Angela raised her eyebrows. "You missed so much already today. I'm just glad you made it for lunch. The president here would have been really disappointed if we hadn't all enjoyed his hospitality. What have you been doing with yourself?"

"It's my cousin," Adam explained.

"Right, your cousin." Angela looked skeptical. "The one you just met, barely know, and have been running around Warsaw with night and day." She looked Adam up and down. "And this isn't about our friendly *Pani* Stanko, is it?"

"Sylvia? No, of course not, it's about Łukasz. He's gotten himself into a little bit of trouble, and he needs my help right now."

"What kind of trouble, Adam? Are you going to end

up in trouble yourself?"

"Not at all, of course not. He's a journalist and he just needs some help getting the information he needs for his story. Given our role here, I'm in a position to be able to help, so I am." Angela looked worried and Adam felt a pang of guilt for not telling her the whole truth. "I'm doing the right thing."

"The right thing for him or for you? You're supposed to be working while we're here, you know? Making your department look good? You shouldn't be distracted like this. Or putting yourself in risky situations."

"Don't worry, it's nothing big. I'm just trying to find the right people who can help him."

Angela stood for a moment and stared at him. He could only guess what was going through her mind, but finally she let out a breath and adjusted her glasses on her nose. "Fine. I guess we all need help sometime."

Adam watched her go with a smile, then turned to the elevator bank at the other end of the hallway. As he turned the corner, he heard Angela's voice carrying over the others.

"*Pan President*, I must extend the sincere apologies of my colleague, *Pan* Kaminski. I'm afraid a family emergency has drawn him away urgently. I know he is very disappointed not to be able to stay for the rest of our tour here."

Adam grinned to himself as her voice faded as the group moved farther away, and offered Angela a silent nod of appreciation.

The sky was clear but the light was nevertheless gray as Adam stepped out onto *Emilii Plater*. Turning to his left, he saw the great Palace of Culture looming ahead. He thought of a joke a university student had told his group during one of their first meetings in Warsaw. From where does one get the best view of Warsaw? From the Palace of Culture. Why? Because from there, you can't see the Palace of Culture.

The view from the Palace of Culture these days was

quite different from when it had first been built. Now gleaming fortresses of business and capitalism slowly encroached on the grand concrete plaza surrounding the palace.

As he approached the area, Adam saw the giant skyscrapers weren't the only sites of capitalism in the space. Within the plaza itself, a makeshift market was set up. Under a tin roof, rows of rickety wooden stalls formed narrow aisles around which shoppers moved, searching for cheap clothes, home goods or electronics. The heavy scent of kielbasa and sauerkraut in the air suggested a food vendor was tucked away in one of the aisles. Stall after stall sold everything from watches to winter coats to books and music. Adam wondered how many of these goods were being sold legally. Probably none.

Pausing to look through a pile of used books in one stall, Adam caught a movement out of the corner of his eye. Turning to see what had attracted his attention, he saw only an old woman, bundled against the cold, digging her way through a pile of woolen sweaters in the next booth over. Seeing him look at her, she smiled uneasily and nodded, then returned to her search.

Adam laughed at himself and moved on to the next stall. Wherever he looked, he saw only buyers and sellers, residents of Warsaw trying to make a living or live on the small income they had. Bartering was rampant and young men moved about between the stalls, keeping an eye on their goods and perhaps keeping an eye out for any police. Though law enforcement was not evident.

Yet he couldn't shake the feeling of being watched. And he couldn't afford to ignore it. He had intentionally attacked his suspects that morning, pushing hard to see if any of them cracked. It was a tried and true technique, and Adam knew results weren't always immediate. Sometimes the criminal mind had to wallow for a few hours before responding to a challenge.

Moving quickly, Adam stepped into a narrow gap between two stalls. Walking behind the booths, he backtracked until he found another passage to the main aisle, this time earning what were probably some fairly crass words from an old woman manning the booth. Apologizing quietly, Adam stepped carefully back out into the aisle. No one noticed him, no one called out.

Walking up the aisle, following the same path he had just taken, Adam watched the people around him carefully, looking for any sign that one of them was paying him more attention than the others. A man in a dark jacket caught his eye, then turned away. A young woman in a trendy woolen coat dropped her handbag and looked at Adam as she bent to pick it up.

This was getting him nowhere. He was just paranoid. Turning to retrace his steps back to the tram and his hotel, Adam caught a glimpse of a man ducking between the stalls. Jogging to catch up, Adam pushed through the same gap, and once again only caught a glimpse of the man's back as he ran up the narrow path between the backs of the stalls. Moving to follow him, Adam felt a heavy arm push against his chest.

"*Nie można go tutaj, proszę pana.*" A large elderly man stood in his path. "This is not for visitors, only vendors." The man's lined face was set like stone, and he took a step forward as he crossed his arms over his chest. Adam contemplated pushing past the man, then noticed the two younger men approaching from either side. There was no way he was getting behind the booths again.

"Damn!" Adam spun and ran back out to the main path, but he hadn't seen enough of his pursuer to know what he looked like. He had only caught a glimpse of what looked like black jeans, black shoes and a dark leather coat. That description fit half the shoppers in this marketplace.

ADAM DROPPED THE JOURNAL back onto the coffee table and sniffed the air. A musty odor, of old books and wool sweaters. Not what he expected in the apartment of a young woman like Basia Kaminski. He turned his back to the bookshelf, ignoring the dead plant that sat, leafless, on top.

Łukasz had been happy to give Adam the key to Basia's apartment. He was looking for anything that would help him get a better sense of who Basia was. And why she might have been killed.

He stood and stared at the apartment around him. Every possible storage space was used, every corner had something tucked into it. Clothes folded neatly and tucked inside a chest that worked as a coffee table. Extra blankets piled under the sofa. Baking pans stacked upright between the fridge and bookshelf.

He dug through stacks of books and notebooks, poked between neatly hung dresses and trousers, rummaged through kitchen cabinets. But so far, he'd found nothing to justify the intrusion.

He knew she had taken care of her possessions, repairing rather than replacing items that were worn or damaged.

Basia must have liked to cook. The kitchen cabinet was stocked with jars of herbs and spices, from curry powder to Italian seasonings, cayenne pepper and teriyaki sauce. They were small jars and nothing was duplicated. Each kept clean and neat, some almost empty but waiting to exhale the last of their contents.

Piles of books, stacked high on the shelf and against one wall, suggested that reading was her other passion. He ran his finger along the spines of books, flipped through handwritten notebooks, shook out magazines and journals. But nothing slipped out.

Adam took a deep breath and focused. There must be something here. Now he knew more about Basia, not only what she liked to do but how she liked her world — neat, organized, simple. The apartment was so small everything fell under his glance. He let his eyes roam over the space in front of him.

Closing his eyes, he took another breath. Stretched his shoulders. Opened his eyes and looked again.

Someone passed by in the hallway outside the front door, but Adam ignored the footsteps.

There. In the kitchen. Two cookbooks stood upright on the counter leaning against a cabinet. Just where they should be. But between them, sheets of paper.

Adam took the two steps that brought him into the kitchen. A few pieces of paper, folded in half, were tucked between the books. Adam's Polish wasn't strong enough for him to read the typewritten pages, but they looked familiar to him. He recognized the standard format of cover letters and resumes.

Skimming the papers, he saw a few names he didn't recognize. A few more that he did. Kapral. Szopinski. Why would Basia have access to other people's job applications, if these were in fact applications?

There could be good reason for it, Adam knew. She might have been helping fill another internship, seeking out the most qualified applicants.

He folded the papers again, shaking his head and frowning. No. If these were innocent, they wouldn't have been hidden in the kitchen. Basia was too organized for that.

Turning back to the living room, he glanced one more time through the notebooks and books that sat on the coffee table and the bookshelf. Grabbing them up, he tucked them, along with the papers, under his arm.

Łukasz would be able to read these, to figure out their significance. But whatever he found, Adam knew it would tie back to Kapral. A man with something to hide. Something Basia must have exposed.

Adam pulled the apartment door shut behind him and listened to the lock catch. This was his last evening in Warsaw, and all he had done was rattle a few cages, dig up a few lost papers. Łukasz would be disappointed, no doubt.

Even as he tried to convince himself he had done all he could, he frowned at the thought of leaving Warsaw without identifying the killer.

CHAPTER TWENTY-NINE

EARLY SATURDAY MORNING, the small van waited in the drive of the Newport Hotel. The day was surprisingly sunny, given the recent weather, though still bitterly cold.

Stepping out into the brisk light, Angela raised her hand to shade her eyes and took one last look at the city around her. Shrugging her shoulders slightly, she stepped into the van where the other members of the team were already waiting.

The streets of Warsaw were crowded, as they always were on All Saints' Day. Some city streets were closed for processions and parades, which meant heavier traffic on the streets that remained open.

All Saints' Day brought out not only city residents but also visitors from around the country, who came to Warsaw to see the famous cemeteries within its boundaries. *Powązki* Cemetery held the remains of some of Poland's greatest figures while *Okopowa* bore memorials to the millions who had been killed on Polish land.

The van made its way slowly through the city streets, winding its way to the airport on the outskirts of town. The driver cautiously navigated the busy streets, weaving through traffic as cars pulled over to let passengers disembark or stopped suddenly to avoid hitting one of the many pedestrians that swarmed over the sidewalks and sometimes out into the streets.

The driver stopped at a red light and glanced in his side view mirror. A black sedan had pulled up next to him, which meant nothing, until he noticed a second, similar vehicle pull up a little too close on the other side as well.

The attack took less than three minutes.

A man dressed in black with a balaclava pulled low over his face jumped out of one of the sedans and reached for the van door. The driver tried to drive forward, but he couldn't maneuver the van around the second car.

The man moved swiftly, professionally. The doors flew open, the man pushed his way violently inside. Witnesses heard the screams, but stood rooted to the ground in fear. In the blink of an eye, the man was back out of the van and in his sedan. Both cars screeched into motion, blowing through the still-red light, forcing other cars off the road.

Within minutes, sirens could be heard approaching the scene. Three police cars surrounded the van, which now sat still and silent at the intersection. An ambulance approached with a little more caution and stopped a few cars back.

By now, a crowd of people stood on the sidewalks and pushed out into the street near the van. Harsh whispers filled the air as people described to each other what they had seen and heard, and what they had not seen.

As the police approached the van slowly, the doors opened once again. The police halted their progress, weapons drawn. Angela stumbled out of the van, her glasses hanging awkwardly from her face, her coat covered in blood. She gasped and fell onto the pavement.

The police and medics jumped into action. One moved forward to support Angela, leading her carefully back to the waiting ambulance. More moved into the van to offer what help they could to the other passengers.

Leaning heavily on the arm of the technician, Angela shook her head. "No, no, I'm all right, I wasn't hurt, just pushed a little. But... he's dead... he's dead."

"Who's dead, *Pani*, what happened?" the young man asked fearfully in English, carefully wrapping a warm blanket around Angela's shoulders and offering her a drink from a steaming thermos. "What happened to you?"

"It was an attack. They were there specifically to kill him. It doesn't make sense... why him?" She started to sob softly, and the technician looked away, back at the van where other passengers were being led away.

The last two police to leave the van stepped slowly down and shook their heads at their commanding officer. "One dead."

Their words carried to the technician, who unconsciously pulled Angela's blanket tighter around her shoulders, as if to protect her from the words. Words she couldn't translate.

"Who is it, what can you tell me?" the senior officer asked.

"American man, reddish-brown hair, tall, more than six feet."

"How was he killed, was it an accident?"

"No accident, he was stabbed in the heart. One stab, strong and sure. The killer took the knife."

"Okay." The commander looked around at the gathering crowd. "We need to start taking statements, talk to all these people. Someone must have seen the attackers, seen the cars they came in. We need a witness who can tell us what he saw."

The police moved off to start their investigation as two medical technicians stepped out of the van. Between them they held a stretcher, the form of a large man on the stretcher fully covered.

Angela gasped and put hand over her mouth. "It doesn't make sense," she said again, "Why him?"

CHAPTER THIRTY

THE BREAKING NEWS story interrupted the regular BBC broadcast in the hotel dining room where guests were eating breakfast. Some sort of attack had taken place on the streets of Warsaw not too far out of the center of town.

Adam put his fork down as he recognized the van in the pictures. When he saw Angela sitting in the ambulance, he rose from his seat and walked closer to the television.

"Can you turn this up?" He gestured to a waitress. "Is there volume?"

She nodded and reached over to adjust the set.

Adam stood transfixed, watching the scene as his friends and colleagues were taken one by one into ambulances and driven from the scene.

All but one of them. All but Jared.

"No," Adam said aloud to the startled diners, "no that's not right. That should be me."

If he hadn't received a note from Łukasz last night, urging him to stay in Warsaw a few more days, he would have been in that van with the rest of them. And there was no doubt in his mind he was the intended victim of that attack.

Adam crumpled, leaning against a table for support, the empty dishes on its surface rattling under the pressure. It had been so easy to change his plans. A quick call to the airline's Warsaw office was all it took to delay his flight by a few days. He had plenty of vacation days to use.

He had spent the evening with his team, watching out for them, keeping them safe — or so he thought.

He was scheduled to meet Łukasz that afternoon in the Polish Army Field Cathedral, on the corner of *Ulica Miodowa*. He had to get to the hospital first. He brushed past another waitress as he ran for the door.

CHAPTER THIRTY-ONE

NOVOSAD'S WEATHERED face and bushy white hair stood out through the dark glass. Even before he stepped into the vestibule, Adam recognized the man walking toward him out of the hospital.

Adam stopped in the narrow entranceway, but Novosad didn't seem to recognize him.

Adam cleared his throat. "Minister Novosad."

"What?" Novosad looked up, his expression distracted. Distant. "Oh, yes?"

"Adam Kaminski, we've met a couple of times. I'm on the delegation from Philadelphia." He paused, watching as Novosad first recognized him, then frowned.

"*Pan* Kaminski. Terrible, this. Terrible."

"I'm glad you're here. Perhaps you've heard something about what really happened?"

"Me? No, no." Novosad's right hand seemed to tremble and he pushed it into the pocket of his coat. "No. Young Laurienty is inside. Perhaps he can help you."

Novosad turned away, walking out the sliding glass doors to a car parked in the curved drive.

Adam watched him go, then stepped into the hospital. Just ahead he could see the admittance desk, the best place for him to find out where his friends were. And how they were. But to his left, down a hallway that ran along the front of the building, Laurienty Szopinski stood shoving a sheaf of papers into his briefcase.

Adam turned left.

Laurienty seemed focused on his efforts, which were not going well. What should not have been a difficult task was taking an inordinate amount of time, as edges of the paper kept getting caught on the side of the briefcase, folding the sheets over. He finally got the last piece in neatly when Adam stopped beside him.

"Laurienty. I'm glad you're here. Do you have any news about what happened?"

"*Pan* Kaminski."

Adam reached out and grabbed the briefcase just as Laurienty dropped it. After the effort he had put into filling it, it would be a shame to have it all spill out over the floor.

"Thank you." Laurienty took the case back from Adam, closed the clasp and tucked the case up under his arm.

"I came to see how they are." Adam thought that should be obvious, but Laurienty seemed surprised to see him.

"Yes, of course. But weren't you with them? In the van, I mean." Laurienty's eyebrow twitched as he spoke, the sweat budding on his top lip.

"I was not." Adam chose his words carefully. "I decided to stay in Warsaw for a few days. With my cousin."

"Right. Right. Of course, your cousin." Laurienty adjusted his glasses and a shaft of reflected light blocked the view of his eyes when he spoke again. "The cousin with accusations of murder."

Adam turned his head, tipping it to the left. "You don't take his claims seriously? You're not concerned about Basia's death?"

"Basia's death?" Laurienty shook his head with quick, tight shivers and the lines on his forehead deepened. "I am always concerned about death, *Pan* Kaminski. Now

Pan White's death. I'm sure you've heard."

Adam closed his eyes and let out a deep breath. "I thought as much." He stepped to a bench that lined the wall and sat heavily. "Jared's dead."

Laurienty said nothing, just watched Adam and fiddled with his glasses, waiting.

Even with his eyes closed, Adam knew Laurienty stood still in front of him. He heard the tread of doctors and nurses at the far end of the hall. He heard the sound of traffic from the street outside, muffled by the thick walls, frosted glass windows, and wafts of disinfectant that hung in the purified air.

"Dammit." Adam punched the bench next to him, sending vibrations that traveled along the wall, displacing two Styrofoam coffee cups abandoned farther up the bench. He opened his eyes. "This was my fault. My fault."

"Yes, it probably was, *Pan* Kaminski." Laurienty nodded violently, his glasses shifting again on his nose. He didn't adjust them. "It probably was your fault. Running around asking about murder. About death." The mottled pink of his cheeks grew darker as he spoke. "You of all people should know we have had enough of that here, in Poland." He paused and took a shaky breath.

"What do you mean?" Adam shot out of his seat, suddenly standing toe to toe with Laurienty. "What's going on here that I don't know about?"

"Hah! That you don't know about? Everything." Laurienty threw his hands up at he spoke, forgetting about the briefcase tucked under his arm. It hit the ground with a thud, its clasp holding tight. "You know nothing, *Pan* Kaminski. Nothing about our country, about our history. You have no authority here, no role. What do you think you can do here?"

Adam's voice was tight, his lips drawn close together. "Then you can tell me."

"Oh, I can tell you. Oh, yes." Laurienty's glasses

shifted again and this time he put a hand up to adjust them. "Murder happens, *Pan* Kaminski. Murder, killings that nobody ever solves. And now nobody even cares."

"What are you talking about?" Adam took a step back.

"I'm talking about murder, *Pan* Kaminski, which you seem so interested in." Flecks of spittle shot out of Laurienty's mouth as he spoke, the patches on his cheeks now a dark red. "You care so much about poor Basia, but what about all the others? Hmm? Where have you been? Safe in America, reading about the deaths in the paper. Something distant. Something that happens to people far away. I know about your family, you see. I know they left the country, sneaking away like cowards."

Adam gripped the windowsill, focusing on the feel of the cold steel in his hands. He took a breath and the scent of lilies faded, the image of a line of three coffins blurred. "What deaths, Laurienty?"

"People died, *Pan* Kaminski, fighting so that I could be here. So you could be here." He took a breath. "People died fighting the government. They didn't run away, they stayed to fight. Fighting for freedom."

"You're talking about the war? About Solidarity? But that was years ago."

"Phaw," Laurienty spit out a sound of derision. "For you, perhaps. But not for us. Not for the survivors."

Adam looked at Laurienty in a new light. "But you're too young, aren't you? You couldn't have been alive during Solidarity. And what do you think you know about my family?"

"I hear the stories, *Pan* Kaminski, and I do my own research when I need to. I know many things. About the war. About Solidarity. It is true, I was young. I did not fight. My grandfather, though..." Thoughts of his grandfather seemed to have purged his anger, and Laurienty sat, staring at his briefcase that still lay on the floor below the window.

Adam sat next to him. "What happened to your grandfather?"

"He died."

Adam waited, thinking. He knew many Poles had fought for political freedom. There may not have been a war, but there was a fight. A battle fought in the newspapers, in the schools, in the coffee shops and bars, and even in the courts. He knew people had been arrested for their activities, but he hadn't realized there had been casualties.

"Tell me what happened." Adam repeated his question.

"He was found. At the bottom of a staircase." Laurienty turned his head to look at Adam, his fashionable tie now loose and twisted. "They said he fell."

"And you don't believe that?"

"He fell. And hit his head three times on the way down. And broke the fingers of his right hand. And somehow took a deep hit in his kidney." Laurienty smiled down at his hands. "No, I don't believe that. Neither did my mother. But what could we do?" He raised his eyebrows. "What could we do?"

"Why do you think he died?"

"He was part of the fight against the communist government. He published articles, using a false name. He helped organize underground meetings. Somehow they knew." Laurienty's frown deepened. "Not just somehow. Someone. Someone who knew."

"Are you saying someone betrayed him?" Adam asked. "Who?"

Laurienty shrugged. "How can I know? I can't. I don't. I will never know." He looked back at Adam. "But someone gave them his name. Someone told them what he was doing. Someone informed to the secret police. And then my grandfather died."

Adam paused before responding, considering. "I'm sorry that happened, Laurienty. I'm sorry you and your mother had to go through that. But what does that have to do with Jared? Or with me?"

Laurienty smiled and blew out a sound that in another place might have been a laugh. "Nothing, I am sure. Nothing. Just more death." He stood, patting off his pant legs and adjusting his glasses. "Just more unexplained death. We all feel guilt, *Pan* Kaminski, over the death of those close to us. We all seek a way to move on. To get away." He smiled again.

"So you want the government to pursue more lustration cases?" Adam pushed, knowing once Laurienty regained control he would be less inclined to talk.

"More? No." Laurienty waved away the suggestion. "We must move on. We must move past this. I simply tell you this so you understand." He leaned forward toward Adam as he spoke, and Adam still saw the glint of anger in his eyes, despite his efforts to calm himself. "You must understand we all have sadness, we all have guilt. We all have deaths we cannot explain. But we must move on. We must. Or we will not survive."

CHAPTER THIRTY-TWO

SPIRES OF GOLDEN stone caught the afternoon light and the Polish flag floated above the Polish Army Field Cathedral. Across the street, mute metal men, larger than life, crawled out of an underground tunnel under the shelter of a concrete curtain. Commemorating the successes — and failures — of the Warsaw Uprising of 1944, the memorial loomed out of the gray concrete surrounding it. This desolate reminder of the bravery and loss of the citizens of Warsaw was no match for the macabre scene waiting to greet visitors inside the church.

Entering the vestibule, Adam came face to face with a memorial to war designed as only those who have faced war's terrors could design. The Second World War had devastated Warsaw. Bombed, tortured and killed, the residents of this city had held on, through it all, to their faith. But the effects of this misery could not be ignored.

Facing the entranceway and almost filling the small space stood a crucifix like none Adam had seen before. A body hung, as on most crucifixes, but this body was one of distress and misery, not life and resurrection. Tattered rags hung off the form, the artist having creatively scraped and distressed the metal that formed the artwork to generate an appearance of torn clothes, shriveled limbs, wasted skin over broken bones.

This figure hung between two stone pillars, themselves cracked and covered in jagged edges.

Embedded within the stones of these pillars lay what appeared to be human skulls, lost souls crying out for redemption. Clearly crying in vain.

Shuddering slightly, Adam walked through the interior doors to the nave of the church, trying unsuccessfully not to think of death. Or the dead.

Hundreds of votive candles flickered throughout the church, their heavily perfumed smoke hanging in the air. Fantastic painted frescoes depicted images of Poland's victories and God's greatness.

Adam turned his eyes from the walls and scanned the pews, searching for Sylvia and Łukasz. A few elderly women still sat in prayer, their heads covered in black lace, their shoulders bowed. It didn't take long for Adam to spot Sylvia, her blond hair shining in the dim candlelight of the church.

Sliding next to her, he put his hand gently on her leg. "Shh," he said as she jumped and started to speak. When she looked up at him, he saw that she had been crying.

"I know, I went to the hospital, I saw the others."

"What's going on, Adam? What happened to Jared?" She looked away from him as she spoke, her eyes moving upward as if studying the display of Polish Hussar armor that hung near them, two long, curved wooden frames lined with ostrich feathers.

The famous wings of the Hussars. Strapped to the back of the armor of the cavalryman, the wings would catch the air as the horse galloped forward, creating a fearsome sound. Adam could imagine an entire unit of cavalry storming forward, the wind wailing through their giant wings. It would be enough to scare any enemy force.

"I don't know for sure, Sylvia," he answered slowly. "I think they were looking for me. I think they got Jared by mistake."

"By mistake?" Sylvia inhaled sharply and wound her hands together around the rosary that lay in her lap. "How could anyone kill someone by mistake?"

Adam nodded and looked down at his own hands. "Łukasz is on to something, Sylvia. Whatever we're digging up, we're scaring somebody. They're willing to kill to stop us. I'm in the middle of this now and I'm not even sure what it is."

Sylvia sat staring at him, her hands finally still. "What are you talking about, Adam?" she whispered. "What's going on? Was Jared involved as well?"

"No, damn it!"

Sylvia shushed him harshly even as the words escaped his lips. A couple of black-laced women glanced back at them from a few pews in front.

"Sorry. No, Jared wasn't involved. I think whoever killed him was looking for me. You know Jared and I look alike, at least to anyone who doesn't know us."

Sylvia frowned and shook her head slightly, so Adam continued, "I was supposed to be on that van, Sylvia. And if I had been, I'd be dead by now." He paused, looking at her closely. "And Jared would be alive."

Sylvia shook her head sharply. "No, I can't believe what you're saying. I don't know what trouble you're in, but it can't be because of Basia Kaminski or anyone at the *Sejm*."

"Are you sure?" Adam watched her, but her expression didn't falter.

She gestured slightly to indicate the grand nave of the church and all of its artwork. "Do you see all this? All this beauty, all this history?"

Adam looked around once again, at the colorful icons painted on the wall, the stained glass that tinted the light within the church. The giant wings of war.

"Yes, it's beautiful."

"But it's not real. It is a reconstruction, like every other building in the Old Town." Sylvia smiled, a sad gesture. "It was all destroyed, you know. First the war. Then the German occupation. Most of the city was rubble by the time it all ended."

She looked around as she spoke, her voice picking up.

"But we reclaimed our land, you see?" She looked at Adam, smiling now. "From all over the country. Children collected tin cans to donate... churches throughout Poland gathered funds... tradesmen donated their time." She smiled. "Warsaw was rebuilt."

"That's a beautiful story, a proud history."

"But that's my point. We have struggled. But to move forward. Not backward." She cast her glance once more up at the apse, then looked at Adam. "Not backward."

Adam glanced at his watch. "We've been here for an hour. Łukasz should be here by now."

Sylvia continued to examine the beauty around them and didn't respond, so Adam continued. "I don't know what Łukasz is digging up, but it must be big. He told me he thought he had stumbled onto proof of corruption in the legislature. He thinks Basia found it, too, and it got her killed. I don't know. I suppose that could be it. It just seems like it must be bigger than simple corruption. Would someone kill to hide that?"

"Perhaps" — Sylvia shrugged — "if the benefits he received from it were important enough to him. Or to her."

"Or to her," Adam repeated. "We need to dig deeper. Łukasz and I — we need to look farther into the past. I'm convinced there's more there, we just need to find it."

"Why?" Sylvia finally looked at Adam. "Why do you need to? I understand that Łukasz wants to find the truth about what happened to his daughter. He believes that truth lies in our history. Perhaps it does. But why is this so important to you?"

"Because I want to know who's really responsible. Even if we catch the person who killed Basia and Jared — or the thugs who attacked Łukasz — I think there's someone else behind this. Someone in a position of power in this government. It's not enough to find the man who pulled the trigger, we need to find the man who's calling the shots."

Sylvia shrugged. "Perhaps. Perhaps that is important. Is it important enough to die for?"

"Whoever it is, he thinks it's important enough to kill for. And right now, that's all that really concerns me."

Adam looked around again. The church was by now almost completely empty. Only two other people remained, one kneeling in front of the votive candles, another hunched low in the last pew.

"We can't stay here forever, we need to move. At this point, we need to be surrounded by people. It's the only way we can be safe. Do you know where we can go?"

"There is somewhere I can take you. Where most of Warsaw will be today, in fact." She glanced up at Adam hopefully. "You know, that's probably where Łukasz is right now."

"Where?"

"*Powązki*. The cemetery."

"What?" Adam asked, confused. "We need to be somewhere public, somewhere crowded."

"Oh, yes, I understand." Sylvia smiled slightly. "You'll see."

CHAPTER THIRTY-THREE

A SHORT DRIVE from the center of town along the avenue named for the Polish Home Army, *Powązki* Cemetery stood wrapped by a red stone wall. It covered forty-four hectares, as large as Vatican City itself.

The road leading to the cemetery was already congested, so Sylvia parked a distance away from the main entrance. The two walked slowly along the wall toward the gate. Church and community groups had set up along the walls with stalls selling flowers and candles, beverages and sweet cakes.

"Every year, artists and actors gather here at the cemetery," Sylvia explained when she saw Adam's confusion. "To meet their fans, put on a concert, to raise money to support *Powązki*. It is our nation's cemetery. Łukasz must be here, I'm sure of it. His editor probably assigned him to cover this event and he didn't have a chance to tell you."

Adam looked skeptical, but he took Sylvia's hand. "Okay, let's go find him."

Voices called out to them as they passed, vendors offering hot drinks, babka, sweet fried dough. A stand with colorful balloons on display attracted the attention of the children while their mothers stopped to buy bread or votive candles, or drop a few coins into the red donation cans.

Inside the gates of the graveyard, the festival-like

atmosphere gave way to a reverent hush. Crowds of people passed along the narrow paths between burial plots. Voices were whispered and muffled.

Though it was still early in the afternoon, the rows of tall gray headstones created dark shadows along the narrow paths that wound through the graveyard, and the flickering lights of hundreds of small candles reflected through the dimness.

It seemed to Adam as if all of Warsaw were here, gathered in the cemetery. Trying to make their way through the cemetery, Adam and Sylvia found themselves brushing past mourners and tourists alike, families and school groups. As they walked, Adam could hear voices of children asking their parents about what they were seeing.

"*A tu*," a young boy's voice carried across the stillness, "and here, who is here?"

"Kieslowski," a father answered, reading from a moss-covered stone.

"Boleslaw Prus," announced another.

Adam smiled as he watched the youngsters, eager to learn more, pulling their parents forward from gravestone to gravestone.

Burial ground for artists and authors, political leaders and leading dissidents, *Powązki's* grounds brought all great men and women buried here to equality. While some graves bore more candles than others, none were untended, not even those of the Soviet leaders buried here but now reviled. All graves were cared for, weeds pulled, flowers planted, candles lit.

Thick oak trees with gnarled and twisted trunks leaned perilously over the tombs and gravestones near the gate they entered by. Farther into the cemetery, pale birches marked an area dedicated to those whose lives were lost during the war. Simple crosses of white birchwood tied together marked sites where Adam suspected no bodies had been left to be buried. Plaques on these crosses listed the names and ages of the young men and women — nineteen, twenty, eighteen years old — who had been killed during the Uprising.

"We should move toward the chapel at the side of the cemetery," Sylvia explained. "That's where the concert is later, and where Łukasz is probably waiting."

"I don't like this." Adam glanced around them as they walked. "He should have been at the church. He's the one who suggested the meeting. I don't believe he would just not show up and not send me a message."

Sylvia shrugged and kept walking, moving quickly past the meandering tourists and kneeling mourners.

As they turned a bend in the path, Adam ducked behind a large stone, pulling Sylvia with him.

"What are you doing? What is it?" She looked at him, then turned to look around them.

They stood behind a giant angel whose marble had become mottled and gray over the years. Its face bent down toward them, an expression of terrible sadness etched into its features.

"I'm not sure, I think I saw someone," Adam explained. Had he imagined the black coat and jeans ducking behind a large gravestone just up the path from them? He was sure it had been the same man who followed him in the marketplace. But he hadn't got a clear look at the guy then, either.

"Who did you see?" Sylvia pressed him, but Adam had no answer.

"Come on, let's find another way to the chapel. We need to find Łukasz."

Sylvia nodded and led them away from the path, weaving among the warped and faded stones that marked the final resting place of Poland's greatest heroes.

After a few minutes of walking, they found themselves in one of the oldest areas of the cemetery. All the ground here was taken, with no room to pass between the heavy stones.

To avoid going back to the main path, they stole

carefully over graves, climbing over the ancient markers. Even here, votive candles marked individual graves, and Adam slowed to avoid knocking any over, his hand running along the icy marble of the long resting stones.

As he put his weight on one, he felt a shock of warmth emanating from the marble. Pulling his hand back as if burnt, he stumbled. Sylvia glanced back to make sure he was all right, then kept moving.

"There, up ahead." Sylvia pointed. An open path lay ahead of them, again crawling with visitors. Farther along the path, beyond a few turns and dips in the ground, Adam could see a small chapel, its lights glowing in the distance. "That's where he'll be. We must follow this path."

Adam nodded and led the way across the last few graves, covered in pebbles, gravel and the detritus of what once had been a green lawn.

They merged into the crowds flowing along the path and turned toward the chapel. They found it harder to move quickly here, as the mass of people was denser. They fell into pace with the other visitors, moving painfully slowly toward the lit door of the chapel. As the path neared each turn in the way, they slowed even more, as visitors had to pause to make room for those leaving the chapel and heading back toward the cemetery gates.

At one of these turns, the ground dipped low, below the level of the stones behind them. A movement behind them caught Adam's eye. Pushing Sylvia roughly off the path, he turned as quickly as he could in the crowd.

Thanks to his turn, the blade slid across his shoulder, slicing through his coat instead of through his back as it had been aimed.

Adam caught the arm that held the knife under his own and spun the man off the path into the gray field of stones where Sylvia already hid. Beyond a few complaints, the crowd hardly noticed the scuffle and kept moving forward at its slow pace.

Coming to rest leaning against a square black stone, he looked at the man who had attacked him. He was older than Adam, maybe in his late fifties. His expression was as still as that of the marble angels; only his eyes shifted below his closely cut gray hair. He bounced on the balls of his feet, switching the knife between his hands as he tried to guess Adam's next move.

Sylvia crouched a few feet away. Adam could see her leaning forward to see around the stone that hid her. She was behind the attacker, and as far as he could tell, the man hadn't seen her yet. He wanted to keep it that way.

He stepped to his right, spinning around a towering marble cross and jumping over the next row of stones behind him. His attacker didn't miss a beat. Jumping agilely over the stones between them, he narrowed the gap between them faster than Adam could get away.

Adam kept moving until there was enough distance between the attacker and Sylvia or one of the innocent visitors on the path to their left. He stopped with his back to his attacker. Holding his breath and counting down, he waited only a few seconds, until he knew the man was closing in. He spun and caught the man hard on the jaw with his left arm.

Knocked off-balance, the man tripped over a low stone, dropping his knife. Bending as he ran, Adam grabbed the knife and moved toward the attacker.

"Who are you? Who do you work for?" he asked as he approached the stranger, who was once again back on his feet and ready for a fight.

The man remained silent, simply watching Adam warily, staying light on his feet and ready to lunge again.

"I'm younger than you, I'm stronger than you, and I have your knife. What do you think is going to happen next, hmm?" Adam asked him, watching him carefully.

The man seemed not even to realize Adam was speaking. His eyes were fixed constantly on the knife without wavering. Finally, Adam moved toward the man.

Adam's opponent leapt forward and to his left, grabbing Adam's arm as he moved and spinning Adam hard against a gravestone. Even as his face crashed into the rough marble, Adam felt his arm bent painfully behind him. He lost his grip on the knife.

Kicking out behind him, Adam managed to pull away, but it was too late. The man had the knife and was smiling now, moving slowly closer to Adam. Adam knew he was outmatched in this fight.

"Stop, or I'll scream." Sylvia's words in Polish meant nothing to Adam, but the attacker stopped and turned.

At the sight of Sylvia, his eyes widened and his posture straightened. It was only for a second, then he resumed the stance of a hunter. Adam had seen it, there was no question. And Sylvia had noticed it, too.

"Who are you?" she asked, this time in English. "Why are you attacking us?"

When the man didn't respond, she picked up a large rock lying on one of the graves. "I am a good shot. If you attack me, Adam will get you while your back is turned. If you attack him, I will scream. And I'll do some damage with this rock, I am sure."

The man smiled slightly. It was the first response Adam had seen him make.

The man looked once more back at Adam, then at Sylvia, then turned and ran away from the main path, through the stones that filled the graveyard to the red brick wall.

Sylvia dropped the stone and Adam could see her hands were trembling. He ran to her and held her hands in his own, pulling her close against his body to stop the trembling that threatened to take over.

"Shh, it's okay, he's gone," he spoke as he caressed her hair, wiping the tears that spilled down onto her cheeks. Only a few yards away, innocent visitors continued their slow march to and from the cemetery chapel, there to remember the dead, blissfully unaware of the deadly attack that had just taken place. When Sylvia finally calmed down, he stepped back and looked down at her. "Who was that guy? Do you know him?"

Sylvia shook her head. "We're not safe here, we should go."

"We need to find Łukasz. That's why we came here, remember?" he asked, shaking his head at her. "We can't leave now."

"No, we must leave. It isn't safe here. I don't know if Łukasz is here or not, but we can't stay."

"Where can we go? There's nowhere we can be safe." Adam held her close again, trying to comfort her, but she pushed away from him.

"No! I know what I am saying. If he was sent to attack us, he will try again. He still has his knife. We aren't safe here. We can go back to my apartment."

"If he knows you, he knows where you live, Sylvia. You must tell me who that was."

"I don't know that man," Sylvia insisted. "He doesn't know me and he doesn't know where I live. This is your problem, not mine. You and that cousin of yours. I am not part of this. And I need to go home."

With that, she pushed past him and strode back to the path, joining the few people who were moving upstream, away from the lights of the chapel. Adam shook his head as he followed close behind her.

SYLVIA PUSHED the door to her apartment open roughly, barely allowing Adam time to squeeze through before she slammed it shut and leaned heavily against it. Adam, too, rested against the wall for a minute. Then he turned, leaning over Sylvia with his hand pushing against the door behind her.

"What's going on, Sylvia? Who was that man?"

"I don't know," she whispered, "I don't know what's happening, I swear." She looked up at him, tears in her eyes.

"He recognized you, you saw that as clearly as I did." As he leaned toward her, he could feel her heart beating in her chest, only inches from his. His own heart was pounding in his ears, the adrenaline still pumping through his veins. "How did he know you?"

"Adam, you must believe me." She put a hand up to touch his face, but he pushed it away.

"I don't know what to believe anymore. I don't know who's behind this, I don't know what's going on. I don't know where Łukasz is." Adam paused, frustrated. "I feel like I'm losing control."

Sylvia reached up once again, placing her hand gently on Adam's face. This time he didn't move. "You must believe me, Adam, because you have no one else to believe. What just happened today, I don't know what that was. I was scared, Adam. I am still scared. I need you to believe me."

Sylvia lifted her face to his and ran her lips gently over his eyes, his cheeks and his lips. He shut his eyes. He didn't know what to believe anymore. Sylvia had been the one person he trusted. He thought he trusted. He pictured her as he had first met her, waiting on the train platform in Toruń, her lavender-scented hair blowing in the breeze.

"No... wait." He pushed away from her and moved deeper into her apartment. "I need to think, Sylvia."

"Think? About what?" Sylvia's voice sounded high and tight. "I know how I feel about you. And I'm sure you feel the same way." Sylvia stepped close behind him, resting her hand on his shoulder. "I'm scared, Adam. I don't know what's going on. Why are you turning away from me?"

Adam turned to face her. He tried to focus on the blueness of her eyes, the scent of lavender that drew him in and surrounded him in a sense of warmth and excitement. But it was as if a veil had come down between them. All he could see in his mind were images of other days, other places.

Sylvia trying to prevent him from talking with Łukasz at the police station and again at the *Sejm*. Sylvia — could it have been Sylvia? — watching him from the third floor office as he and Łukasz left the *Sejm* together. Sylvia sharing a look with Laurienty... whispering with Malak... sharing a laugh with Kapral.

"What do you know that you're not telling me?" He tried to keep his voice low and calm, but even to his ears he sounded harsh.

Sylvia stepped back. "What do you mean, Adam? There are many things I haven't told you. What do you want to know?"

"About Basia. About why she had to die. About the man who just attacked us in the cemetery." His voice was coming out as a hiss now, and he took a deep breath, trying to calm himself. Sounds of traffic from the street outside carried faintly into the apartment. Light from the lamp in the corner painted shadows across the ceiling. Time stood still as Sylvia looked up at him, her expression fathomless.

The moment broke.

Her eyes flashed and she threw her hands up in the air, turning and moving about the apartment as she spoke. "This again! I have told you already, I did not know that man." She turned back to him, her eyes narrowed. "And I will not answer that question again, Adam Kaminski. I am done with this."

She walked close to him, her chest almost touching his, and looked up into his eyes. "Do you trust me?"

Adam paused. He took a breath, then another, waiting as his heart rate slowed, his shoulders relaxed, his anger receded. As if the veil were lifted, he once again saw her face, her eyes. He ran his hand gently along the curve of her cheek.

"I do," he whispered.

Her whole body shuddered and she laughed gently, her head bowed. "I am relieved to hear that."

She looked back up at him, the anger in her

expression replaced with concern. "Adam, please believe me. Are there things I have not told you? Of course. About my work, my school... about my life, about past loves." She smiled gently. "These are things we can talk about in time. But not tonight."

"I just know that I'm missing something. Something important, that links these killings together."

Sylvia nodded. "I understand. If I knew what I could tell you that would help, I would. Where to start? There are things in my past that I'm not proud of. Of course. Just as I am sure you have hidden secrets from your own past. Doesn't everyone have secrets?"

Adam leaned his head forward, resting his forehead against hers. "Yes. We all do." He lowered his face more and kissed her gently. "I do trust you."

"And I, you." She laughed again. "I have followed you into this nightmare because I trust you, you idiot." She hit him lightly on the chest. "Never doubt me again."

He kissed her again. Sounds from the street receded, light from the apartment faded, until it was only them, together, alone in this small room.

CHAPTER THIRTY-FOUR

HE HAD no idea how long they stood there. It seemed like only a moment and a lifetime.

"I know where we can go for help." She pushed herself away from him. "There is someone who may be able to help us."

"Sylvia." Adam watched her as she quickly gathered her coat and purse. "What are you thinking?"

She stopped moving around to look at him. "It's okay, Adam. We're okay. I know I can trust you, and I needed to know that." She kissed him lightly. "And you can trust me. Trust me now, because I have an idea."

The knock on Sylvia's door startled them both. They froze where they were, Sylvia on the sofa zipping up her boots, Adam near the door buttoning his winter coat.

Sylvia looked up at Adam, the fear that had been temporarily kept at bay creeping back into her eyes.

Adam put a finger to his lips, nodded at her, then stepped silently toward the door. He leaned against the door jamb, putting his ear close to the wall, but shook his head when he heard nothing. With one more look at Sylvia, he stepped back only slightly.

Pulling the door open with a jerk, he moved forward simultaneously, hoping his forward momentum would be enough to catch their visitor off guard.

It was.

Łukasz fell back against the wall of the hallway as

Adam stepped into him. He said something softly in Polish — Adam could only assume it was a swear — as his skull slammed into the wall. Putting his hand up, he touched his fingers to his head.

"I have already suffered enough damage, Cousin Adam. This does not help."

"Sorry, Łukasz, I couldn't know it was you. You're just in time — come."

The trams were mostly empty, though still running frequently. Adam watched the streets of Warsaw lurch by, the densely built city center gradually giving way to more spacious buildings.

"I was in the church earlier." Łukasz spoke under his breath, though there was no one nearby to overhear. "You were not there. I was later than I intended, I'm sorry." He looked at Adam, who sat in the seat behind his. "I went to the hospital first, of course. I thought you were dead."

Adam nodded. "I think a lot of people thought I died this morning. And some of them were happy about it." He turned slightly to look out at the evening sky. "I stopped by the hospital, too, to see what had happened. Once I realized the knife had been meant for me, I left. I can't stay near my colleagues. I can't risk putting them in more danger."

"Ah, so you came to me. I see." Sylvia's voice was lighthearted, but she frowned as she spoke and clung tighter to Adam's arm.

"I guessed you would turn to *Pani* Stanko here, cousin," Łukasz explained, "so I have been checking her apartment occasionally throughout the day. There and at your hotel. I have been waiting to talk with you."

"I had nowhere else to turn, Sylvia," Adam answered Sylvia's accusation. "I knew I could trust you. And you did help me — you came up with the idea of looking in the cemetery."

"*Powązki?*" Łukasz raised his eyebrows. "Why were you there?"

"Sylvia suggested that you might have been sent there by your editor, to cover the concert tonight."

Łukasz nodded but frowned. "Yes, it was a reasonable guess, I suppose, but Adam, you must realize that at this point, I would not have trusted my editor enough to go where he sends me. I fear that we are all in danger, after what happened to your colleague this morning."

"You're absolutely right about that, Łukasz." Adam watched Sylvia as he spoke. "We were attacked this afternoon, at the cemetery. A man with a knife. And I think I've seen him following me before. Yesterday, in the market. I'm sure he's the one who killed Jared. I just don't know who he is." He paused, still watching Sylvia, but she made no response. He glanced back out the window.

They had passed through the still urban neighborhood of *Ursinów*, nearing the affluent suburb of *Wilanów*. Houses here were newer, almost all built in the past ten years. Older buildings that still remained had been renovated and updated. Streets were wider. Sidewalks newly paved.

After a minute's silence, Łukasz spoke. "I have some more information that may be helpful in figuring this out. That's why I wanted to meet with you today."

"What is it, what do you know?"

"The books and articles you took from Basia's apartment," Łukasz explained. "I have been reading through these."

"You think they're connected with her murder?"

"Most, no, they are books about politics — in Poland, in Europe. She was always studying, always learning. She liked to read about men she admired, to learn from their personal stories. Jacek Kuron, for example."

Sylvia nodded. "He was a hero for Tomek Malak, as well. A man who was a strong leader, who people followed."

Łukasz continued impatiently, "Then there were other articles, other stories. About Novosad, for one, Basia's mentor." Łukasz looked back and forth from Sylvia to Adam. "You have heard the stories, I'm sure, but did you know they are true?"

"What do you mean, true?"

"He has connections to the Russian mafia. I found an article, in Basia's notebooks, about a cousin of Novosad's. He was arrested not too long ago for his criminal activities. He is not accused of being a mastermind. Far from it." Łukasz snorted. "But he is connected. And that means Novosad is connected."

"That could be a motive. Something he doesn't want people to know. I understand he already faces a tough reelection, people thinking he's too closely connected with Russia. This would put the nail in his coffin, I suppose."

Sylvia shrugged. "Perhaps, perhaps not. I think the rumors you heard about Novosad's reelection were exaggerated. You heard these from Laurienty, perhaps?" she asked Adam.

Adam nodded.

"He is bitter," Sylvia continued, her voice a whisper. "Because of his own struggles. He assumes that everyone is as mean as he is. He does not see things clearly. Novosad's switch in parties did not hurt him, it helped him. He now is in a party that more closely aligns with his own personal opinions. People trust him. I do not think he has as much to worry about as you suppose. Or to hide."

Łukasz shrugged. "Okay, then there's this: Nelek Kapral."

"What do you have on Kapral?" Adam perked up.

"Laurienty Szopinski," Łukasz answered. Adam and Sylvia both nodded.

"There's something not right there, I know it," Adam agreed.

"Kapral hired Szopinski two years ago. Fresh out of university. He had advertised the position within the school, looking to hire a young person."

"He actively supports youth involvement in politics, I know this," Sylvia said.

"Why Szopinski?" Łukasz asked. "Basia had the files from Kapral's office. Records showing the applications from the many who applied and the reviews offered by Kapral's other staff. Szopinski wasn't even part of the original applicant pool. Kapral had narrowed his selection down to two very qualified candidates — either would have been better than Szopinski — then suddenly, Szopinski's application appears."

"He is not unqualified," Sylvia pointed out. "I complain about him, sure, but maybe it is not unreasonable that Kapral hired him."

"If Szopinski was the only applicant, no. But he was by far the least competitive of the three. Why him? Why did Kapral even accept the application?"

"And why was Basia looking into it? What did she think she had found?" Adam asked. "And what was she going to do with that information?"

"Novosad... Kapral... Szopinski... these are not killers. They may have secrets, problems of their own. But to kill... to, what, to push Basia over the bridge? I don't believe it," Sylvia said.

"Killing isn't always a hands-on job," Adam said quietly. "Sometimes it's as easy as ordering dinner."

"Hiring a killer to do the job for you, you mean?" Łukasz asked.

Adam nodded. "The man who attacked us in the cemetery. He was an expert, I'm sure of it. He had no hesitation, no interest in talking. He was there for one thing. And I believe he was paid to do it."

"Tell me about this man," Łukasz asked, "what did he look like?"

Sylvia shuddered. "I don't want to think about it. I don't want to think about him." She turned away from Adam, as if trying to ignore the two men, then jumped up. "Come."

They followed Sylvia. Adam didn't answer Łukasz's

question until they were standing in a tight circle on the next tram, holding onto the overhead leather straps.

"Short, older, closely cropped hair." Adam spoke under his voice, though again there was only one other passenger. "He was fit, in great shape, and he had an intensity that would be hard to beat."

"How old?" Łukasz asked.

"In his late fifties, maybe sixties?" Adam guessed. "But fit. Very fit."

"There are many men who were involved with the Polish secret police or the KGB," Łukasz said. "When the regime fell, these men had nowhere to go, nothing to do. Some of them moved on to Russia, where their particular skills were still needed. Some stayed here, in Poland. And let themselves out for hire. For whoever was willing to pay."

Adam nodded, thinking. Łukasz's explanation made sense, fit with the facts.

Łukasz rubbed his chin, his eyes deep in thought. "I have some ideas for who may still be in Poland from that time. There are records, articles I can review. I just need some time to look into it."

"If it was a hired killer," Adam pointed out, "how did he get Basia to the bridge? I'm sure he took her from her home. Knocked her out there. Maybe drugged her, maybe hit her."

Łukasz shivered.

"I'm sorry, Łukasz, I know it's hard for you to think of that. But we must. How could a hired killer get such easy access to her? Would she have let him into her apartment?"

"No, of course not." Łukasz's eyes flashed. "She was much too smart for that."

"Then someone she trusted introduced them. Maybe came to her apartment with the killer, invited him in."

"And left her. Alone with him," Łukasz's voice dropped. "Someone left her alone with a killer, to die."

Sylvia put her hand on Adam's shoulder and turned to Łukasz. "You have found nothing, really. You have more questions, but no answers. You are no farther along solving this puzzle, and now we are all in danger."

"We have motives, Sylvia. And we have opportunity," Adam explained. "One of these men is evil and must be stopped. Someone you work with. Surely you want to stop him?"

"If it is someone involved in the government at all..." Sylvia frowned and pushed a loose strand of hair back behind her ear.

"Will you help us, *Pani* Stanko? Will you help us find the truth?" Łukasz asked.

Sylvia nodded slowly. "Perhaps. We are going now to someone who would be even more help to you than I." She looked at Łukasz and Adam. "Tomek Malak. He knows everyone who works for the city and the national legislature. He may be able to help us."

"You think he knows more than he's telling?" Adam asked.

"About these murders? No." Sylvia shook her head and frowned again. "If he knew someone had such a dark secret, he would have already reported him. He would have gone straight to the legal authorities. No. But he may be able to give us more information about these men. Not just these guesses." She looked meaningfully at Łukasz.

They stayed on the tram until it passed through *Ursinów* then crossed *Zygmunta Vogla* to catch the bus that would take them the rest of the way. As the bus moved through *Wilanów*, the streets were better lit, houses fewer and farther apart. Sylvia grabbed Adam's sleeve as the bus neared *Ulica Uprawna*, and he and Łukasz jumped down after her, heading into the well-kept suburban neighborhood.

Sylvia stopped and pointed at a large white house set back from the street. Lights shone from almost all the windows and Adam could see figures moving behind the thin curtains.

"There. Tomek's house. And it looks like he and his family are still up. Good."

With that, she moved determinedly up the path and knocked loudly on the ornately carved wooden door.

CHAPTER THIRTY-FIVE

SYLVIA'S HAND had barely moved away from the door when it swung open and Tomek Malak stood facing them. He was dressed in a suit, as he had been when Adam met him at the *Sejm*. But it was creased, as if he had been wearing it since the day before. Malak wore no tie. His hair was disheveled, his eyes red.

"Sylvia," he said with a start, "oh... yes?"

"Sir," she responded with a smile, "I am sorry to bother you at home like this. We need help, and I am hoping you can offer it."

Malak looked at the two men standing behind her before nodding and stepping back from the doorway. "Of course, of course, come in, please."

Sylvia stepped through the door into the well-lit house, Adam and Łukasz following close behind her. Once they were in, Malak peered briefly out into the dark street, then shut the door behind them. "Please, come through to the living room. We were just finishing our dinner."

A tall blond woman rose from a blue satin couch when the group entered. "*Dobry wieczor*," she said, smiling, with a questioning look at her husband. "Tomek?"

A young woman moved through the room, gathering cut crystal wine glasses that rested on various surfaces in the room. Adam counted five glasses and couldn't help but wonder who else had been here. Or was still here.

"Maria," Malak answered her in English, "you remember Sylvia, of course." The two woman smiled and shook hands. "And may I introduce Adam Kaminski." Adam offered his hand as his name was mentioned. "*Pan* Kaminski is visiting us from Philadelphia, in the United States, as part of a sister cities program."

Malak turned to Łukasz. "And Łukasz Kaminski, one of our city's finest journalists. I admit I am curious as to your role here, sir."

Adam offered the explanation. "*Pan* Kaminski is my cousin, *Pan* Malak."

"So this is a chance to visit with family." Malak smiled and shook Łukasz's hand. "How nice."

"Yes. Something like that," Adam left it at that, not knowing how Sylvia thought Malak could help them.

"Please, please, have a seat." Maria Malak indicated the carved wood, satin-lined chairs that dotted the room. A wooden chest stood against one wall, its inlay created from multihued varieties of wood plus what looked like ebony and ivory. Two Chippendale chairs sat together around a Queen Anne table.

It looked beautiful, but Adam would be afraid to live in a house like this, in constant fear of breaking things. "Our daughter is just clearing up after our post-dinner drinks, she would be happy to bring you something. Sonja!" This last she called out to the young woman, who could be heard moving about in another room.

"*Słucham?*" Sonja called back, walking into the living room where the group still stood.

"No, no, thank you," Sylvia answered for all of them. "Tomek, we have something we must discuss with you. Work related," she added, glancing at Maria.

"Ah, I see." Malak leaned over and kissed his wife on the cheek. "It appears that I must leave you briefly, my dear. This won't take too long, I hope?" He looked at Sylvia.

"No, no," she assured him, "just a few moments of your time."

Malak guided the group up the grand staircase that dominated the entranceway then down a short corridor. The air was heavy with a musky scent, and Adam couldn't shake the feeling they were going deep underground, even though they were on the second level.

At the end of the hall a door stood closed. Malak opened it and ushered them in. The room was clearly used as his study. Brown wood paneling lined the walls. The thick carpet was Persian, in deep hues of red and blue. A marble statuc of the Virgin Mary held pride of place against one wall, smiling benignly down at the room from its perch on a seventeenth-century Dutch *kussenkast* display cabinet. Brown leather chairs that looked significantly more comfortable than the ornate furnishings in the room below created a cozy place to have a private conversation.

Malak closed the door firmly and gestured to the chairs. While the others sat, Malak moved over to a wooden cabinet, its doors inset with tortoiseshell, pulling out a bottle of vodka and a few small crystal glasses.

"Drink?" he asked, raising the bottle.

"No —" Adam started to answer, but Łukasz cut him off.

"Thank you, yes," Łukasz answered for all of them. Adam shot him a look, but didn't say anything more.

As Malak poured the drinks, Adam looked at him closely. He looked exhausted. Perhaps this was the end of a long day for him. The change was enough to get Adam's attention. Just a day ago in his office, he was calm, in control. Now his hands shook slightly as he poured the drinks, his smile was weak, unsure.

"Gentlemen." He put the bottle down on a side table. "What can I do for you? *Na zdrowie.*" The last words he said as he raised his glass in a toast. The others followed suit and downed the vodka he had provided. They each lowered an empty glass.

"This is not an easy subject to discuss, *Pan* Malak," Łukasz started. "I am writing a story for my newspaper. It is a story about corruption in our government. And it is a story about murder."

As Łukasz paused to pull together his thoughts, Adam watched Malak's face. He couldn't be sure, but it almost seemed as if Malak's expression softened. As if he had been expecting something different. Something worse.

Malak leaned forward and refilled their glasses, then placed the bottle down gently. "An admirable story, *Pan* Kaminski. It is good to root out evildoers in our government. I am the liaison between the city and the national legislature. If you believe there is corruption in the legislature, I am glad that you have brought these concerns to me."

Łukasz smiled briefly, then looked down at his glass. "I believe you might be able to help us."

He tilted his head back as he downed the clear liquid in a smooth motion, replacing his glass on the small table.

"I believe the criminal has already attempted to cover up his crimes with murder. He killed a young woman who found him out, and now he is trying to kill Adam and myself."

Malak shook his head in surprise. "No. That is not possible. If there had been a murder in the *Sejm*, I would have heard about it."

"Basia Kaminski."

"Ah…" Malak nodded and looked at the ground. "I understand now." He paused. "But that was ruled a suicide, was it not?"

"It was murder. I'm sure of it." Łukasz spoke quickly.

Malak shrugged and his face showed his indecision.

"Don't you want to know if it is true, Tomek?" Sylvia said, leaning forward.

Malak stood, replacing the bottle on its shelf and carefully closing the door of the armoire. He walked over to her and placed his hand on her shoulder. "Of course I want to know. I simply do not believe it is possible."

She smiled up at him and nodded. "I know how closely you work with everyone in the *Sejm*. I know how important this is to you."

Adam frowned and jumped into the conversation. "Yes, but what if there's more? Digging into Basia's death has led Łukasz to believe there is corruption within the legislature. A minister, or ministers, are using their positions for personal gain."

Malak smiled at Sylvia one more time, then regained his seat. "Perhaps" — he shrugged — "it is possible. This is politics." He raised a hand before anyone could utter a protest. "I agree, if there is someone stealing from the people of Warsaw, from the people of Poland, this would indeed be a horrible crime."

"That's not all. Whoever it is, he or she has tried to stop me several times. My life has been threatened. And now another life has been taken."

"What... what are you saying?" Malak asked, his concern clear on his face. "Has someone else been killed?"

"Jared White, whom you met the other day," Sylvia answered softly. "He has been killed. In a vicious attack."

"My God!" Malak stood again and paced around the room, once again coming to rest near Sylvia, his hand on her shoulder. "This is terrible. And he was here as an ambassador, seeking a closer relationship with the United States. This cannot be."

"It is, Tomek. He is dead. He died this morning."

"How could I not have heard of this?" Malak wondered aloud.

Adam was wondering the same thing, but kept his answer brief. "It was in all the papers, sir, and on the TV news. I am surprised you had not heard."

"You must have been locked in committee meetings

all day, Tomek; you mustn't feel bad about this," Sylvia tried to comfort him.

"Not meetings, a hearing." Malak seemed distracted as he answered her. "We are moving forward with action on a lustration case. Very rare. It has taken all of my focus."

"What case is this?" Adam asked. "I hadn't heard about it."

"Oh no, you would not have. It's too sensitive, we are keeping quiet about it. Once the legislative committee makes a decision, it will be passed on to the courts. It only becomes public information at that point."

He looked around the room. "I should not have shared as much as I just did, it was very unprofessional, I apologize. It's only this news that you bring me — of criminal activity, murder even — has upset me very much. I love this country and I love this city. I have given so much to it, I cannot stand the thought of it slowly crumbling apart under the weight of corruption and crime. This has happened to too many countries. Not Poland. No!"

Sylvia looked as if she had been brought to tears by Malak's speech. "It is a horrible thing, but we think you may be able to help. You can help us find out who is behind this and bring that person to justice."

Malak nodded absentmindedly as the others stood and prepared to leave. "Two murders, then. Two."

"You must look into this yourself, Malak," Łukasz explained, "you must find out who has committed a crime so heinous that he is willing to kill to cover it up. We need your help."

"Of course," Malak responded, "I will help you in any way I can. But I cannot let it take time away from this other proceeding, you understand. We must not look indifferent in our response to this accusation of collaboration."

"There is a criminal working in this government, sir. Isn't a criminal investigation more urgent? This is about the present, not the past."

"Yes, perhaps." Malak said. "Some people believe that we must resolve problems from the past in order to move forward, that lustration is really about the future, not the past. It is important for the lustration process to proceed. The citizens must be fully informed. They must trust the system."

With that, Malak guided them back down the elegant staircase to the heavy front door. "I will help you, do not worry," he said as he stepped onto the path that led down to the sidewalk.

Adam and Łukasz shook his hand. Sylvia gave him a quick kiss on the cheek. The three of them turned to head back to the bus stop.

Adam paused at the sidewalk and looked back at Malak. He had turned his face to the black sky, where only a handful of stars were visible through the light streaming upward from the city's many buildings. He heard Malak say something under his breath and he grabbed Sylvia.

"What did he just say?" he asked.

Sylvia stopped and watched Malak. "He is expressing his hope that he can regain control, that he can take action and not simply be a victim." She looked at Adam. "This is something that he believes in, I know. Too many Poles are willing to let others handle their problems. They become victims to other people's desires instead of being in control of their own."

Adam pulled Sylvia toward him, wrapping his arm around her shoulders as he turned back to the street. "We will stop these guys, Sylvia. Whoever they are. We will take control."

CHAPTER THIRTY-SIX

ADAM SLEPT with one eye open that night, listening for anything out of the ordinary. On the few occasions when he left Sylvia's bedroom to look out the window and check the hallway, he saw Łukasz lying awake on the sofa. They were both too worried to sleep.

Sylvia nevertheless insisted on going in to work that morning. As a result of the time she'd spent shepherding the group from Philadelphia, she was sorely behind in her regular work, she explained. Not to mention her coursework. One way or another, she needed to get things done, either at her office or at the university.

"No. No way," Adam said, his voice quiet but firm. "I'm not letting you out of my sight. Not until we've figured out what's going on and who's behind it all." His tone softened when he saw the anger building in her eyes. "I'm just worried about you, that's all. Surely you can understand that?"

"I think you should be more worried about yourself." She smiled, but her eyes were sharp. "I was not in any danger before you brought it into my life, you know."

Flinching as if slapped, Adam took a step back. "You know what, you're right about that. I guess it is my fault that you're involved in all this. Which is exactly why I feel responsible for protecting you. And I can't do that if I can't see you, if I'm not there with you."

Sylvia flung her arms up in despair.

"Friends... friends." Łukasz walked between them. "We cannot turn on each other. We need each other right now. Cousin." Łukasz turned to Adam. "Think about it. Isn't her office the safest place for *Pani* Stanko right now? A secure building... with guards protecting her?"

Adam couldn't argue with the logic. "I suppose that's true."

"Thank you, *Pan* Kaminski." Sylvia started gathering her coat and bag. "As if I need permission from either of you to go to work."

"Good, that's settled," Łukasz said. "I have a few more places to look at the newspaper archives, so I will continue my work there. Shall we meet for lunch?"

Sylvia frowned. "If I can make it, I will. We shall see."

Adam followed her out of the apartment, calling to her as she walked away. "Be safe. Please." She simply waved in response, without turning around.

The day was cold, but clear and bright. Even the wind had lessened, as if willing to give the residents of Warsaw a short reprieve before launching them into the depths of winter. Adam's breath hung in the air around him as he walked quickly to the Hotel Newport from Sylvia's apartment.

Adam's thoughts were on his friends when he entered the hotel lobby. It was a rookie mistake. He let his guard down.

When she jumped at him from the side, he was caught by surprise.

"You! So you are still alive. I was hoping you weren't."

"Angela." Adam took a step backward, but Angela matched his stride.

"Jared's dead. We're stuck in this country until the police tell us it's okay to leave." She brushed a hand roughly over her cheeks, wiping away a tear as if embarrassed by it. "And where have you been? Do you even know what's going on?"

"Calm down." Adam put a firm hand on her arm and guided her over to a discreet seating area against the wall. "You're angry, I know. Don't make a scene here."

Anger flashed in her eyes and she twisted her arm out of his grip. "Why the hell not? Why shouldn't I make a scene?"

"I'm so sorry, Angela." Adam shook his head and lowered his face so he could look her in the eye. "This is my fault. It's my fault Jared is dead. And I am so sorry. I wish I could take it back. I wish I could change things." He closed his eyes and ran his hand over his face.

His obvious concern seemed to mollify her slightly, but she was still breathing quickly when she asked him, "What do you mean? What did you do?"

Adam nodded as he gathered his thoughts, trying to keep his emotions in control. "I've gotten involved in an investigation, Angela. With my cousin."

"That's what you told me before. That he was researching a story and you were helping him. What kind of story is it that it got Jared killed?" Even as she spoke, the tears came once again to her eyes. This time she didn't brush them away. "Adam, I'm scared."

He took both her hands in his and held them close to his chest. "I know. I can understand that. I'm scared, too. I really believe you'll be safe, as long as you stay away from me."

"Oh, fine!" Angela stood up, jerking her hands away from him. "Stay away from you. You're the only person who seems to know what's going on. It seems like you're the only person who can protect me, and you're telling me to stay away from you."

Adam stood as well. "I will protect you Angela, as best I can. I promise you." He glanced around the lobby. "You just need to stay out of sight for a while. And not be seen with me. What did the police tell you to do?"

"The police told us we needed to stay in Warsaw for another day or two, to answer questions. They're coming back to the hotel later today and they want to meet with each of us." She lifted her chin toward Adam. "They'll want to meet with you, too, you know."

"I have no doubt of that. Look, you need to take care of yourself. Go back to your room. Go to the gym. Just stay in the hotel today. You'll be safe here. No one is after you. It's me they want. And I'm not going to hang around here."

"No, of course you're not. You're going to leave us alone again. Leave me alone again." Her eyes flashed as her tears caught the light from the window. "You just leave, then. See if I care."

With those words, Angela ran toward the stairs that led back to her room. Adam lifted his hand as if to reach out to her, but he didn't call out.

CHAPTER THIRTY-SEVEN

SILENT ROWS of pale metal shelving marched forward as far as the eye could see, filling the vast hall that comprised the newspaper's old archives. Brown cardboard boxes stacked on the shelves seemed to absorb the white lights that shone down from the ceiling, creating strange shadows along the narrow aisles.

Łukasz grunted as he raised his arms to pull down another box, shifting his posture slightly to keep his weight on his left side. A puff of dust escaped from between the boxes and Łukasz sneezed.

He carried the box back to the table along the wall, placing it next to the five other boxes he had already gone through. Some of the material he was looking for had already been digitized, and scanning through that had been quick. The archivists were working their way backwards through the old materials. Anything from within the past five years was digital, anything before that was still in the boxes.

Łukasz sneezed again as he lifted the lid off the next box and started rifling through the papers neatly filed inside.

Adam hadn't supported Łukasz's decision to come back to the newspaper archives this afternoon, and Łukasz fumed as he thought of Adam's comments over lunch just an hour earlier.

"Cousin, we need to find out who's behind this. Without support from the police, we have no other choice. We cannot simply sit back and wait for the next attack." Łukasz replaced his spoon in his soup bowl and wiped his lips.

"I know you're right, Łukasz. I just know that you're putting yourself in unnecessary danger. Wait until tomorrow. Wait until the offices are open and there are other people with you. There's safety in numbers. Today is not the day to go wandering into closed, empty spaces, is it?" Adam raised his spoon to his lips as he spoke and his face puckered at the first sour sting of the barley and kielbasa soup.

Łukasz grinned. "And what will you do while I am hiding away, trying to stay safe, hmm? Will you also be protecting yourself? Staying in hiding?"

"I want to go back to the embassy. I think that's the only place I can find help at this point." He glanced at his watch, then looked up at the entrance. No one came through. "I just don't know if I'll be able to get hold of anybody on a Sunday afternoon."

Łukasz considered his cousin. "It's not your fault. You can't protect everyone. You can't control everything." He paused, but when Adam didn't respond he continued, "If anything, this is my fault, for dragging you and your colleagues into my investigation."

"I should have seen it coming." Adam's response was sharp. "I should have been able to protect Jared. Now I have to protect Sylvia."

Most of the tables in the milk bar where they ate were occupied and the noise of multiple conversations grew as the lunch hour progressed. The hum of voices surrounded them, covering up their conversation. Łukasz put his spoon down in his *żurek* and looked at his cousin over the plastic table.

"Was your work this morning not productive?" he asked.

"Ha." Adam's laugh came out as a bark. "I got ahold

of my partner, Pete, at home, so that was good. He hadn't even heard about Jared's murder yet. Can you believe that? Our friends at the State Department didn't see the value of bringing the Philly PD into the picture."

"You told him, so now he can help?"

"I hope so." Adam shrugged. "He'll be able to reach out to the folks at the Philadelphia International Council, too, to see if they can help me get into the national archives."

"And is there something else bothering you?" Łukasz pressed, as Adam continued to frown down at his soup.

"I caught Pete at home because of the time difference... it was still early morning in Philly." Adam spoke softly. "But Julia, my sister, I couldn't reach her. I guess she wasn't at home."

"You cannot protect everyone, cousin," Łukasz repeated, shaking his head. "No one can."

"I can't stop you, can I?" Adam asked, looking up. "From continuing your own research?"

"No, cousin, you can't. You know I must find the truth, simply for this to end. I cannot stop now. I will not."

Adam nodded. "Fine. Do what you have to do. But be careful. Please."

As they left the restaurant, Łukasz turned right toward the newspaper offices. It was a long walk, but he needed the time, and the air, to focus his thoughts and figure out the best way to organize his search through the paper's archives.

The walk had worked for him. He arrived at the archives with a mental list of exactly which old stories he should start with, which files he needed to revisit. As soon as he had entered the darkened building, he moved quickly to the room that held the files he wanted, turning on only the lights he needed.

Cones of white light tapered off into pools of

darkness, highlighting sections of shelves, parts of tables. In the darkness, Łukasz could hear the floorboards settling. A book shifted on the shelf, finally succumbing to someone's placement earlier in the day. Muted sounds of traffic filtered in from the street outside.

Łukasz focused on his work, ignoring the sounds of the empty building.

Three hours later, cardboard boxes were piled high on the floor around the table. He jerked his head at a noise hinting of a door closing in the distance. He waited, but no footsteps followed. No colleague appeared out of the darkness that surrounded him.

Łukasz returned his gaze to the table and squinted his reddened eyes as he read the last of the files.

A series of articles covered the table in front of him. Some were stories that had been run years before in the paper. Others were notes from stories that had never run. They each had one element in common: Tomek Malak.

"Stavos Foundation Announces Malak Fellowship" announced the first headline, ten years after the fact. The Stavos Foundation had opened their Warsaw offices twelve years ago. The nonprofit supported an international exchange program for university students and ten years ago, two years after arriving in Warsaw, had created a scholarship in Malak's name.

The story covered a press conference held by the organization to announce the new program. Malak was being recognized for his efforts to help the foundation. Buried within the article was the fact that the organization had succeeded in a tight competition against other institutions, each looking to acquire a government grant for their work. Whoever had written the article hadn't gone into detail about that competition, but it caught Łukasz's eye. Mostly because he knew one year after this story had been published, Malak's daughter Sonja had spent a year at Oxford on just such an international program.

Other articles Łukasz had pulled included the headlines "Hilltop Hotel Announces Expansion and New Hires" and "Ener-Tech to Open Warsaw Branch." Each article was an example of a new, successful business venture in Warsaw, an international company making its way through the murk of the government bureaucracy. Each also mentioned Malak as instrumental in their success. The article about the Hilltop expansion listed Jerzy Malak, Malak's son, as a new manager. Ener-Tech had hired Sonja Malak as a vice president.

Five articles covered the successes of a series of corporations lucky enough to have established their businesses in Poland only days before acquiring lucrative city contracts. Malak was involved with each of these businesses. A real estate company had purchased land, cheap, immediately after Malak led an effort to rezone the land.

There was no evidence of graft, yet each article included subtle hints — gifts given to the city of Warsaw in return for its support, for example. CEOs saying they were pleased with the cost of doing business in Poland. Łukasz knew enough about the "cost" of doing business in Poland to read between the lines.

Łukasz could picture the Bernini statue of the Virgin Mary, the Chippendale chairs, the Wedgwood cut crystal glasses in Malak's house. These were the "gifts" these companies had offered, he was sure. That was the cost of doing business in Warsaw.

Łukasz rubbed his eyes and glanced at his watch. It was already after five. He had been lost in these files for hours. He had found suggestions that Malak might be corrupt, might be accepting inappropriate gifts. So what? None of this was truly criminal, nothing that couldn't be explained. Or justified. It was corruption, yes, but hardly worth killing over.

He closed his eyes to focus on what he had found. Could Basia have been killed because she threatened to expose Malak as a thief? As using his power for personal gain?

He sighed and shook his head. It wasn't likely. Worse, he wasn't sure Basia would have even tried to expose this. There was too much corruption in Poland now for her to be worrying about small gifts like these. Exposure might generate some bad publicity for Malak, and it might not. There must be something more. But what?

He turned his attention back to a second pile of papers on the table. These were newer records. They would never be digitized. These were notes collected by journalists who had tried to cover stories about lustration. The *Sejm* and the courts were strict about keeping the details of these cases out of the public eye, and journalists were not free to cover them or write about them. Every journalist worth his salt did anyway. And the notes slowly started piling up, notes of stories they each hoped they would be able to write one day.

Page by page, he started reading.

As he read about private individuals whose lives had been ruined by neighbors' lies or friends' indiscretions, Łukasz was reminded of the power of the previous regime. Its tentacles still reached into Poland, even now.

What had become of the people who collaborated? Some were good people, Łukasz knew. Some were trying to do the right thing, others were just trying to save themselves. But their lives were ruined, jobs lost, friends gone, when the truth about their collaboration came out.

And the agents of the secret police who would listen to these lies, to these secrets, where were they now? Some had gone to jail, convicted for their crimes against the people of Poland. Some had gone to Russia, to join forces with comrades there. And others had simply vanished, hidden themselves deep within Poland, anonymous and dangerous.

Łukasz shook his head and kept reading. Someone had a secret, a secret he had killed Basia to protect, and

Łukasz would keep reading, keep digging, until he found it. He focused on the papers on the table, ignoring once again the sounds of the darkness that surrounded him.

CHAPTER THIRTY-EIGHT

"SIR, THAT'S simply not possible. Please step back." The guard repeated his warning, clearly annoyed at Adam's persistence.

The American embassy loomed behind the guard standing in a small gatehouse at the main entrance. Its windows were dark, but Adam hadn't seen much light in them when he had visited during the week either.

"I have to see Sam Newman, sir. An American has been killed and I need Sam's help." Adam didn't care how stubborn the guard was, he wasn't giving up. And the guard seemed to realize it.

"I can give him a message from you, sir, that's the best I can do. He doesn't work on Sundays, I don't even know where he is."

Adam thanked the guard and told him he'd wait for the answer, then walked back down to the sidewalk. It was a bright winter afternoon and even in this quiet neighborhood, pedestrians roamed the streets. Some strolled, window shopping, while others moved with determination toward whatever outdoor activity awaited them. The cold wind that had returned to cut across the Sunday afternoon wasn't going to stop the residents of Warsaw from enjoying sunny November weather.

He was still considering his next step when he heard footsteps jogging down the drive behind him. Turning, Adam saw the guard coming toward him.

"Mr. Newman asked me to give you a message, sir," the guard called. "I caught him at home, and he said he'd meet with you."

"Thank you," Adam responded with feeling, "I really appreciate this. Thank you." Adam took the note the guard was waving. It listed a place and a time — an hour away. Adam didn't wait. He headed for the tram that would take him to Łazienki Park, the meeting place Sam had suggested.

The sounds of children playing carried across the lawns. Even bundled against the November chill in their thick, puffy parkas, the children ran and jumped, making the most of this afternoon outdoors, not locked behind warm walls. Tiny marshmallow people bounced up and down on the swings and merry-go-round in the playground.

Parents, also bundled in darker, woolen coats, waited patiently around the borders of the playground or walked along the paths that ran around the lake and through the trees. Łazienki Park was a place for children to play and a place for grown-ups to see and be seen. Women in high-heeled boots sashayed along the paths, their short skirts exposing more leg than Adam expected in November. Men walked beside them, a proud arm resting on their backs, smiles on their faces.

Young couples stopped to throw breadcrumbs at the giant carp that bubbled at the surface of the pond in front of the small palace. Teenage girls skipped and laughed, pointing at the teenage boys who sulked against the stone walls of the gardens.

Adam waited under the gray marble statue, its solid bulk carved into gently waving willow branches hovering lightly over the figure of Poland's best known composer, Frederick Chopin. A concrete patio stretched out before him, a space filled during the summer with residents enjoying piano recitals and ice cream. Today, the concrete pad sat empty, and Adam watched the people flowing by.

A family passed, a man and a woman wrapped in scarves and coats pushing a pram as a second child walked slowly next to them. The walking child paused periodically to pick at the rocks along the path, and the man spoke gently to her, encouraging her to run ahead to the playground to join the other children.

As she ran, the man looked over at Adam and caught his eye. Adam nodded at Sam, who leaned over to say something to his wife, then walked to where Adam waited.

"Adam, I was so sorry to hear about Jared. This is terrible, simply terrible. How are the others on your team holding up?"

"About as well as you can imagine," Adam responded. "They're scared, confused, and they're being told by the police they can't leave the country."

"I know, we're working on that," Sam assured him. "We've been in constant contact with DC since this happened, and we'll get you all out of here, safely back home, as soon as possible."

Adam nodded. "Thank you. I appreciate that." He looked out at the playground, where Sam's daughter had joined the other bouncing marshmallow men. "You have a beautiful family."

"Thank you." Sam smiled. The smile faded again as he turned back to Adam. "Why did you need to see me, Adam? Were you just checking that we were involved, looking out for you?"

"Perhaps." Adam frowned. "And perhaps because I need you to know that I'm looking out for me, too. I need to know who did this." He looked at Sam. "Because I believe they were aiming for me."

Sam looked at Adam, surprised. "That's quite a statement. What makes you say that?"

"I told you, I've been helping my cousin on an article he's writing."

"About political corruption. Yes, I remember."

"Corruption, yes… but there's more to it than that.

We're going to find out who killed his daughter."

"We?" Sam raised an eyebrow.

"Me. Łukasz. Sylvia."

"Ah... that was ruled a suicide, Adam. How can you blame someone else for that?" Sam asked quietly.

"It wasn't suicide. Łukasz knows it, I know it, and at least one other person knows it — the person who killed her. We're going to find him, Sam, and expose him."

"This is a dangerous game you're playing, Adam." Sam's voice held a note of warning. "Jared White is dead now. Is that really because of you?"

Adam let out a long breath of air and it floated visibly in front of him before slowly dissipating. He felt the weight of what he was about to say sink heavily down upon his shoulders. "I believe so, yes."

Sam frowned again, becoming much more serious. "What have you done? You must leave this. You must."

"I can't, Sam. I have to know the truth. The police aren't looking. You're not looking. Sylvia is the only Polish official willing to believe us. Willing to help us."

"We're looking now, believe me. We are offering the Polish police any assistance we can to find whoever killed Jared. It's a horrible crime. We cannot let this go unpunished." Sam looked over at his family. "I'm telling you nicely, Detective Kaminski, leave this alone. Let us do our job. Let the police do their job. Keep your cousin and your new friend safely out of this."

Adam followed Sam's eyes to where his wife sat with their infant son on her lap, bouncing him up and down, laughing with him. "I can't, Sam. Łukasz's daughter is dead. You have children, you can imagine how that must feel. He can't let it go, so neither can I."

"You don't know what you're doing." Sam's voice was as harsh as his words now. "We have relationships, carefully built relationships. You could jeopardize these."

"Yes, relationships. You told me this before. And I still don't like it. Do you know the men you have these relationships with, Sam? Really? And don't you want to know if one of them is a criminal, maybe even a killer?"

"People make difficult choices for difficult reasons, Adam." Sam's eyes were hard as he stared at him. "I don't always support those choices, but if their choices help the United States, I accept them. Without question." He paused, licking his lips. "Stay away from our connections, Adam, don't go digging into things you don't understand. If we have a source in the *Sejm* willing to help us achieve our goals, that's important. More important than you."

Adam raised his eyebrows at the words, but Sam was smiling again, his genial facade once more in place.

"You'll only make it worse, Adam." Sam's voice was kinder now. "I understand how you feel. Stay out of it. Don't make things harder than they already are."

CHAPTER THIRTY-NINE

"WORSE?" ADAM wondered to himself as he waited outside the newspaper offices for Łukasz. "How could it be worse?"

He had come straight here from Łazienki Park to catch up with Łukasz. If he couldn't talk Łukasz out of doing this research, the least he could do was keep an eye on him.

Adam watched as Łukasz peered out into the dark courtyard. The door closed with a distinct click behind him. A wide paved path lay before him, lined with narrow flower beds. No plants grew at this time of year, but small statues punctuated the brown rectangles of earth. Łukasz frowned and mumbled softly under his breath as he moved toward the wrought iron gate that separated this enclave from the *Aleje*.

The entranceway to the newspaper offices was in almost complete blackness, lit only by the few lights marking the street beyond the main gate. Łukasz didn't stop to check the lampposts that lined the pavement but remained unlit, instead moving swiftly toward the gate.

Watching from the sidewalk beyond, through the bars of the black fence, Adam could tell that Łukasz wasn't thinking about his environment. His focus was on whatever it was he had found — or not found — in the archives inside. Adam didn't make the same mistake. As he watched Łukasz moving through the courtyard he also kept an eye on the sidewalk around him, stamping his feet and shivering. He had been waiting out here far too long.

"Łukasz... hey!" Adam called out when Łukasz made it to the sidewalk.

The other man turned. When he saw Adam, he walked over quickly.

"Cousin, it is good to see you. I believe I have more information that is important to us."

"What did you find?" Adam asked.

"I'm not sure. I have hints... clues... some maybe pointing in one direction, some in another."

"Tell me, maybe I can help figure it out."

"There is the corruption, as we suspected. Tomek Malak is taking bribes, 'gifts' as he calls them, from companies willing to play the game." Łukasz grimaced. "And those companies are succeeding where others are still fighting the bureaucracy."

"Is that it? The motive behind Basia's murder?"

"No, it can't be. Think about it, look around. There is corruption everywhere. And who is Malak helping? Non-profit foundations, green energy providers. These are not the acts of an evil man. These are the acts of a man frustrated with how slow the system is and willing to take risks to work around it."

"And make a tidy profit in the process."

"Yes, but there is something else," Łukasz insisted, shivering and folding his arms across his chest, the folder of papers he was carrying pressed tight against his body.

"About Malak?"

"No, not Malak. Novosad. I dug some more into his past, his connections with Russia, the records kept about him by the previous regime."

"How can you have access to his files from the previous regime? I thought those were all locked away safely in the national archives."

"They are. Here I have access to notes taken by other journalists. Notes for stories that may never be written. The newspaper is holding onto them, just in case."

"And what did you find about Novosad?"

"Kuhl was right. He is Russian. And it's as bad as I suspected. His cousin is definitely part of the Russian mafia. A small player, it seems, but nevertheless a part. That is certain, there is no doubt."

Adam kicked at a small rock at his feet, moving to keep warm. "Would Novosad kill to keep that secret? And is that something Basia might have found?"

Łukasz nodded. "I think we should ask Novosad that."

"Oh no, this is something real. Something we can take to the police. Maybe this will be the push they need to dig a little deeper into Basia's death."

"You are right, of course." Łukasz laughed out loud. "Thank God. I have been so focused on being in this alone. I can't tell you how valuable it has been to be able to share this with you, to work on this with you."

"You're not alone anymore. I'm here. And once we take this to the police tomorrow, they'll take over the investigation."

Łukasz's body sagged and Adam could see the tension leaving him. "This is good, cousin. Thank you. The end is in sight." He flipped through the papers in his hand. "But there are some... Yes, here they are."

Adam took the few wrinkled papers Łukasz handed him. "What's this? Why can't these go to the police?"

"These are not for the police, cousin. Only for your eyes." Łukasz shook his head as he spoke. "You said you wanted to learn more about your great-grandfather." He gestured toward the papers Adam still held out as if afraid to take. "These are letters. I had them in my office."

"Whose letters? I don't understand."

"Read them. When you have time. Then you will understand. Hopefully. Something about your family and mine. About the past."

Adam nodded, glancing at the papers for just a moment before folding them neatly and sliding them into his inside coat pocket.

Łukasz tucked the papers he was still carrying absentmindedly into his pocket. "I'll be okay now, I'm going to head home. I need to see my apartment again, it's been too long."

Adam watched Łukasz walk away, then turned to go himself, back to his hotel. After only one step, he paused, frowned, and turned back to Łukasz. A dark sedan up the street had caught his attention.

The driver had pulled the car up to the curb about a hundred yards ahead. It was in a parking lane, but at this time on a Sunday night there were no other cars parked there. The car was idling, its headlights on. Adam couldn't get a clear look at the car or the driver.

"Hey," he called out. Łukasz looked back. Seeing Adam, he raised a hand slightly, lifting his chin and shrugging as if to ask Adam what he was yelling about. His breath hung on the air around him, illuminated by the lights of the car.

Adam never got a chance to answer. As soon as Łukasz's back was turned to the car, it started moving. Fast.

As it neared the spot where Łukasz waited on the sidewalk, the driver swerved. The car tilted precariously as it weaved onto the sidewalk, its left tires still on the street.

"Look out!" Adam called out.

Łukasz turned, but didn't step aside. He never had the chance. The car picked up speed as it closed the distance with Łukasz. By the time it hit him, the driver was already turning the wheel to swerve back out onto the street.

"No!" As Adam ran toward Łukasz, he saw his body slam into the front of the car, then fly over the hood into the street.

As Adam watched, the driver turned his head for an instant, to see where Łukasz had landed. To make sure, Adam supposed. It was a dumb move.

The driver didn't swerve back onto the street quickly enough. As the car turned toward the street, the right side of the car caught a streetlamp. The whole car jerked violently and started to spin. The driver had lost control.

Adam ran back toward the sidewalk, away from the spinning car. He watched, helplessly, as the car skidded to a stop across the street, the smell of burnt rubber filling the air. Horns blared as other drivers turned to avoid the black car, then turned again to avoid Łukasz, lying motionless in the middle of the lane.

Finally, Adam moved. He started running toward Łukasz, but a movement from the black car caught his attention and he turned. The driver had pushed the door open and was hanging out of the car with his hands resting on the street, shaking his head.

Figuring the driver wasn't going anywhere, Adam ran toward Łukasz. Bending over him, he felt for a pulse. It was there, but it was weak. Blood streamed out of a wound on Łukasz's head. Adam knew how much head wounds bled, and knew that it didn't necessarily mean the wound was fatal.

He leaned over Łukasz, afraid to touch him more or move him. "Łukasz... Łukasz... can you hear me?"

Łukasz didn't move.

The driver of the black car did. Adam turned to look just as the driver struggled to his feet. He glanced toward Adam and Łukasz, then turned away and started walking, uncertainly, in the other direction.

The sounds of sirens carried over the air, moving closer. Help was on the way. There was nothing more he could do for Łukasz now. Except catch the man who'd hurt him.

With a quick nod to himself, Adam took off after the fleeing man.

CHAPTER FORTY

SOUNDS OF THE SIRENS were weaker now. Adam followed the fleeing driver off the main street into a neighborhood lined with narrow cobblestone alleys and old stone houses. His footsteps echoed in the tight space and he intentionally tried to step onto the thin layer of snow that coated the edges of the paths in the hopes that it would muffle his steps. It did muffle the sound, but it also made walking more treacherous and he had to move carefully to avoid slipping.

He kept his eyes on the dark figure ahead of him. He had recognized him immediately as the knife wielder who had attacked him in the cemetery and hadn't lost sight of the man since he had run from the crime scene. He had clearly been hurt in the accident and as he ran, he kept one arm tucked inside his coat. Adam didn't know if the injury was to the arm, to the ribs he was holding, or to both. He didn't care, except that he would use that information against the man once he caught up to him.

Adam was in no hurry to catch the man. A better bet, he thought, to follow him, see who he reported back to. If he just ended up drowning his pain in a local bar, then Adam would take him. Use his injuries as a weapon against him to force him to tell Adam the truth. If Adam got lucky, the driver would lead Adam to the person behind all this. If Adam got lucky.

So he kept his distance, walking carefully on the slippery path, staying out of view as the man stopped periodically to check behind him. Adam walked holding his arms tight against his body, against air that froze his face, his hands, his feet. Each breath felt like inhaling ice, and he did his best to stay calm and keep his breathing slow.

He tried not to think of Łukasz lying bleeding on the city street. The ambulances would have made it to him by now. He was probably already safely on his way to a hospital, where they would bandage his head wound, patch up any broken bones. Łukasz would be fine, he'd live through this. Adam kept repeating this to himself as he walked. To convince himself it was true. That he had made the right decision to chase the attacker instead of staying with Łukasz.

The man's uneven footfalls echoed from ahead, and Adam could tell he had turned off into another narrow alley to the left. Adam followed not far behind. Light from the lamps on the main streets didn't reach back here. The only light came from windows of the apartments that lined the alley, filtered yellow light sneaking out between chinks in lace curtains, casting figures of yellow and white over the snow-covered bricks of the path and creating shadows that scuttled up the yellowed stone walls.

It seemed like they had been walking for hours, though in reality Adam knew it hadn't been more than ten minutes, when he heard a door open ahead. The low murmur of voices spilled out into the night air along with a shaft of bright light. Adam turned the corner just in time to see the door closing again behind Łukasz's attacker.

So he was going to drown his pain. Not report back to his boss. That was all right, Adam had considered this possibility. He just needed to get the man back outside where he could question him thoroughly.

Adam pulled open the old wooden door and stepped

into the bar. It might have been his imagination, but the room grew stiller when he entered. The conversation didn't stop — a loud bark of laughter followed his entrance — but something about the tenor of the conversation changed.

Adam glanced around. The man he had been following was not in sight. Spotting a door just to the right of the stained bar, Adam moved toward it. A short bald man stepped in front of him as he rounded the bar.

"*Slucham*? Can I help you?" the man asked in a surprisingly high voice. "Are you here for a drink?"

The man planted the bottle of vodka he was holding firmly on the bar, his arm barring Adam's path to the door. A sliver of light bounced off the chain around his neck. A medal of Saint Casimir.

Adam shuddered, but stayed calm. "I need to go that way." He waited, not pushing.

The man looked at him for a moment, then shrugged and stepped aside.

Adam walked by him and grabbed the handle on the door. It didn't move. He pulled again, but the door was clearly locked. He turned back to the short man with the Casimir medal.

"Did you see that man who just came in here? Where did he go?"

"Sorry? My English not so good, not understand." The man's accent seemed to be getting stronger.

Adam leaned against the bar and looked around the room. There was no other door, except the one Adam had come through. Everywhere he looked, dark, sullen faces looked back at him. One customer smiled, baring his teeth.

Adam turned from the bar and walked back out into the dark alley. There was no side door to the bar, no path leading to the back of the building. Up and down the street, houses and stores stood side by side, like sentries guarding hidden realms with no chinks in their armor. Adam walked past six buildings before he found a break between them he could pass through. As he walked along it, though, he saw there was no way he could work his way back to the rear of the bar.

He spun around in despair, hoping to see some access point he had missed. Some way to get to the back of the building. But even as he waited, he knew his quarry was getting farther and farther away.

The driver was gone. Adam had lost his best lead.

CHAPTER FORTY-ONE

THE WARMTH and light of the hotel lobby greeted him like a comforting embrace. One he really needed right now. He also needed help from home. Stretching his neck and relaxing his shoulders, he glanced around the lobby, then walked over to the lobby phone.

His conversation with Pete was short but effective. For every question Adam asked about the suspects in the case, Pete had the answer. Background information, family information, birth dates, incomes.

"And there's one more thing, Kaminski," Pete added when Adam had finished pumping him for information. "A message from the captain."

"And what's that?" Adam asked, his voice dropping.

"Make sure this case is solved. Fast. It doesn't look good, a member of a US delegation killed right under the nose of one of Philly's finest."

"Don't you think I know that?" Adam's voice dropped even lower, his eyes closing as he spoke. "Don't you think I feel responsible for Jared's death?" He felt the tension in his shoulder creep back. The guilt burning at the back of his neck.

"Calm down, partner. I know, I'm just passing on a message."

"Sure. Right." Adam took a deep breath. This call wasn't as comforting as he had hoped. "So where do I go from here?"

"Motive?" Pete asked. "Always a good place to start."

"I like Łukasz's take on this." Adam nodded as he spoke. "Someone with something to hide. A secret Basia uncovered."

"Until you know that secret, you don't know the motive." Adam could tell Pete was thinking out loud. "So opportunity, then."

"Not that easy." Adam shook his head. "I think this could be a hired killer. He seemed like it when I met him."

"Interesting..."

"What are you thinking, Pete?"

"A wise man once said, three men can keep a secret — if two of them are dead."

"Let me guess, Raymond Chandler?" Adam asked.

"Close," Pete answered. "Benjamin Franklin."

Adam smiled despite himself. "So it's the 'no honor between thieves' approach. If the goal of all this is to keep a past secret hidden, they may be each other's weakness."

Pete's voice carried calmly and quickly over the line. "And maybe you can use that against them."

Adam hung up the phone and looked around the lobby. An open doorway across the room led to a dimly lit bar and Adam headed that way seeking liquid solace.

The sharp, heady scent of whiskey mixed with a hint of cinnamon floated from the room. What little light the electric candles hanging from the chandelier produced bounced off the gleaming cherry bar. Pale green wallpaper reflected in the gilt mirrors that lined one wall. A rack of spotless glasses and mugs hung over the bar. Thick curtains over the windows kept the cold air outside. The room was dim yet cozy, comfortable.

The first people Adam saw when he entered were Angela and Ray. They sat on high stools up against the bar, both nursing mugs that had stopped steaming long before. As he walked toward them, Adam saw the dry tears on Angela's cheeks and a twinge of guilt brought his shoulders back up into a tense hunch.

Adam pulled up a third stool next to Angela. "Can I join you?"

"I thought it wasn't safe. I thought you were going to abandon us." Angela's words were sharp, but her voice didn't carry the anger it had held earlier.

"Yeah. I'm sorry about that. Angela, Ray, I'm doing the best I can to protect you. To protect my cousin. Hell, to protect myself. I don't want anyone else getting hurt. At this point, I have nowhere else to go."

Ray reached around behind Angela and patted Adam on the shoulder. "Have a drink with us, then. It's a hot toddy — at least, some Polish version of hot toddy. It's vodka, that's all I know."

"Looks like you could both use fresh drinks, too. I'm buying." Adam finally managed to catch the attention of the bartender, who was seated on a low chair at the far end of the bar absorbed in a newspaper.

"Good to see you again, Kaminski. It's been a while." Ray winked as he spoke. "Chris is shitting bricks worrying about you."

"I'm sure he is. I'll talk to him tomorrow. I'm too tired right now."

"And how is your investigation going?" Angela asked. "Has your cousin found anything new?"

"I don't think so." Adam spoke quietly. "I don't really know, to be honest. He was in another accident. He's in the hospital." He paused to take a quick drink from his steaming mug. "I don't even know how he's doing, they won't tell me anything."

"Oh, Adam, I'm so sorry." Angela put her hand on Adam's leg. "I'm so sorry."

Tears started to well up once again in her eyes, and she moved her hand and turned her head away.

"It's okay, Angela. It's okay to cry. Sometimes I wish I could just let it out. These are sad times. To Jared." Ray lifted his mug in a toast. "To our lost team member, may he rest in peace."

The three drank in silence for a few minutes.

Adam knew that Angela was right. He shouldn't have come back here. These guys were after him and he was putting her and Ray in danger just by sitting with them. Where else could he have gone, damn it? The hospital had refused to give him information about Łukasz. Sylvia hadn't been at her apartment, and that worried him even more. Was she just working late? Was she in danger? Or worse, had she gone somewhere she didn't want Adam to know about?

Angela's hand touched his leg again and Adam looked over. Ray was standing up, patting his pockets to find his room key. "Time's up for me. I'm heading upstairs." He glanced over at Angela and Adam. "Take care, you two. Don't do anything I wouldn't do."

"We have tickets to leave Warsaw tomorrow, Adam. I don't know if you knew that?" Angela asked him. "The police have determined it's okay for us to leave."

"I didn't know. I'm not scheduled to fly out until Wednesday." He laughed under his breath. "I thought that would give me plenty of time to figure out what was going on, to help Łukasz. And instead I've just made things worse."

His hands tightened around his glass mug, soaking up its warmth. He fought to ignore the sounds of grief in his head, the crying mothers. He blinked and shook his head.

"Don't" — Angela leaned toward him — "don't beat yourself up like that. You're doing all you can. I know you are. You can't be responsible for everything. For everyone." She stared at his face, but he looked away. "Where are you? Sometimes your eyes, they're so far away... where do you go?"

He didn't answer, and she turned back to her drink. After a moment, she tried again. "Tell me about your students. The reason you left teaching."

Adam stayed silent.

"They died, didn't they?" Angela asked, looking at

Adam closely. "Were they killed?"

Adam nodded, his eyes on his hands. "Drive-by. They weren't even involved. Just hanging out in front of their home. Three dead, one injured too badly to come back to school. They were good kids, they didn't deserve that. Their parents didn't deserve that."

Angela closed her eyes, nodding, her thick mahogany hair sliding forward over her glasses, hiding her face. Her expression was strained when she turned back to him, her normally wide eyes narrowed, her lips taut.

"It happens, I know." She paused, then added, "I'm sure there was nothing you could do about it."

"No?" He looked up at her. "I was their teacher. I was supposed to protect them. I didn't." He shrugged. "Now I'm a cop. It's a little more clear-cut." His lips turned up into a mockery of a smile.

She shivered and looked down at the mug in front of her. "I'm sorry I lost it this morning. I was just angry and scared about what was happening. I wasn't really mad at you."

Adam considered the woman next to him, her face pale and drawn, her fingers tapping on her mug. He took a breath and put his arm over her shoulder. "Thank you. I really appreciate hearing that. So, what have the police told you?"

Angela let her breath out in an angry hiss. "Nothing, that's what. Nothing. I don't know if they don't know anything or if they just won't tell us." She shrugged. "The police still don't know who killed Jared and I suspect they never will."

The two paused as they absorbed this fact and what it meant for them.

"I'm just furious," Angela finally burst out. "The police have given up. Don't they care?"

"They care. I'm sure they care. A murder was committed and they will keep working at it until they figure out who did it and bring those people to justice. I'm sure of it."

Adam spoke confidently, but his own thoughts were closer to Angela's. It was possible that the police really wouldn't solve this case, either because they couldn't or because they wouldn't. Was it just because Jared was a foreigner, or was it because they were afraid of what they'd find if they really investigated this murder?

Adam put his arm around Angela again and she leaned into him, resting her head on his shoulder.

Adam raised his other hand. "Bartender, another round," he called out.

The young bartender slowly rose from his seat and moved back toward them.

CHAPTER FORTY-TWO

THE OLD WOMAN'S stare told Adam all he needed to know. She wasn't going to let him into the building. He had been waiting outside Sylvia's apartment again. She still wasn't responding to the doorbell. At this time on a Monday morning she was most likely at work. But why hadn't she been home last night?

His common sense told him she was probably fine, but he also knew she was still in danger. He couldn't help worrying. If she was just working, why hadn't she left a message for him at the hotel letting him know she was all right?

His fear for Sylvia's safety had been with him all night. Even as he and Angela got more and more comfortable with each other at the bar last night, he couldn't let go of it. Angela had noticed.

"You're here, but your mind is elsewhere. Where are you? And who are you with?"

"Sorry, Angela, it's everything going on. I just need to work through it, figure out what all the evidence is pointing to. Łukasz thinks he knows, and he was hammered with a car because of it. I just have this feeling there's something more."

"Uh-huh." Angela looked sideways at him. "Once a cop, always a cop, I guess. It must be tough for the women in your life."

Adam smiled. "Maybe that's why there is no particular

woman in my life."

"And yet, I have the feeling you're thinking about one right now. And it's not me."

"I'm sorry, Angela." Adam smiled at her sadly. "You are a great woman, and in another time, perhaps. But you're right, right now I'm worried about Sylvia. I got her involved in all this and now I don't even know where she is."

Angela nodded, but she frowned. "We all have to make choices, Adam. And sometimes that means living with the choices someone else makes." She finished her drink and stood. "I wish you luck, Adam Kaminski, I think you're going to need it."

Adam smiled and looked up at her.

"Maybe I'll see you in the morning before we leave?"

"Maybe, but let's say goodbye now."

Angela smiled one more time and put her hand on his shoulder. "Goodbye, then."

Standing that morning outside Sylvia's apartment, Adam could still see the image in his mind of Angela walking gracefully out of the bar. She would soon be safe at home, back in Philadelphia. Now it was time to worry about Sylvia's safety. He had dragged her into this mess. He couldn't live with himself if she had been hurt because of him.

His attempts to get into Sylvia's building as other tenants left were not getting him anywhere. Even if he could get into the building, he still hadn't figured out how he'd get into her apartment anyway.

Finally giving up, he turned his collar against the chill and started the fifteen minute walk back up *Ulica Miodowa* to *Aleje Jerozolimskie* and his hotel. Hopefully, Sylvia was at work. He could call from the hotel to confirm that.

Adam worked his way around groups gathering on the sidewalk. Parents with small children, another group of university students, a cluster of middle-aged women all stopped along the sidewalk and turned to watch the street. Weaving through the crowd, Adam couldn't at first identify the cause of the gatherings.

As he moved farther up *Aleje Jerozolimskie* and the crowd grew denser, he started to hear the music. A faint thread of a traditional Polish fiddle carried over the air first, followed by the sounds of the rest of the small musical group marching at the front of the parade.

It wasn't a huge parade. As Adam watched, the quartet passed by, followed by men and women dressed in the garb of Polish *górali*, or mountain folk. Next up were a group of men and women in what appeared to be military gear, carrying flags of Poland, Warsaw and the regions around Warsaw.

Craning his neck to see over the crowds, Adam could just make out the banners carried by the rest of the participants. SLD. The parade was supporting the candidates of the party to the national legislature.

Parade participants walked in groups, divided by the region of Poland they were from and holding signs that identified the labor groups they supported: nurses, teachers, truck drivers. Adam watched all this with interest, surprised to see such an overtly socialist parade.

The number of university students gathering around him grew. Turning, Adam found himself surrounded by young men. One of the young men raised a hand and shouted toward the parade. Adam didn't recognize the words. Soon other young men were shouting, and it was clear they were not calling out their support for the parade.

As the shouting grew more intense, Adam leaned over to one of the students. "Hey, do you speak English?"

The young man blinked in surprise and looked up at Adam. "Of course."

"Good." Adam nodded, ignoring the man's arrogance. "What's going on, what are you shouting?"

"They are the SLD. They want the government to pay them even when they don't work. They want to go back to the old way of doing things, where the government took care of us, but we had no power, no control."

"So this is a political statement?" Adam asked.

"Of course." The man shrugged, then turned away from Adam. Cupping his hands around his mouth he shouted, "*Wracaja praca!*" Turning to Adam with a smile and a wink, he shouted again, "Go back to work!"

Adam moved a little way up the street.

As the number of students grew, police showed up on scene. They formed a line between the protesters and the parade participants, ready to block any attempts at aggression on the part of the students. Looking around the crowd, Adam didn't think there was going to be trouble. The students who were shouting were smiling and laughing. They were having fun — at the marchers' expense, perhaps, but fun all the same.

The young man Adam had questioned ran across the street, followed by a small group of friends. They entered a university building that looked out over the parade route. A few minutes later, a white T-shirt flew out of a second-story window and dangled in the air. The shirt had a crude painting on the front in red ink. "SLD," it read.

The students who had flung the shirt out the window had taken precautions to ensure that anyone watching knew they were not supporting SLD. The shirt dangled from the window on a rope, and the rope was tied with a hangman's noose. It was literally hung in effigy.

When the audience saw the shirt, everyone laughed. It seemed like a congenial atmosphere. One older woman walking by commented to her friend that the students were being stupid, and some of the marchers made rude gestures toward the students, but there was no threat of violence that Adam could pick up.

After a few more minutes, the marchers passed by and the police moved on with the parade.

That was when the fighting started.

A man from the audience jumped up onto the outside of the university building and tried to grab at the T-shirt, climbing precariously up the outside of the building. He lunged at the shirt but failed to catch it. Others from the crowd surrounded him, chanting, some encouraging him and others trying to stop him.

The man lunged one last time at the shirt, catching it with both hands. Losing his grip on the building itself, the man swung from the building holding onto the shirt. Holding onto the hangman's noose.

Adam stepped forward. Someone was going to get hurt and there were no police around. As he moved, his eyes were on the young man hanging from the building and the group of students surrounding him. He didn't notice the person coming up behind him.

The first punch hit him hard in the kidney. He grunted and fought the urge to bend forward, instead stepping fast to his left. The second punch landed on his arm.

Adam turned to face his attacker and recognized him immediately as the man who had attacked Łukasz in the alley behind *Pod Jaszczurami*. Adam saw his own handiwork in the nasty cut still healing across the man's nose. Make that men — his smaller companion was standing just behind him. Glancing quickly over the crowd, without taking his attention from the large man facing him, Adam thought he caught a glimpse of his third friend with the knife. This wasn't going to be a fight he could win.

The shouts from the group of students got louder and angrier. The man who had been hanging from the building had finally let go, landing with a thud onto the hard pavement. Some of his friends had come to his aid; other students were coming forward with anything but aid in their minds. One was brandishing a wooden pole, taken from the signs that had been carried by the marchers.

Adam looked back at his attacker and the man grinned. His teeth were gray and uneven. He ran his tongue over them roughly as he smiled.

"Shit," Adam thought to himself.

He turned and ran toward the group of students, intentionally knocking over the man brandishing the stick. The man stumbled, then turned toward Adam, anger plastered over his face.

"*Hej, kurwa*," he spat out and stepped menacingly toward Adam.

Adam ducked and ran past him into the crowd of students. His preference was always to face anyone attacking him. Running was rarely the right idea. In this case, however, given the odds, he figured it was his only option.

The young man with the stick started to follow him, but was blocked by another group of students busy dumping out a trash can onto the street. Glancing back, Adam saw his attackers trying to move through the crowd of students. By hitting and pushing the students out of their way, they were only managing to get involved in the brawl that was starting on the street. For each young man they pushed out of their way, two more stepped up to confront them.

Adam turned away again and slipped down a side street, then another, and kept going.

CHAPTER FORTY-THREE

LEANING BACK against the rough brick wall of a small grocery store, Adam looked back the way he had come. The street was empty. The sounds of the fighting a few blocks away carried over the air, and any residents or shoppers who might otherwise have been out were safely tucked away at home or behind closed doors.

Adam waited, thinking. He couldn't just hide here. He needed to find out if Sylvia was safe. Was she simply at work, behind locked doors and armed guards? Or had something happened to her?

Rather than retracing his steps, Adam moved forward. Narrow cobblestone streets filled this old part of the city, each occasionally taking an unexpected twist or turn. As he walked, he checked doorways and gaps between the houses to make sure no one was hiding, waiting for him. He also kept an eye out for good hiding places if he needed them.

Eventually, Adam found his way back to *Aleje Jerozolimskie*. Stepping onto the sidewalk, Adam saw the group of people to his right.

The police had finally gotten involved in the fighting, it seemed, and had managed to calm everyone down. Now Adam could see a number of uniformed officers taking control of the crowd. He didn't see his attackers in the crowd, but he knew they'd still be looking for him.

The hotel stood just across the street. Moving quickly, Adam skirted around a bus shelter, leaned into a parked van, staying close to any structure he could find in an attempt to stay hidden. It didn't work. He should've known he was too big to hide.

A shout from the crowd to his right got his attention, and he turned to see a young man pointing directly at him. He recognized him as the man who had tried to tear down the white T-shirt. He was pointing at Adam and speaking excitedly to one of the police officers in the group. That officer starting walking toward Adam.

Knowing better than to run from the police, Adam changed directions and went to meet the officer with a slight feeling of relief. Perhaps someone had seen the attack and the police were finally ready to help him. He was tired of trying to do this on his own without any official help. He wasn't used to working around the law.

As he approached him, the Polish officer put his hand on his nightstick. Adam saw the movement and tensed. Something was wrong.

Another officer had seen Adam as well and was talking into a radio. As that officer stepped to the side, Adam saw the body.

The small man, part of the team who had attacked him, lay in the street, blood pooling around his back. The knife still sticking up out of the wound.

Adam stopped moving. This wasn't right. How could that man have been stabbed? He knew who had had that knife. He assumed they had been working together.

As Adam paused, uncertain, the Polish officer grabbed him by the arm and swung him around, pushing him against a car parked along the street.

Adam twisted as he fell, trying to see more of the crime scene, to figure out what had happened.

"You are an American, no?" the officer said in broken

English. "You think our law does not apply to you?" He spat on the ground at Adam's feet as he spoke.

"No, officer, there's been a mistake. I didn't hurt that man. I don't even know that man."

Even as he spoke, Adam thought about the night in the alley with Łukasz. He hadn't hit the small man, had he? Would they find his blood on Adam's coat? His eye fell again on the knife, and Adam understood clearly.

He had held that knife the day before. He had picked it up off the ground in the cemetery. Adam knew without any doubt that when the police tested it, they would find his fingerprints all over that knife.

"You will come with us now, Mr. American," the officer was saying. "You will not be going back home to your America now."

Adam was no longer listening. His eyes had focused on the small piece of metal pinned to the officer's uniform. A tiny version of a medal. Saint Casimir. Just like the Philly cop at the funeral.

All of Adam's muscles tensed and his vision started going black, heat rising in his face with his anger. He had to keep control. He couldn't let himself go back to that cemetery. Back to the guilt.

His thoughts flashed to Łukasz, still in the hospital. Was he alive? Was he safe? He thought of Sylvia. God only knew where she was, who was with her.

He couldn't let himself get arrested. There was too much at stake. Too much out of control. No way he could trust this cop.

Adam took a deep breath then let himself relax. He leaned forward into the car. To his right, he saw another officer approaching, pulling out a pair of handcuffs. Adam nodded to himself, braced himself, and kicked out backwards.

He caught the officer by surprise and the man stepped back. He didn't release his hold on Adam, but he gave Adam enough space to twist to the left. Adam grabbed the officer's arm as he twisted and, with a sharp movement, threw the officer back against the car. It had only taken a few seconds. The second officer started running toward them and Adam took off, back up the alley he had come from.

CHAPTER FORTY-FOUR

THE HUMMING was soft but constant. Eventually overwhelming. He lay still, first trying to ignore it, then trying to identify it. He couldn't block it out. Whether he focused on the sound or tried to think about something else, there was only room in his head for the sound.

Humming, buzzing, broken on regular intervals by a squeak and the sound of air escaping.

It grated on his ears, rang in his head. He just wanted to go back to sleep. His arms, his legs, his whole body ached. But the sound was too much. He couldn't take it any more.

Łukasz opened his eyes and tried to sit up in the bed. Hospital equipment surrounded him. Cables and wires stretched from digital displays, pumps and IV bags into his arms and his chest. He looked like a machine himself. He felt like he was tied down.

The room was dim, the hallway beyond his room dark and quiet. All he could hear was the constant humming. Buzzing.

He pulled at a thick cable that lay near his pillow and a remote control slid toward his hand. At least turning the TV on blocked out the maddening humming. Barely.

Łukasz kept the volume turned low. He was alone in the room and he liked it that way. No reason to alert the nurses he was awake. He needed to think.

Someone had tried to kill him. Again.

He had seen the driver of the vehicle before it hit him. He shivered as he remembered the man's face: hard, rough, flat, uninterested. Adam had been right. This was a killer for hire. He had no interest in Łukasz, he had no anger or joy. He was simply doing a job.

The screen of the TV lit the room in shades of blue and gray, as if the whole room were underwater. Łukasz watched the shadows dancing across the foot of the bed, not paying attention to the images on the screen that were creating the shadows.

Novosad, he thought. It must be Novosad. With his connections to the Russian mafia, he would have had the opportunity to hire a former member of the Polish secret police. Or even KGB. The man had looked like KGB. Would Malak or Kapral even know how to contact such a person? Łukasz thought it unlikely.

"Kaminski." The word cut through his thoughts, bringing him back to the present.

Łukasz heard the name and glanced around, but the room remained empty. Then his eyes turned to the TV and the news announcer who was speaking. "The police are looking for Adam Kaminski, an American visiting Poland. He is wanted for questioning in connection with this murder."

The image behind the anchorman showed the scene earlier that afternoon along *Aleje Jerozolimskie*, the crowd of students, the ambulance carrying away a stretcher covered in a white sheet.

Łukasz focused on the TV now, absorbing every detail the media was sharing. Grabbing the remote, he flipped through channels, hearing other versions, other perspectives.

A man had been killed, that much was clear. Stabbed that afternoon during a parade. The man had been declared dead on arrival at the hospital. And Adam Kaminski was wanted for questioning in connection with the stabbing.

Łukasz dropped the remote. He thought *he* had problems. He had only been hit by a car. Adam had been hit by something much worse.

He grunted and swung his legs off the bed. Grabbing at the wires and lines that snaked across his body, he pulled. Some came away easily, tiny detectors glued to his chest, back and arms popped off. The IV line was harder. He grimaced as the line came out, like bugs crawling under his skin.

Finally free, he slapped at his arm to stop the itching as he stood cautiously, holding onto the bed. Then he waited.

Nothing happened, no one came running.

He heard another TV, distant, the sound faintly carrying down the hall. The nurses were otherwise occupied, he assumed. Not overly concerned about their patient.

Łukasz took that as a good sign. No one was expecting him to die of his injuries any time soon.

His left arm was in a cast, and with his right he could feel a thick bandage stuck to his forehead. His chest and sides hurt when he breathed, but by holding his arm tight against his body, he could move without too much pain.

He walked softly to the open door and peered down the long hallway. Flickering lights six doors down revealed the room the nurses were using as their break room. He stepped out of his room and turned in the other direction.

He was a few yards down the hall when someone came around a corner ahead, walking directly toward him. A doctor, dressed in the green scrubs and white lab coat of his profession. The man walked slowly, reading notes from a clipboard as he walked. He hadn't even noticed Łukasz yet.

There was nowhere for Łukasz to hide, no open door to duck into. Instead, he stood up straight, pulled his hospital robe tighter around his pajamas, and picked up his pace. He walked confidently past the young doctor.

The doctor looked up as they passed in the hall. Łukasz smiled briefly and nodded, then kept walking. The doctor returned his gaze to his clipboard.

As he turned the corner, stepping out of view of the doctor, Łukasz breathed again and curled into himself. His heart was pounding and his side hurt. He was getting too old for this, he told himself. This was a young man's work. He should be covering horse races and school concerts, not doing investigative journalism.

This would be his last investigation, he decided. The last, and the most important.

Not many people roamed the halls at that time of the evening, but there were some. Some Łukasz avoided, ducking into empty rooms, stepping around corners before he was noticed. Others he confronted with confidence, as he had the first doctor.

He was just relaxing, feeling confident, when he heard soft footfalls approaching from behind.

"Sir, sir," the young nurse called.

Łukasz stopped and turned to face her.

Her cherubic face, surrounded by dark brown curls piled into a messy knot on top of her head, was furrowed with a look of obvious concern. "Sir, are you all right? Can I help you?" She looked over him, still in his pajamas and robe, the red marks clear where he had pulled out his IV line. "You should be in bed, I think, shouldn't you?"

Łukasz smiled kindly at the young woman, so obviously concerned and taking her job seriously. "Thank you, *Pani*, yes. I should be. But my back, you know..." Łukasz leaned forward slightly and put his hand on the small of his back. "If I lie in bed for too long, it pains me."

"We have painkillers for that, you know," she responded. "I can contact your doctor and get approval to give you one."

"Oh no, no," Łukasz shook his head and frowned. "I do not need anything that drastic. I just need to walk around for a few minutes. I will be fine. In fact, I'll head back to my room right now."

The nurse took his arm and stepped forward with him, looking as if she had every intention of walking Łukasz back to his room. He was trying to figure out how to get away from her when a loud buzzing sounded from the nurses' station just up the hall.

"Oh, dear. *Pani* Małgosza. She always needs something. She can never sleep for more than thirty minutes at a time." She looked up at Łukasz. "I do have to go to her, I'm the only one on duty on this floor. Are you sure you can make it back to your room on your own? I could call someone else to come and help."

"That's simply not necessary, my dear." Łukasz smiled down at her. "I will be fine. You hurry and help *Pani* Małgosza, I'm sure she needs you more."

Łukasz watched as she turned and trotted back up the hall, then stepped quickly to the stairwell to put as much distance between himself and this caring nurse as possible.

It seemed that he had wandered across the entire hospital when he finally found the room he had been looking for. The main surgical office was guarded by a nurses' station, but only one tired-looking nurse waited there. Behind her, he saw the closed door labeled "RECORDS." He needed access to those medical records.

He waited. His legs grew cold as drafts of air blew up his pajamas, but he waited. Eventually, that nurse would have to check on her patients, abandon her guard of the records room.

Eventually, she did. As soon as she stepped out of view, Łukasz ducked behind the desk, then through the unlocked door. He knew exactly what he was looking for.

HE HAD been twenty-six when he covered his first murder. Łukasz remembered it like it was yesterday. The body being carried out on the stretcher, red and brown stains over so much of the room that Łukasz could see them from where he was standing, trying to get a view over the heads of the detectives gathered inside.

Murder by sword. A lethal stabbing with a *shashka*, the single-edged sword used by the Cossacks. Two men fighting over the love of a woman, one man grabbing an artifact that hung on the wall and using it as it had originally been intended to be used. Bringing it back to life for one vicious, bloody moment.

That story had been a big hit. It had everything Łukasz could want: violence, history, passion. He had reveled in it. His first story made the front page, so he followed it up with a second, and then a third. Each time digging deeper into the lives of the killer, and the victims.

It hadn't bothered him, at the time. The blood. The hate. The killing. Or the exposure that hurt the victims, bringing their petty jealousies and secrets to light. He had been doing a job, and he did it well. He wrote with enthusiasm, adding a layer of thrill to a story that hardly needed it.

He used that skill again and again, moving on to other, new stories. Bringing people, crimes and passions to life on the page. So that readers would look for his byline and know they'd find a good story.

He'd covered the violent crime desk for many years, making a name for himself as the journalist willing to go to any scene, talk to any witnesses, to get his story.

The change had been gradual, subtle. He hadn't noticed it at first. Friends would comment on the change in his writing, a new perspective he brought to his stories. Where before he had brought excitement, titillation, now he started bringing tears to the eyes of his readers. Where once editors sought him out because he would write an entertaining story, even about something as grisly as a murder, now editors sought him out because he could plumb the depths of the victims' emotions — and the killers'.

Over the years, he had developed empathy. He no longer looked at a crime scene and saw a robbery or a beating or a stabbing. Now he saw only victims, innocent people whose lives would never be the same.

His stories had changed, and he had changed. And the empathy that at first gave his stories depth and meaning eventually took his stories away from him all together.

After ten years of covering the violent crime desk, Łukasz had lost the stomach for it. Not because of the gore, or even because of the tears, but because he could see both sides of the story.

By then, his career had taken off. He was no longer the rookie reporter, fresh out of university. He had made a name for himself and he built on that. His articles on politics and corruption were hard-hitting and accurate. Łukasz would spend more time investigating each story than the criminal he was investigating had probably spent thinking about the crime.

He never forgot where he had come from. He would stop and chat with the young men and women who now covered stories of violent crime. He would compare notes with them on how best to avoid the smell of blood at a crime scene or how to describe an attack so the reader could practically feel the hits himself. And he read the newspapers. All of them. He knew every story about every crime that had taken place in Warsaw for the past twenty years.

So it was no surprise that, as he read the description of the wounds received by the victim of that day's stabbing, he recognized the technique.

The records had been easy to find. Once he knew the victim had been brought to that hospital, where he was declared dead, Łukasz knew the medical report would be stored in the surgery records room. He had spent enough time buttering up the nurses in the emergency room, back when he was on the crime beat, to know that all ER records were stored temporarily with Surgery, before being filed permanently in the hospital's main records archive.

When he entered the room that evening, the boxes of ER files were clearly labeled, waiting on a rolling cart tucked under the window. Łukasz threw the lid off the box, not caring where it landed, then rifled through the files. He didn't know the name of the victim, but each file was clearly marked by date and time.

The news reports had not been detailed enough in their reporting of the time of the attack, and Łukasz had to wade through ten other reports before he found it. The fatal stabbing.

The victim had died of internal bleeding, the report read. The wound was small, the blade used was narrow, and death had occurred within five to seven minutes after stabbing. The victim would have been immediately incapacitated and would have bled out quickly. There would have been no struggle.

Only one clue stood out as to who might have committed this violent act. One detail included in the medical report that immediately caught Łukasz's eye. The victim had been stabbed in the back, the knife angling in to the right. Until the very end. The killer had twisted the knife slightly just as he hit the deepest point, turning almost imperceptibly to the right. The ER doctor who had noted this had good eyes, and a mind for details. The twist itself wouldn't have caused any additional damage, it was too insignificant. There was no clear reason why the killer would have done it, and the doctor was confused by it.

For Łukasz, it made everything clearer.

THE CAST on his arm was itching, but that bothered

him less than the fact that it prevented him from working more quickly. Getting back to his room in the hospital had been the easy part. Finding that the doctors had cut his clothes off him made it more difficult, but he found a pair of scrubs in the closet near his room and felt no qualms about stealing them.

Sneaking out of the hospital in the scrubs took time, precious time. It would have been obvious to anyone who saw him that the old man in a cast and multiple bandages didn't belong in scrubs and didn't belong out of the hospital. He was an adult, he could check himself out if he wanted to, he reminded himself as he stuck his head out into the hospital's main entrance area one more time to see if the guards had looked away yet.

He just didn't have time to wait until the morning, then deal with all the paperwork he knew would be required of him to leave. The hospital bureaucrats could chase him down tomorrow for his paperwork. Tonight, he had more important things to do.

As soon as the guard headed back up the hallway, Łukasz dashed across the lobby — as much as he could dash while holding his bruised ribs with his broken arm, shuffling slightly to keep from tearing the stitches in his right thigh.

He gritted his teeth and forced himself to move. Just until he was outside. Just until he had flagged down a taxi. Just until he was sitting, painfully, in the lobby of the newspaper building.

Then he breathed. Then he cried a little.

Eventually, the pain subsided, as physical pain always did. He was onto something, though, he had a story in his grasp, and his familiar drive kicked in, lifting him up off the bench, dragging him to the elevator and down, back to the newspaper archives.

He breathed a light sigh of relief, knowing the articles he was looking for were all from within the past five years and available on the computer. He didn't have to lift any boxes this time. He sat at the closest machine, waiting for it to come to life, then started reading.

About murder. About shootings. About stabbings. About brutal robberies and accidental deaths. He skipped over all the emotions, all the pain, all the blood, looking for the detail that mattered to him now.

Finally, after going through more than three years' worth of violence and gore, he found it. A stabbing. The killer had been found to be left handed. And a very bright doctor had identified a clue as to the killer's identity: when he stabbed, he shifted his hand just a fraction as the knife hit the deepest point, causing the blade to twist. Ever so slightly.

Another doctor might have missed it, but not this one. Not only did he see it, he knew what caused it. An injury to the wrist, he had explained to the police. The killer did not have full motion in his left wrist. Look for a killer with an injured wrist.

Not the perfect identification the police might have hoped for, but it was something. The article Łukasz was reading went no further. The killer had not been found, nor any suspects identified. Now Łukasz was on the trail, he knew there was more. He kept reading.

A year later, another stabbing. Another left-handed killer, another slight twist in the stab. This time, the doctor hadn't identified the cause of the twist, and apparently the police hadn't made the connection with the stabbing the year before. Łukasz did. And this time there was a suspect — Stefan Wilenek. He had known the victim slightly, the friend of a neighbor.

Or perhaps the enemy of a neighbor.

Wilenek had not been charged. Not enough evidence pointed to his guilt, no motive, no trace evidence found at the scene. He had only been questioned because someone had seen him in the area at the time. The police had questioned a few more people, some as witnesses, some as suspects, but no arrests were made.

Łukasz kept reading. Two more years' worth of murder and violence. Then another stabbing. Then another. In each case, no arrest had been made. In each case, someone was suspected, someone found to have a motive, but no evidence existed to place that person at the scene of the crime. Sometimes the suspect had an unbreakable alibi. Sometimes there was simply no proof he or she had been in the area at all.

A hired killer, Łukasz knew. That's how they could kill from a distance. Why there was no evidence putting them at the scene. Łukasz smiled wryly. A left-handed hired killer with a bad wrist. Stefan Wilenek's name came up only once more, but once was enough for Łukasz. He knew what he was looking for, and Wilenek fit the bill.

Łukasz changed tracks. Leaving the archives behind him, he took the elevator back up to his office. Once there, he went straight to his desk and pulled out a pill bottle. It was half-empty. Grimacing, he shook two out into his hand and swallowed them. He limped down the hall to wash them down at the water cooler.

Back in his office, wearing the change of clothes he kept handy for those occasions he needed to work through the night, Łukasz stood in front of his bookshelf. Histories of Poland, writing style guides, biographies of American presidents next to psychoanalyses of serial killers, his books were in no order and seemed to fit no pattern. Łukasz read widely, based on whatever story he was working on at the time.

This time, he was looking for a book on recent Polish history.

"Aha," he said aloud as he pulled the thick volume from the shelf. *Miller's History*. The book was bound in cloth, published in someone's basement, not a publishing house. It was a story that would never make it in a commercial sale, but it served as a bible of sorts for Łukasz. It was a first-hand account of life under the Polish secret police during the communist regime.

Łukasz had known Thaddeus Miller for only a few

years, when Łukasz was at the height of his profession and Miller was just starting out, a young student eager to find a big story. Łukasz had helped him; he was happy to nurture such talent and enthusiasm. And in return, Miller had helped him. Miller had given him the book.

Compiled over a period of ten years, the book had many authors. Individuals who had written down for Miller what they knew, whether it was long, flowing details or just a few short sentences.

Miller had fit the pieces together. Descriptions cobbled together from different sources eventually yielded clear pictures. Pictures of corruption among the communist leadership in Poland. Pictures of men and women who were willing to share information, to sell out their colleagues just to save themselves. And pictures of the men and women who paid for that information.

Stefan Wilenek was one of those men. There was no photograph available, but as Łukasz read the description Miller had compiled, he once again saw those hard black eyes staring at him through the windshield, aiming not to hurt but to kill.

Wilenek had worked for the *Służba Bezpieczeństwa*, the Polish secret police. He had followed people, lied to people, tricked them into giving him information, sometimes paid them to give him information. Łukasz knew no informant ever really benefited.

The information they provided was used to arrest, torture, even kill the ones they knew, the ones they loved. Half the suicides in Poland in the late 1980s were the end result, people who couldn't handle it when the reality of what they had done sank in, when they saw the true cost.

Wilenek was one of those men. And he was back in Poland now, a killer for hire.

Łukasz looked at the clock. This wasn't proof that Adam was innocent, but it was certainly enough to make the police look closely at Wilenek and ask some hard questions. Łukasz knew better than to run to the police with this. There was a more powerful way to get this information to them. The power of the pen.

CHAPTER FORTY-FIVE

SUNLIGHT GLINTED off the large storefront window. Adam squinted against the glare. He kept his head tucked low into his collar, moving every so often so as not to attract too much attention to himself.

The night in the shelter had been uncomfortable, to say the least. The nuns working there had been welcoming, though, even offering Adam a hot meal. They had spoken no English, and if they wondered why an American was living rough on the streets of Warsaw, he hadn't understood their questions. But the church shelter was there to help those who needed it, and God knew he needed help last night.

The police seemed to be everywhere. He knew better than to try to gain access to his hotel room, but his approach to Sylvia's apartment last night had been equally unsuccessful. He had approached from the river, walking up *Ulica Długa*, past the cafes, school and small shops that dotted the cobblestoned street. From a block away, behind the protruding facade of the Polish Army Field Cathedral, he could see Sylvia's window.

The curtains were pushed open, and every so often Sylvia's form passed in front of the window. Even from this distance, Adam knew it was her. The tension in his back lessened as he let his breath out. She was safe. Thank God.

As he watched, she paced back and forth in the small

apartment. She kept her hand to her head, and Adam guessed she was on the phone. Looking for him, perhaps? If only he could go to her. Tell her that he was safe. And innocent.

From where he hid, he could also see the uniformed officer, waiting, watching guard over her home. They knew about his connection to Sylvia, knew he might turn to her for help. He couldn't approach without getting arrested.

Despite his inability to contact Sylvia directly, he was glad to see the police there. Whoever had framed him might still be after her. At least this way she'd be safe. He hoped.

So he had spent the night in the church shelter. And while a hot shower and change of clothes would have been heaven just then, Adam was only grateful that he hadn't had to spend the night outdoors, exposed to the freezing temperatures. He might not have survived that.

He put his hand out again to block the glare, but kept his eyes on the drive that led out of the *Sejm*. Sylvia would have to come out eventually, and hopefully she could help him find out how Łukasz was doing. If he was even alive.

He was just stepping away, moving to stare into a different shop window, when a familiar figure caught his eye leaving the drive, walking toward the stretch of restaurants and cafes that ran along the street.

Changing his mind, Adam strolled in the same direction, stepping into the small cafe a few minutes after his quarry.

Kapral almost jumped out of his chair as Adam's hand fell on his shoulder.

"Sit. Stay," Adam commanded, sliding into the seat next to him at the small table.

Kapral replaced his espresso cup into its saucer with a shaking hand. "You are wanted for murder, *Pan* Kaminski. You cannot keep me here, I will simply call for the police."

"I know about Laurienty." Adam didn't have many options, and he was willing to take a gamble.

Kapral eyed him carefully, but didn't crumble. "Really? You think you know?"

Adam considered the man before him. "Here's what I know. I know I didn't kill that man. I know whoever did also killed Basia Kaminski and Jared White and tried to kill Łukasz Kaminski. And I know whoever did that has a secret. A secret he's willing to kill to protect."

"Ah, secrets. Yes." Kapral nodded, finishing his coffee with a final sip. He raised a finger to catch the attention of the barista, and Adam heard the familiar sounds of the grinder, the water passing through the freshly ground beans. The heady aroma followed the tiny cup to the table, and Adam waited until Kapral brought the cup first to his nose, then to his lips, before he spoke.

"You have secrets, minister. Secrets you want kept hidden. Secrets Basia Kaminski found."

"She had no right." Kapral's words were sharp, bitten off by his effort to control his rage. He closed his eyes briefly, took a breath, and continued. "She didn't know what she was doing, what she was looking for. It was not her concern. She should not have become involved."

"But she did. And she found the truth." Adam spoke quietly, hoping to encourage Kapral to continue.

"She was helping me, she told me, you know." He smiled mirthlessly at the table. "She apologized. She came to me and said she thought she was helping."

"You didn't want her help."

"I wanted my privacy. I wanted her not to get involved." Kapral shrugged. "But she did. There was nothing more I could do."

He looked at Adam. "I did not kill her. I was angry at her for prying, but I did not kill her." His voice held a note of disbelief that rang true.

Adam watched him, waiting, saying nothing.

Finally Kapral continued. "She thought Laurienty was

blackmailing me. Hah! She couldn't understand why I had hired him when there were others so obviously more qualified. So she decided it was blackmail. As if Laurienty would have the brains to do something like that."

"She came to you when she found the truth."

"Of course she did." Kapral's pride reemerged, his chest puffed out. "I am a leader in the *Sejm*, she came to me to seek answers from me and to tell me my secret was safe with her." His eyes wavered and the look he gave Adam was drowning in doubt. "And then she died. And I thought... I thought, what did I say to her? Was I too harsh? Did I drive her to kill herself?"

"She didn't kill herself, sir. She was murdered. Was it because of what she found about you?"

"That is not possible." Kapral smiled again. "I would not kill, not for this or any other reason, and Laurienty... well" — Kapral raised his eyebrows — "Laurienty, I am ashamed to say, wouldn't have the brains to kill anyone, either."

"Ashamed?" Adam asked.

"Ashamed, *Pan* Kaminski, because Laurienty is my son."

Adam thought back to the information Pete had found on Kapral. He was married, had been for twenty-eight years. His wife served on the board of the school their daughters had attended. His daughters were both in university now, doing well and making their father proud. His two daughters. There had been no mention of a son.

"I see you are surprised, *Pan* Kaminski. So no, you did not know about Laurienty. Perhaps you thought the same thing Basia believed. That I had committed some horrible act in the past, and Laurienty was using it against me, blackmailing me to hire him?" Kapral laughed under his breath.

"In a way, that is true," he continued. "Not a horrible act, perhaps, but an indiscretion. An affair, *Pan*

Kaminski, nothing worse. Simply an affair."

Adam nodded. Affairs had brought down politicians before Kapral, Adam knew. Some men could carry them off, their loving wives standing by their side, telling the world she forgave him. For other men, the scandal meant the end of their career, the end of the people's trust.

"My wife would not have forgiven me, had she found out," Kapral said, as if reading Adam's mind. "It was over almost as soon as it had started. A secretary, of all things. How cliché of me. After only a few nights, I knew I had made a mistake. I recommended her for another position — a promotion — and she went. And that was it. Or so I thought."

He pushed his espresso cup away on the table, resting his hands on the polished wood surface, playing with his napkin.

"I had no idea there was a child. She never told me, and I didn't keep track of her or her career. Then Laurienty showed up." He looked over at Adam. "And what was I to do? Send him away? Deny that he was mine?"

"So you simply accepted his word that he was your son?" Adam asked with disbelief.

"Bah, no, of course not. Don't be absurd. I required that we have tests done. I could not believe it at first. I was sure he was lying. Then his mother contacted me as well, and I thought perhaps it was true. So we did the tests, and I was his father." Kapral nodded, remembering.

"And you hired him because you wanted to help him. Because you felt you owed him, after all these years?"

"That is true." Kapral frowned, nodding. "I did owe him." He looked out over the coffee shop, filled with the midmorning coffee crowd from the neighboring offices and stores. The hum of conversation filled Adam's ears as he thought about what Kapral had told him.

"You were also afraid. You were afraid that if you didn't help him, he — or his mother — would tell your wife. And the scandal could ruin you."

"Of course it would ruin me," Kapral hissed, glaring at Adam. "How do you think that would look? Not only had I cheated and lied, I had fathered a child out of wedlock. Then abandoned him." Kapral grunted. "No one would care about the truth. That I didn't know about Laurienty. Politics is not about truth, *Pan* Kaminski, it is about appearances. Reputations. And I had to protect mine."

"Better to look like you're willing to give a chance to a struggling young man than to look like an adulterer," Adam agreed.

"It was nobody's business but my own. When Basia Kaminski came to me, I was furious. What had she done? She had stolen the records showing the other applicants for Laurienty's position. She had lied to the clinic where we had the test done and succeeded in getting a copy of the results. *Kurwa,*" Kapral cursed softly, "she had no right. No right."

"What did you do, minister?"

"What could I do? I lost my temper. I yelled at her. I swore that if she ever told anyone, I would see to it that her career was ruined. Finished. No matter how long it took, I would make sure she never worked in politics again." He looked at Adam. "I told her to leave my office, and I never spoke to her again. That was it. I swear."

Adam nodded, looking down at the table. This was a motive, a strong one. Would Kapral have admitted it if he really had Basia killed?

"You must believe me, *Pan* Kaminski," Kapral said again, "I did not kill her." He frowned, thinking for a moment. "When we last met, you asked me for access to the national archives. Do you still want that access? Do you still believe you can find the answer to who killed Basia in those records?"

Adam looked up at Kapral, surprised. "Perhaps. I know Łukasz was looking there just before he was attacked the first time. I know somebody was worried about what he found there. And now someone has tried to kill him again, and I don't even know if he survived."

Adam rubbed his hands over his face, the exhaustion and worry finally catching up to him as the adrenaline of confronting Kapral faded.

"Let me help you." Kapral reached into his briefcase. "Your cousin is alive, *Pan* Kaminski. I happen to know he was back at work this morning, at his newspaper. I spoke to his editor only this morning on another matter, and he mentioned it. Do not worry about him. Do the investigation you need to do at the national archives. If you can find the truth there, you will know I am telling you the truth when I say I did not kill her. Here."

Pulling out a sheet of his letterhead, Kapral wrote out a quick letter. Signing and dating it, he handed it to Adam. "This will get you into the archives, and it will give you free access to review whatever materials you want. You will not need to request documents or make an appointment."

Adam took the letter, still wondering about Kapral's motives. "Thank you, this will help." His eyes as he looked at Kapral grew dark. "I will find the truth, sir. I have no choice now. I need to find the truth to prove my own innocence."

"Then you know how I feel, *Pan* Kaminski. We both need the truth to come out."

CHAPTER FORTY-SIX

WANTING NOTHING more than a hot shower and to burn the clothes he was still wearing, Adam wrapped his hands around his bowl of barszcz and huddled low over the table in the milk bar. As bad as he felt, he knew he blended in with the other customers, a dark, bundled mass leaning over a warm bowl of soup. He blew on the soup and waited.

This was Łukasz's favorite haunt for a quick, cheap lunch. And he could wait here without attracting attention. Every few minutes, the scent of wool and mothballs would carry in on a cold draft, signaling the entrance of a new customer. Each time, Adam looked over his shoulder expectantly, then back down at his soup. When he finished his first bowl, he purchased another.

Just when he thought he couldn't stand the thought of yet another bowl of beet soup, he recognized the lavender scent on the cold air and turned with a smile to see Sylvia entering with his cousin.

"Cousin" — Łukasz grimaced as he turned a little bit too fast toward Adam's table — "I cannot tell you how good it is to see you."

"You too, you're a sight for sore eyes." He smiled at Sylvia. "Both of you. I was so worried."

"*You* were worried?" Sylvia's voice seemed to carry more anger than concern, but Adam hoped he was imagining that. "How do you think it felt for me... or for *Pan* Burns, who is responsible for you while you are in Warsaw... for you to... to..." Her hand waved in the air as her voice trailed off, as if feeling around for the right words.

"I didn't do anything, Sylvia. It wasn't me."

"You ran, cousin." Łukasz spoke as he eased into a chair at Adam's table.

Sylvia stood for a moment looking down at both men, hands on her hips, but eventually took the other empty chair. "When *Pan* Kaminski suggested we meet, I had no idea we would be seeing you, Adam. You should have told me." Sylvia directed this last complaint toward Łukasz. "I should inform the authorities right now that I am with you."

"I had no idea, *Pani* Stanko, I assure you. This was not part of my plan."

Adam backed up Łukasz's denial. "This was my plan. I figured of anywhere in the city, this is where he was most likely to turn up. Sylvia, you must realize I've been trying to reach you. Where have you been?"

"What?" Sylvia frowned, her furrowed brow puckering her beautiful face. "I have been home, I have been at work, I have been at school. And all the time I have been worrying about you." She looked confused, unsure of herself for just a moment, then her expression firmed. "You are wanted by the police, Adam. They were at my home, looking for you."

"I know." He shrugged. "They're still watching your apartment. That's why I couldn't come over. I've been trying to reach you. There, and at the *Sejm*."

Sylvia shivered. "I was at my office at first." She nodded. "I felt safer there. On Monday, when the police arrived, looking for you... well, I've been there ever since. Waiting for you." Her blue eyes softened and her voice quieted. "I haven't been able to work or to study, I was so worried about you."

"I'm sorry. I'm just glad you're all right. Both of you."

Łukasz grinned. "You should know by now, cousin, I do not kill that easily. Nor do I stop digging. I have news."

"So do I," Adam said. "Now get some lunch and we can compare notes."

"Just like that?" Sylvia's tone was now one of incredulity. "You are wanted for murder. You run from the police. But we should chat over a warm meal as if nothing had happened?"

"Sylvia," both men said at once.

Łukasz nodded his head toward Adam, who continued, "Do you trust me?"

"Yes... yes." Sylvia's response was tentative at first, then firmer.

"And do you think I killed anyone?"

Now Sylvia smiled. "No, of course not."

"Then we must work together to prove Adam's innocence," Łukasz finished for Adam. "Come, food will be good for us, I think."

"It must be Novosad," Łukasz stated a few minutes later over bites of grilled kielbasa and pierogies fried in onions and mushrooms. "He has the connection to Russia, and Wilenek was part of the former secret police. You know he must have connections to the KGB. To Russia. It would be easy enough for Novosad to put the call out to his contacts and for Wilenek to respond."

"That's just a guess, *Pan* Kaminski," Sylvia cautioned him. "I can see why your editor told you to rewrite the article."

"Bah..." Łukasz waved his hand dismissively, "I cannot understand any of his actions. This is urgent, vital, and he wants to rewrite, to revise, to have others review it before he publishes."

"He's right, Łukasz. Don't put in writing anything you can't prove." Adam shook his head. "And I'm not sure I agree with you. I still don't trust Kapral. He may have given me access to the archives just to throw me off track, to stop me from finding out the truth about him and his relationship with Laurienty."

Łukasz moved his head slowly from side to side. "I don't know, Adam. His story has the ring of truth. There was a rumor at the time, you know, speculation about how his secretary was promoted so quickly. She succeeded in her new position and no one thought about it any more. He could be telling the truth — about Laurienty and about his ignorance of his own son."

"We need more information. If we can't even agree between us, given what we know, we need to know more."

Adam patted his pocket where the letter from Kapral was safely tucked away. "For me, that means the archives." He looked at Sylvia. "Are you sure you're okay? I know you're probably taking some heat because of me. As our official liaison, I mean."

Sylvia shrugged and smiled at Adam, who couldn't help but smile back. "Do not worry about me, Adam. I will not tell anyone I saw you here."

"Even if that puts your career at risk?"

"Even so. You do what you need to do. Find the truth. And then my career will not be at risk, you see?"

Adam nodded, paused. "Łukasz."

"Yes, cousin?"

"I read the letters you gave me."

"What letters?" Sylvia asked.

"Ah yes." Łukasz nodded. "I provided Adam with some old family letters. About his great-grandfather. Who left Poland in 1940."

Sylvia frowned. "That was a difficult time. I'm surprised there are any records preserved of people escaping."

Adam shook his head. "They're not official records, just family letters. Written not long after the fact. They suggest..." Adam shrugged and looked down at the table.

Sylvia and Łukasz watched him, but he didn't

continue. Finally Łukasz added, "They imply, *Pani* Stanko, that Adam's great-grandfather was a coward who left his family in need. An able-bodied man who could have fought, but instead packed up his wife and children and escaped, leaving his brothers and sisters and their families behind."

"Well... But..." Sylvia struggled for words. "That is just one perspective. It was a difficult and dangerous time. Every man had to make decisions to keep his children safe."

She turned to Adam and her voice softened. "Adam, this is terrible that you should read such letters. But you understand, do you not, that everyone has his own perspective? These letters cannot be the whole story, just one side of it."

Adam smiled across the table at her, her eyes blue and earnest. "Thank you, Sylvia, of course you are right. And I can't let ancient history bother me now, anyway, can I?"

He pushed his hands against the table as he stood. "I'm off to the archives. If I can get there without getting arrested. Police are everywhere."

"Perhaps I can help with that, cousin." Łukasz smiled up at him.

CHAPTER FORTY-SEVEN

ADAM COULDN'T help but smile as he pushed open the oak door and walked into the main hall. He could hear the voices behind him, Łukasz's voice rising above the others, until the heavy door clicked shut with finality, blocking out all outside sounds.

Łukasz's diversion had worked perfectly. The picturesque, round building of pale golden stones waited quietly on a tree-lined street in *Ochota*, an area in the south of the city, not expecting any trouble. Storming through the doors of the *Archiwum Akt Nowych*, the Central Archives of Modern Records, Łukasz had demanded immediate access.

The nervous young woman working behind the desk hadn't known what to do. She glanced at the armed guard standing near the main entrance, but his attention was on the street, not her desk. Seeing her discomfort, Łukasz had soldiered on, demanding to be allowed to review the documents from the secret police that were still housed there, claiming the right of the journalist to free access to information.

When at first the young woman hesitated, and almost seemed like she was about to grant Łukasz the access he wanted, he switched tacks, raising his voice and spitting out insults about the archives, their management, and the people who used them.

Finally realizing this was not something she could

handle herself, the young woman picked up the phone and called her supervisor, the director of the archives himself. He appeared from a back room, a portly gentleman with a sour face. Too many hours peering at faint documents, Adam supposed.

He took one look at Łukasz and promptly called over the guard. Which was the moment Adam had been waiting for.

While the director and the guard were engaged in quieting Łukasz and trying to drag him off to a side room, Adam approached the young woman.

Smiling apologetically, he said, "I'm sorry, I don't speak Polish. But I have a letter granting me access to these files. Is that okay?" Looking over at Łukasz, he added, "Should I come back another time?" He smiled again.

The woman smiled gratefully back at him from behind the brightly polished, lemon-scented desk. "I am sorry, sir, this does not usually happen. I appreciate your understanding." She glanced at the letter Adam held in his hands. "Let me see that, perhaps I can help you."

She read through the letter carefully, then looked back up at Adam. "This is from Minister Kapral. He says you are here on his authority and require free access to all of the records. This is very unusual."

Adam shrugged. "I understand if this isn't something you can help me with. Perhaps we need to ask the director?" He gestured toward the portly man, now turning bright red in the face as Łukasz turned his venom onto the man's innocent family.

"No, no," the young woman answered quickly. "I think it would be best not to bother him. This is clearly an important request. Of course we will honor it."

She smiled as she returned the letter to Adam, pressing a button underneath the desk. Adam heard a click as the oak door to his right unlocked. He thanked her as he headed through it, but she had turned her attention immediately back to the director and to the police, who had just arrived.

Following signs for the public reading rooms, Adam took one flight of stairs up, stepping out into a narrow carpeted hallway that followed the circular curve of the building. On the left, windows looked down into the paved central courtyard, where a few benches waited for spring and warmer weather. Walking along the hall, Adam carefully pushed doors open, checking the rooms on his right.

One was a large conference room, lined with artifacts and displays of Polish history — paintings, historic documents, mannequins in earlier versions of army uniforms. The air was stuffier in here and Adam suspected this was a ceremonial space, not often used.

Other doors opened onto reading rooms, as Adam had supposed they would. Readers occupied small wooden desks tucked away under looming shelves. Each reader had an assigned desk, and as the materials he or she had requested became available, archivists would stack the materials, clearly labeled and numbered, on the shelves above the desks.

Fewer than half the available desks were occupied and the rooms were painfully quiet; only the occasional turning of a page or stifled cough could be heard above the hum of the dehumidifiers. Tall, rectangular windows that looked out over the city allowed in only limited light, and dust motes danced across the rooms in the narrow beams that reached into the musty space. Adam was surprised to catch the scent of roses in one room, lingering traces of a woman's perfume. The quiet young woman at the front desk, perhaps.

He continued his way around the hall, heading toward the main storage building, when he spotted something he wasn't expecting. A stroke of luck.

A lone pay phone hung in a booth at the end of a short corridor jutting off of the main hallway. He stepped in and slid the doors closed behind him.

"Pete, don't say anything, just listen to me." He spoke

quickly before his partner could say anything to let the others in the squad room hear who was calling. It was risky bringing Pete into his problems like this, but he had no choice. He was only glad his credit card still worked and hadn't been cut off already.

"What the hell have you gotten into, partner?" Pete's words were muffled, preventing others in the squad room from overhearing. "The captain's getting calls about you left and right. You killed someone? What the hell?"

"Cut it out, Pete, you know I didn't kill anyone." Adam smiled despite himself, glad to know that Pete still trusted him. "And you know what's going on here. Whoever's behind Basia's death wants me out of the way. I still need to figure out who it is. Did you find anything else that will help?"

"Not much," Pete answered softly. "I'm still looking into the names you gave me, but they each seem to check out. I gave you all the background I had last time you called. Without going through the captain, there's not much more I can find."

"Better not alert the captain you're working on this. Not yet, anyway. He'll have your skin."

"I think you should be more worried about your own skin, Kaminski. He said he wanted you to solve the murder — not get convicted for it."

"I know, partner, I'm working on it, believe me. I'm pretty sure I know who killed them. A man named Stefan Wilenek, former Polish secret police. Killer for hire. Nasty character."

Pete whistled. "Good work, Kaminski. Do you have enough proof to go to the Warsaw PD?"

"Almost. Łukasz is writing up what he does know."

"Writing up? Like for the police, or for the paper?" Pete asked quickly.

"For the paper. I know…" Adam cut off Pete's objections. "But we still don't have enough to stand up in a court of law, just our own testimony — and you know what my testimony is worth right now. His editor wouldn't even publish what he wrote the first time. He's working on revising it now, making sure it's defensible against a libel suit. Meanwhile, I need to find out who hired Wilenek."

There was a pause on the other end of the line as Pete thought about what Adam was saying. "What can I do to help?"

"I need you to reach out to the rest of the team from the Philadelphia International Council. Did they all make it back safe?"

"Yeah, they came back yesterday. The captain has already called each of them to let them know we're still on the case to find out who killed Jared."

Adam felt himself relax. "I'm glad he did that. He's a good man. I still need you to visit them, Pete. They'll be hearing things about me now, and I need you to let them know I'm fine. That I'm on the case, too, and I won't leave here until I solve it."

"Kaminski..." Pete started to say something, then cut himself off. After a pause, he continued, "You need to know this is hurting our case against Luis."

"Luis? What does he have to do with this?"

"Nothing, partner, absolutely nothing. But it's not just him. All your recent arrests are going to come under scrutiny."

Adam said nothing, thinking about the truth behind Pete's words.

"Luis is only locked up on our request that the judge wait until you're back in Philly. And if you can't testify..."

"Or if my testimony isn't worth crap..." Adam took a breath. "I get it. I know. I'll figure this out."

"I know, partner. And I'll talk to the people who were on your delegation. What about Jared White's family? What can I say to them?"

Adam shut his eyes, picturing Jared sitting on the train drinking coffee that was far too strong for him, talking about teaching, dreaming of a future he would never see. "Tell them I will catch whoever did this. And tell them I will explain everything I know to them in person when I return."

"Uh-huh. And Julia? Anything I can tell her?"

Adam realized with a start how all of this must look to his little sister. Her brother accused of murder, running from the police. He couldn't even call her himself without implicating her in his alleged crime. He shook his head in the dark phone booth. "Take care of her, Pete. Just take care of her for me."

"Will do, partner," Pete answered. "And you take care of yourself."

CHAPTER FORTY-EIGHT

THE METAL DOUBLE doors leading to the glass enclosed bridge were closed, but not locked. Adam followed the bridge over the driveway through to the main storage facility behind the genteel public space of the archives.

This building was simple and square. No windows exposed its contents to the sun's potential damage. The air was dry and purified, dehumidifiers and air conditioners humming away actively in the background. No dust motes would be permitted to dance in the air here, Adam thought, seeing the fluorescent lights reflected sharply off the spotless tile floor, the gleaming metal of the modern shelving units stacked against each other throughout the large open space.

The room filled half the floor of the large building, and down a long hallway to his right Adam saw another similar room. Silver and gray shelves, pushed up close together, back to front and front to back, created narrow aisles for archivists to squeeze through.

Each individual shelf had its own metal wheel that, when turned, would slowly shift all the shelves in that unit, gradually exposing the desired contents. The room was clean but an earthy scent lingered, as if someone had tried but failed to wipe away the last traces of the outside world within this protected space.

Adam walked through the long, narrow aisles, reading

the small labels on the end of each shelving unit. These archives held over two thousand archival collections of records of central state institutions, social records, political records and records from the interwar period of Polish independence.

On the labels that he could read with his limited Polish, Adam saw records of institutions including the Civil Chancellery of the President of the Republic of Poland, the Ministry of Foreign Affairs and other ministries from the period between the wars.

The records were kept in a variety of formats, holding for posterity not only written documents, but images and sounds as well. Copies of old slides filled a series of boxes while another held old tape recordings. Slide viewers and tape players had been placed strategically throughout the space, easy to hand for archivists responding to requests.

He paused when he came across a series of labels noting the location of documents from the Polish Underground State from the period of World War II. These included documents of underground institutions and military units active during German and Soviet occupations of World War II. If he had had more time, he could have spent hours, days, discovering the secrets held within these historic files.

He searched the shelves, working through years of history. Eventually, he found the more recent records, records of social institutions, labor organizations and political parties from within the last thirty years.

He leaned in to the metal wheel at the end of the unit, and it slid smoothly around. The shelves silently shifted, opening up to Adam's touch. As they moved, a whiff of the musty scent of the documents stored here floated out, then lost itself to the air purifiers above.

Adam walked slowly along the shelf, running his hands across the file folders and books, breathing in the feeling of walking through history. He closed his eyes and could almost hear the din of the marches and parades, the shouts at labor union meetings, the anger at the student protests. The sounds of gunfire as the Polish people were attacked by their own government. The cries of joy as the truth was realized, that the communist state was no longer in control. The cheers, and cries, as Lech Wałęsa accepted the position of president of a free Poland.

As Adam pulled down file after file, box after box, his shoulders sagged. He was searching for a needle in a haystack. A very large haystack. He had to find a way to narrow his search. He knew there was something in these records that implicated one of the men involved. It had to be something Basia Kaminski would have come across on her own.

He narrowed his search to records of political activities in the Warsaw area, but even that would take him all night to work through. This wasn't going to be easy. He had to trust that Łukasz would successfully talk his way out of his confrontation with the police. And he had to trust that Sylvia would keep his plans secret, even knowing the risk to her political career.

With a deep breath and a glance at his watch, he got started.

CHAPTER FORTY-NINE

ADAM GRIMACED as he stretched his back, his neck cracking as he turned it from side to side. He put a hand on the shelf to his right and pushed himself up off the ground. Realizing that carrying the files he wanted back and forth to small tables on the far wall was taking too much time, Adam had resorted to squatting on the floor between the shelves as he read, pulling out one file, skimming through it, then replacing it and pulling out another.

So far, he had found records showing Kapral's involvement in a variety of political institutions since the regime fell, as well as documentation of Tomek Malak's involvement in student protests throughout the 1980s. None of this was secret, however, and none of it a motive for murder.

Looking around him, he realized with a start that beyond the narrow aisle he occupied, the rest of the room lay in darkness. Only weak red light from emergency exit signs lit the paths between the metal shelves.

Łukasz's distraction must have worked even better than they expected if the young woman at the front desk had forgotten to mention to anyone else that Adam was in here.

He stretched again, his back screaming at him. He ran his tired eyes over the shelf one more time, then stepped out into the aisle to turn the wheel for the next set of shelves.

He froze at a noise coming from the next room.

The whirring, grinding sound grew louder as Adam moved toward it. He slid through the doorway to the next room and crept toward the sound, keeping his back against the steel shelves. He moved slowly, cautiously, closer.

He was so close he could see the yellow light escaping from a room only a few aisles away when he recognized the sound. Such a familiar sound, he heard it at the precinct all the time. He just hadn't placed it because it was so unexpected, in this place, at this time.

He was listening to someone using a document shredder.

The waist-high machine sat in a small room off the main floor. The door to the room was closed, but the wall facing the main records floor was lined with windows, and both light and sound escaped through these.

Peeling around the last shelf, Adam saw a man standing at the shredder. A pile of files lay on a table to his right, and he systematically pulled them apart into thin sheafs then fed them into the hungry machine. And unless the national archives had taken to hiring thugs to clear out their unneeded files, these were not documents that should be shredded.

Stefan Wilenek focused on the work at hand, not looking around, not even reading the files he was destroying.

"Shit," Adam thought to himself. This was not good. He glanced around, but saw nothing but rows and rows of dark metal shelves. Looking back at Wilenek, he was not surprised to see the hilt of a knife peeking out from a sheath on his belt. Adam couldn't attack him. That was a fight he would lose.

Closing his eyes, Adam pictured the halls he had roamed through that evening. Tried to think of something he could use, some weapon or tool.

He ran back up the silent aisles, through to the other room. First going to the files he had already reviewed, he set up the tools he needed there then moved on to the far door. Just beyond that door, he found a small metal cabinet built into the wall. Fingers crossed, Adam pulled it open and saw what he was hoping to see: light switches.

Pushing all the switches to the "on" position, Adam ran again, almost sliding on the spotless tiles, back to the second step of his plan.

Here, he turned on the tape player to its highest volume. The sound of voices, students debating the merits of an arcane law, filled the room as the bright overhead lights slowly kicked on, one after another.

Running ahead of the sequence of lights, Adam returned to the small office where Wilenek had paused in his activity. Looking up, he could see the lights slowly moving toward him, as each connection in the sequence caught the power and kicked on with a flash. The voices were dim from this far away, loud enough to be heard but not, Adam hoped, to be understood. As if a group of people had just entered the archives and were slowly moving this way.

Wilenek frowned and looked at his watch, then back up at the aisles where the lights were coming ever closer. With a snarl, he grabbed the sheaf of papers still in his hand and shoved it carelessly back into a cardboard file box.

Moving quickly, he carried the box to a rolling cart, one of several pushed up against the wall, each storing file boxes of different sizes. Wilenek pushed his box to the back of a larger pile, arranging the boxes in front of it so it couldn't be seen. Leaving the files somewhere he could find them easily when he returned, Adam assumed.

With one more look out into the main room, Wilenek left the small office, killing the lights as he left, and slipped out through an unmarked metal door. Adam heard his footsteps ringing on the steps, fading away, as the last of the overhead lights kicked on.

Adam stood there, exposed under the bright lights, listening for any sound of Wilenek's return.

Leaving the students' voices playing, Adam moved into the room Wilenek had vacated. Going right for the box the other man had tried to hide, Adam pulled out the papers Wilenek had been so eager to destroy.

At first, Adam wasn't sure what he was looking at. Flipping through three folders, he saw a word or two he recognized, but nothing that helped explain why Wilenek had been destroying them.

Finally, he saw a word stamped on the front of one of the folders: *Służba Bezpieczeństwa*. These were the records from the secret police. The records that could be used to verify someone's lustration statement, if necessary.

Whoever had hired Wilenek to kill Basia and Łukasz had also paid him to destroy the evidence.

That's what this has been about all along. Not corruption, not connections with the Russian mafia, not illegitimate children. *It was all here, if anyone had taken the time to dig. It was only a matter of time before it came out.*

Only one name Adam recognized appeared consistently on all of the sheets: Tomek Malak.

These were the records of Malak's meetings with the secret police. These were proof that he had acted as an informant under the previous regime, meeting with the secret police, sharing information on the activities, plans, even thoughts of his friends and comrades. Exposing them to questioning, arrest, torture.

Why would he have done it? Adam asked himself this question as he stuffed the papers into his coat to take them to Łukasz for translating. Had he been forced? Was he a willing informant, seeking recompense for his knowledge, or just another victim of this deadly history?

He paused as he realized that for him, the more

important question was, did Sylvia know? She worked with him so closely, she must have at least suspected.

Shaking his head, Adam pushed the thought away. He needed to get to Malak before Wilenek did.

CHAPTER FIFTY

LIGHTS GLEAMED from every window in the front of Malak's house, just as they had the first time Adam had been here. But he saw no figures profiled in the windows.

He approached the ornate wooden door. Someone was moving around inside, making small noises that Adam could just hear over the pounding of his own heart. He raised his hand in the air, then held it there, balled into a fist, while he took a breath. The air was heavy with the scent of juniper and burning wood.

He knocked, loudly. The noise inside the house stopped.

Adam waited.

Ten seconds later, the door opened. Malak stood in the entranceway, this time dressed in a dark blue track suit, a silver streak running down the sides of his legs. He held a thick crystal tumbler in one hand, and he used this to wave Adam inside. As it moved through the air, fumes from the scotch trailed behind.

Malak led the way into his opulent living room, then turned to Adam without sitting. Adam stood near the doorway, and the two men faced each other.

"You've done well for yourself, *Pan* Malak." Adam gestured around the gaudy room.

Malak nodded. "Yes."

They fell silent again, and Adam considered his

options. They weren't many.

"You knew Stefan Wilenek." Adam finally spoke. "From your time in university."

Malak nodded and took another sip of his drink. He didn't speak, so Adam continued.

"He was your contact. With the Polish secret police. He was the one you would give the information to. When you were informing on your colleagues. Your friends."

Malak glared at Adam, the contempt and hatred in his eyes so strong Adam felt them physically repulsing him.

"You provided information in return for what — security? Because you believed in the cause?"

No response from Malak.

"Money?"

Malak blinked and Adam knew he had hit home.

"You informed on your friends, turning them in when they were standing up for what they believed in, fighting for what they believed could really happen here in Poland. And you did it for money?" Adam grabbed the back of a chair, squeezing his fingers around the carved wood, its solidity helping him keep his mind in the present, ignoring the sound of dirt hitting a coffin.

Malak's anger, which had been barely controlled, flared. "Yes, I did it for money. They were ridiculous. Ideologues. What they believed, what they wanted, that could never happen. How could a labor union succeed against the mighty communist regime? Their cause was already lost. I was not hurting them. I was looking to the future."

"Your future."

"Yes, my future. I enjoyed the politics, I enjoyed the thrill of feeling like we were doing something big. But I am practical. I knew that in the end it would not succeed. And I would be on the side of the winner. And I would be rich."

"They did succeed. And you were so ashamed of what you had done, you lied on your lustration form."

"I was on the side of the winner after all, it turned out. No one needed to know the truth. They saw me as one of them. A compatriot."

"You had betrayed them."

Malak's voice softened, took on a whine. "Who could have expected this? Who could have expected Solidarity to succeed? No one... even the sharpest academic minds of the time thought it impossible. It *was* impossible. No, I made the right choice."

"So you prospered. You rose in prominence in the political circles within the student movement of Solidarity. And at the same time, you were bringing in extra cash by selling out your friends. When Solidarity won, you must have been quite disappointed. Your secret well had dried up; how were you going to make a living?"

Malak laughed without humor. "There are always ways to make money for someone who wants it badly enough."

"Small things. Taking a little bit here, a little bit there. Not enough so anyone would complain, even if they did notice."

"And all the time, I have been doing great things for Warsaw. Look at the business I have brought in. Look how the economy is thriving under my leadership. Look how the people are happy. We are a democracy. And I am a hero to them."

"If the truth ever came out about your past, you would lose all this. You would lose your job. You would lose the respect of the people. You would lose everything."

"I could not let that happen, you must understand." Malak sounded almost apologetic. "I cannot let that happen."

The sound of a door closing from a connecting room was as soft as a puff of air, but it set Adam's hair on end. Keeping his eyes on Malak, he moved cautiously to the door leading into the kitchen and listened. Footsteps, he was sure of it, in a room beyond the kitchen.

Malak took another long drink from his scotch then sat heavily in one of the silk chairs. He raised his eyebrows and dipped his head toward Adam. Adam stepped through to the kitchen.

CHAPTER FIFTY-ONE

ONLY A SMALL light over the sink was lit, the kitchen in semi-darkness, looking out over an even darker back yard. Behind him, lights shone through the doorway from the living room he had just left, casting shadows from the table and chairs midway through the room. On the far wall, another doorway, another room in semi-gloom.

A shadow moved in that room. Adam heard a door open and shut. He saw the shadow moving in the dark yard.

He followed with caution, stepping slowly into the side room, seeing the back door resting lightly on its latch, not fully closed. More shadows loomed here, bizarre shapes created by the distant light blocked by high-backed carved mahogany chairs, marble busts on turned wood pedestals, a dark porcelain vase on a low shelf that jutted out into the room.

He pulled the door toward him, then leaned to the side, careful not to stand in the doorway, exposed to whoever might be out there. Though he had a pretty good idea who he was following.

Stefan Wilenek scared him, Adam could admit that to himself. A man trained to kill, a man with a lot of experience to back up that training. He had never killed a man. And he didn't want to start now — not when he was acting as a civilian. A civilian already wanted by the police for a different murder.

Seeing nothing in the shadows outside, Adam stepped quickly through the door. He paused with his back up against the house. The rich scent of the juniper again caught at his throat and he coughed.

"I could kill you right now." A voice floated out of the darkness, thick, Russian, menacing.

"I have no doubt," Adam responded in an even voice. "That's what you have been paid to do."

"But where's the fun in that?" The voice carried a smile in its tone.

Adam shivered involuntarily and stepped to his right, away from the door and deeper into the shadows cast by the large bushes that lined the walkway away from the house. The cloying scent grabbed at him again. He listened carefully, but the silence was broken only by the distant sound of a bus on the main street blocks away. So far away.

Adam heard a footfall. Soft, treading in the dirt that lined the path. Only a few feet away.

Adam moved again, crossing the path in front of him in a single stride then moving through a dormant flower bed to a grove of small trees that stood off to one side. Blending in, he hoped.

"What do you think is going to happen here tonight, *Pan* Kaminski?" the voice asked.

"I think we are both going to live through this," Adam answered. "I think you are going to walk away and I am going to expose Tomek Malak for what he has done. For what he is."

A sharp laugh like a brief explosion. "Why would I walk away, when I have you now?"

"Because the truth is out there. I found the documents that you failed to destroy in the archives. They prove Malak's guilt, his trail of lies. They are safe, and they will be published. No matter what happens to me."

"Ah yes, your cousin. The journalist. The one who refuses to die."

"It's too late, Wilenek. The truth is out. You can kill me... kill Łukasz... keep killing, but it won't matter. It won't be hidden any more."

"And what if I just want to kill you for the fun of it? And walk away."

Adam shrugged. "I guess that's your choice. It will be one more murder to hold against you when the police finally catch up with you."

"One more... I have killed so many, *Pan* Kaminski, one more will make no difference to me. No difference to the court of law."

"When Malak is arrested — and he will be arrested, I assure you — he will squeal. Just like he informed on his compatriots before the fall, he will inform on you. He will tell everything he knows just to save his own skin." Adam spoke quickly. "You know him. You know I'm right."

There was silence. Adam took this as a good sign.

"He will be arrested soon — tomorrow, probably. You need to get away, to save yourself. And you need to go, now. Every minute counts. The police will track you. They know your techniques, they know your style. They will find you. You can't afford to waste any more time here, serving a master who is already destroyed."

Silence. No response. Then Adam heard the light puff of air that he knew was the back door being gently opened and closed.

CHAPTER FIFTY-TWO

HE MOVED carefully. Slowly. Too carefully, it turned out. He was too late.

Malak lay back in the same gilded chair. He leaned awkwardly to one side, one arm dangling down to the ground, the other propped on the arm of the chair pointing toward the heavens.

His tumbler had come lose from his grip and rolled uselessly on the ground. The scotch seeped into the thick woven fibers of the carpet and the room reeked of it.

The knife was still there, protruding from his side, as if one of the dark branches from the garden had somehow materialized here, in this room of wealth and safety.

Adam paused at the doorway, seeking out the shadows in the corners of the room, listening for Wilenek's breathing. He saw nothing, he heard nothing. Malak blinked, and Adam moved.

He went first to the phone on a polished walnut desk beneath the window. After calling for help, he went back to Malak and knelt at his side.

Malak was moving his hands, without full control, trying to grab at the knife. "Wilenek," he mumbled, "Wilenek."

"Stop, leave it." Adam put his own hand gently on Malak's arm. "You should leave it in, until the medics arrive. They'll take care of you."

Malak shifted and grimaced with the pain, then turned

his blood-red eyes to Adam. "It is better this way, perhaps. I could not have lived with the truth. I could not have looked my people in the eyes knowing that they knew what I had done." He groaned slightly and licked his lips.

"People will know, Malak. The truth will still come out."

"Perhaps." Malak spoke softly. "Perhaps."

"Łukasz will publish what he found. He's seeking justice for his daughter — a daughter you had killed. He'll make sure everyone knows what you did. The people of Warsaw, the people of Poland. The people you work with — Sylvia..."

Adam stopped himself when he saw a light smile play on Malak's lips at Sylvia's name.

"Sylvia," Adam repeated, almost to himself. His chest constricted. "She knows?" He whispered the question.

Malak smiled. "My Sylvia. She trusts me. She has always trusted me." His eyes sprang open and he stared madly at Adam. "You must protect her. My Sylvia. You must take care of her. She is an innocent. She will only be hurt by this."

Adam's thoughts were flying wildly. He stood from where he had been kneeling by Malak's chair and paced around the room.

"How much does Sylvia know? Does she know you killed Basia?"

Malak groaned again, and once more reached for the knife. Adam grabbed his arm, more sharply this time. "Tell me what Sylvia knows."

"You must protect her," Malak said, "she knows nothing, you must protect her from this, from what will happen when the truth is told. No one will believe that she is innocent, no one will believe her."

Sirens cut through the night, growing louder as the ambulance approached the house.

"I can't protect her if I'm in jail." Adam spoke slowly, watching Malak.

Malak nodded his understanding. "It was Wilenek. Wilenek killed Basia. Wilenek killed small Jurij in the street, to try to frame you. And now Wilenek has killed me."

The ambulance pulled into the driveway. Adam heard running steps on the path, then hands on the door. He stepped quietly out of the room, heading for the backyard.

As he rounded the side of the house, he saw Malak carried out on a stretcher, two medics by his side, a uniformed police officer following closely behind, his notebook open.

"Stefan Wilenek," Malak was repeating, "you must find Wilenek."

CHAPTER FIFTY-THREE

THE SKY hovered low overhead, a dark gray pressing down on him as Adam moved through the city streets. He shivered beneath his coat and dug his bare hands deep into his pockets, but he kept moving.

Trams and buses had long since stopped running for the night and wouldn't start up again for a few more hours. He picked up his pace, knowing it would take over an hour to cover the distance back to Sylvia's apartment.

He stayed on the main streets and hugged the buildings as he walked. The rough gray concrete that covered most of the city reflected the Soviet-era regime's plan to create a city that would withstand the tests of time. They had thought only of wind and rain, snow and ice, not of the disdain of architects and artists.

Square block after square block of apartment buildings, stores, schools, barely distinguishable one from the other. Here and there, new construction stood out, colorful, round, angled, glimpses of joy and creativity against the dull background.

As Adam walked, he felt the hope of the city around him and he thought about his own hopes. He hoped that Sylvia was safe at home, away from the danger he had faced that night. Hoped she wasn't part of Malak's plot. Hoped she hadn't known of his attempts at Łukasz's life, his success at robbing Basia of hers.

The wind bit into his face and broke through the

defenses of his woolen coat. He turned his shoulder as a cold blast blew across a wide intersection, stinging his ears with its bitter chill.

As he got closer to the Old Town, the buildings gradually changed. More and more new construction stood along the street, blotting out the dull grayness of the older architecture. Buildings designed to look like historic structures, designed according to the tastes of Poles generations ago. Buildings reclaiming Warsaw's identity and style.

The sun had barely tinged the sky with streaks of orange and pink when Adam reached *Ulica Miodowa*, when he saw the giant metal men crawling out from their concrete bunker. Pausing, he searched for the police guard that had been present the past few days. He finally found the uniformed officer, sitting in a doorway a few doors down from Sylvia's, his head lolling against the stone wall. Asleep.

He ran the last few yards to Sylvia's door, then leaned on the bell. Glancing up, he saw that her apartment was dark, the curtains pulled tight.

He rang again. And again. And again.

Still there was no response.

He leaned on the bell for almost thirty seconds. He saw a curtain twitch in the apartment above Sylvia's, but he didn't care. He leaned on the bell again.

He was still pushing it when the front door flew open. Sylvia stood there wrapped in her pink robe. She started shivering as soon as she opened the door. Glancing quickly up and down the street, she grabbed Adam's arm and pulled him into the building.

Without saying a word, she turned and ran up the stairs to her apartment. Adam followed closely behind.

Inside, she threw herself onto the sofa and wrapped herself in a thick, sheepskin rug. When all Adam could see was the tip of her head, she spoke.

"Well? Where have you been? What have you found?" she asked quietly.

Adam looked at her — at what he could see of her. He trusted her, he told himself again. She had helped him. She had been the one who suggested going to Malak for help. She wouldn't have done that if she had known he was involved. Would she?

"Tell me about Malak, Sylvia. Tell me what you know."

She peered out at him over the blanket, her blue eyes questioning. "What do you mean? You know Tomek, you know about him."

"Do I? Do you? What do you really know about him, Sylvia? You must tell me, this is important."

He sat on a blue-striped chair near the head of the sofa and leaned toward her. "Do you know about his past?"

"Ah… You are interested in the past. Yes, you always have been, haven't you? Why is Tomek's past of concern to you, Adam?"

He paused before responding, considering the answer. Why was Malak's past important to him? The United States government seemed okay with it, willing to deal with him and his party, even knowing that Malak had been siphoning off profits that weren't his. Businesses were happy to work with him, knowing he would ask for a little bit extra when the deal was done, gifts for himself or his family. No one else seemed to care, so why did he?

He didn't, was the simple answer. He cared only for the present. For the people Malak was hurting now. Basia. Łukasz. And Sylvia.

"Tell me, Sylvia, how much do you know?" he asked again.

She nodded. "I know. I know that he has made some difficult choices. Choices that have helped him support his family even while he was helping Warsaw. Bringing good businesses into Warsaw. Perhaps leaving some of his history out of his lustration statement… it is not so unusual, we all have secrets. Like you" — she peered out at him — "like your great-grandfather."

"What are you talking about? What does my great-grandfather have to do with this?"

"Nothing, Adam, nothing." Sylvia's voice was soothing. "I simply point out that we must all make decisions. Using the resources we have available."

"Resources?" Adam's mind was swimming. Malak. Wilenek. Sylvia. And now his grandfather's father.

"Do you not see how difficult it would have been to leave Poland during the war? To leave safely? Difficult, that is, unless you had connections."

"What kind of connections? What are you suggesting?"

She shrugged, a gesture burdened with meaning. The blanket shifted up and down with the movement. "Connections with people in power. Connections with the occupying forces. Connections with people who could make things happen, who could get him and his family out."

Adam took one step back, shaking his head. "No, I don't believe that." He shook his head again. "No. And it doesn't matter, that's not why I'm here. This is about Malak. About what he's done. And how much you know."

Sylvia's lips turned up into a weak smile. "About Tomek? I know, yes. I don't care. It is done, you see. That is how business in Poland is done. The first time had been a mistake, he told me. He wished he could give it all back. But he couldn't. No one can, you know. You can't take back the past and do it again. He was sorry for what he had done. Once it had happened once, it was easier to do again. And again. These were small mistakes, a small price to pay for what he has to offer. His ideas. His strength. His dedication to this country. Yes, I know, but I am proud to work with him anyway."

She stopped and took a breath, as if the speech had worn her out. "Now that you know of Tomek's corruption," she asked, "what will you do? And remember, my career is linked to his. What you do to him, you do to me."

"There's nothing left for me to do, Sylvia. Malak has done it to himself."

She saw the sadness in his eyes and jumped from the sofa, still holding the blanket around her shoulders. "What's happened? Where's Tomek?"

"He's in the hospital, Sylvia. Wilenek turned on him, finally. One killer turning on another."

"What are you talking about?" She was almost crying. "What are you saying? Tomek was attacked? What did he have to do with any of this?"

"It was Malak all along, Sylvia. He was the one who killed Basia. He was the one who attacked Łukasz."

"That's not possible, I work with him. His crimes are only on paper. He is not violent, he would not attack anyone."

"Not personally, perhaps. But he was responsible. He was a desperate man, Sylvia. The truth was becoming too dangerous for him. He couldn't risk being exposed for what he really was."

"For his corruption? No, I don't believe that." Sylvia shook her head. "The people will understand. He will explain to them the way he explained to me, and they will understand."

"Maybe he could have, Sylvia. Not now, it's too late. It wasn't just corruption. It was his past, what he did. He hired a killer."

"What he did? What does that mean? No..." She shook her head and looked at him as if he were an alien just landed from Mars. "That wasn't Tomek."

"It was Malak. He's responsible for Basia's death. He was trying to hide the truth, and he went too far. His killer —Wilenek — turned on him in the end."

"Where's Tomek, Adam?" Sylvia whispered. "I must go to him."

"I told you, he's in a hospital. I don't know which one. They came and took him from his home."

Sylvia nodded and moved toward the bedroom. "I know where he is. I will go to him."

"Sylvia." Adam grabbed her arm as she passed and the blanket fell down around her feet. She hadn't asked him why — why he would be willing to kill, what secret he was trying to protect. "Sylvia, you really didn't know about this, his role in the killing?"

She looked up at him in wonder. "How can you ask me this? Do you really not know me?"

She leaned in toward him and kissed him gently on the cheek. "I have worked with Tomek for so long, he is like a brother to me. A brother I care about. I hear what you are saying, that he has done terrible things. But I must go to him. I must see him."

With that, she walked into her bedroom and shut the door. Adam let himself out of the apartment.

CHAPTER FIFTY-FOUR

WITH A SATISFIED grunt, his editor handed the article back to Łukasz. "Okay. Now it's okay."

Łukasz grabbed it and ran out of the office, not even waiting to thank him. It had taken him hours, precious hours, to get the man's approval, and he was ready to tear somebody's head off.

He had written the article quickly, drawing heavily from the records Adam had stolen from the national archives. Saved, not stolen, Łukasz reminded himself. Saved, not stolen. He filled in more blanks with the information unearthed in the hospital records and the newspaper archives, drawing connections between Malak's past as an informer and his present involvement with Wilenek, formerly of the secret police.

His editor was not so open-minded about it. "We cannot publish anything we cannot verify. Publicly. Period." He tossed the first draft back at Łukasz with a snort. "What is this? Gossip, stolen records? We would be sued, and we would lose. No, we can't publish this. Not about Tomek Malak."

His final words were the only part of that rebuff that rang true for Łukasz. He knew his editor had taken risks before, published news that had only been verified through anonymous sources, relied on "gossip" as he now called it.

Not when writing about Tomek Malak. And that was

the rub. The man was powerful. He was also well-liked. Any paper publishing such accusations about him would have to have solid, verified and verifiable sources. Łukasz had stolen medical records, borrowed archival records that he wasn't even supposed to have.

So he watered it down. He left in only the bare facts that were supported by the written records, nothing more, then went back to his editor.

And again it was rejected. "Find a source," his editor said. "Find someone who can back up what you're saying."

"The source is dead," Łukasz responded through gritted teeth. "The source was my daughter, and Malak had her killed because she found out the truth."

His editor looked up from his massive desk, a sheaf of papers in each hand. "I'm sorry, Łukasz. I really am." He put the papers down. "I know you want to expose this guy. I need a story I can stand behind. You know that. You would know that if you weren't letting your emotions get the better of you." He looked at Łukasz, tired, unshaven, still wearing bandages from his recent accident. "You shouldn't be the man writing this story, Łukasz. Give your notes to Michał. He's a good man, a good journalist. He'll write the story the way it should be written. He'll get justice."

"Not a chance," Łukasz growled as he left the office yet again.

His editor watched him storm down the hall back to his own office and shook his head.

Thirty minutes later, Łukasz was back. "This is it. You can publish this. These."

The editor held his hand out and Łukasz handed him one sheet. It listed the exact records that had been saved from the national archives, records that were almost destroyed. It quoted the records verbatim, listing dates and times that Tomek Malak was described as having met with Stefan Wilenek, a member of the secret police.

The story added no further details, simply laid out the facts that could be researched. And that could be plumbed at length by other papers, other journalists, other politicians.

The editor nodded and handed it back to Łukasz. "This will work. You took out all mention of the murders."

Łukasz said nothing, but handed over a second piece of paper.

The editor glanced at it. This one made no mention of Tomek Malak. It reported the findings from the stabbing on *Aleje Jerozolimskie*, findings that could be verified by medical records. It reproduced details from previous investigations, details easily available in the newspaper archives, details that drew links between the recent stabbing and past cases. Cases in which a former secret police agent, Stefan Wilenek, had been considered a suspect, but never convicted. It reported that the previous suspect, Adam Kaminski, was no longer considered a suspect by the police, who were now focusing their efforts on finding Wilenek.

It wasn't the exposé Łukasz wanted to write, but it might be enough, he hoped. At least it gave fodder to Malak's political opponents, enough that he would never succeed in a run for the presidency. Enough to raise questions about his past that could be difficult for him to answer. Enough to put pressure on the police to find Wilenek and determine if there really was a link between Malak and Wilenek. Enough. It would have to do.

The editor grunted and handed the sheets back to Łukasz. "Okay. Now it's okay."

Łukasz grabbed them and ran for the copy room. There was still time to make this morning's paper edition as well as get them online.

ADAM WATCHED the river flowing by as he walked slowly along the brick path that lined the water's edge.

The water moved quickly, a green-brown swirling mass that had been flowing here since before Warsaw was built. This river had seen wars won and lost, dreams built and savaged. It had seen love and it had seen death.

An American jogged past and waved at Adam, perhaps recognizing a fellow American. Adam waved in response, then tucked his hand back into his pocket.

He had been wandering for over an hour, running thoughts over and over again in his mind. Sylvia hadn't known, he reminded himself. She knew about Malak's corruption, but not about his past. She had forgiven him his mistakes, without realizing he was making them all over again, just in a different way.

And she cared about Malak. He couldn't hold that against her. She had listened to what Adam had told her, then had gone to see the man himself. Which is exactly what Adam needed to do. He needed Malak to clear his name, once and for all.

Turning to walk up a street that ran uphill back to the Old Town Square, Adam slipped on the damp pavement, just catching himself against a rough stone wall. He shivered at the thought of slipping into that cold, dark river. He thought of Basia and how her last moments must have been. Prayed to God she had never regained consciousness.

He passed a small store, recessed into one of the larger buildings and selling cigarettes, milk and chocolates. His eye fell on a newspaper piled against the door. The front page article had Łukasz's byline.

Adam stooped to grab a copy of the paper, staring at it until his head ached. Much of it he couldn't read, but he could understand the basics. The article had been written by Łukasz, and it was about Tomek Malak. That much was clear.

Adam tossed the paper back on the pile, ignoring the angry call from the shopkeeper, and switched directions. He turned toward *Ulica Wilcza*.

EVERYONE IN THE ROOM WAS GLARING except for Adam. And they were all glaring at him.

Adam smiled his most diplomatic smile and offered a small shrug. "It was just simple police work, that's all. You would have gotten there eventually yourselves." If you weren't blinded by your own prejudices and ambitions, he thought to himself, looking around the unfriendly faces.

Warsaw's Chief of Police, Janek Matuś, had come in from home and invited Officer Szczepański to join the hurriedly called meeting as a translator. Szczepański was not happy about this, not happy to have to admit that Adam had come to him first, seeking help, but that Szczepański had turned him away.

Szczepański translated Adam's comment, but Adam wondered what else he had added in of his own thoughts, as Matuś frowned and glared at Adam again.

Sam Newman was smiling, the only one of the group. "This is good news, gentlemen, as surprising as it is." He slapped the newspaper that lay on the table in front of them, causing Szczepański to start. "This reporter has done significant work, a good investigation. I don't think we can doubt that this man" — Sam leaned forward to read the name from the paper — "Wilenek... Wilenek is the man you are looking for. Not Mr. Kaminski."

Sam's words made it clear how pleased he was that an American had been cleared of any wrongdoing. But something in his eyes, behind the smile and the grateful words, conveyed to Adam his great displeasure that Adam had ignored his warning.

Whatever Malak's crimes, he had been helping the US government, Adam was sure. A man like that would have found a way to make it profitable. Looking for an easy payoff, he had probably been happy to sell information to anyone willing to pay for it. Some people never change.

Adam smiled happily back at Sam. "Thank you, Sam,"

he said out loud, "for your support."

"How can we pursue this Wilenek without also compromising the legacy of Tomek Malak?" Matuś' bushy eyebrows were knotted together over worried eyes. "He said he was innocent, his dying declaration. That is what the people will believe. They loved Malak and everything he stood for."

Malak had almost made it to the hospital, but not quite. He had died in the ambulance, declared dead on arrival by the doctors anxiously waiting for him. Before he had breathed his last, he had also made his last confession. And his last lie.

The police officer who had traveled with him, noting everything he had said, once more glanced through his notebook. "He was very clear, sir." Szczepański translated for Adam's benefit, still looking unhappy about his role, "Wilenek attacked Malak. Stabbed him. Malak didn't know why, he assumed Wilenek was crazy."

Matuś harrumphed. "Crazy, yes. But smart. He killed for money, we cannot doubt this. Which means someone paid him." He looked one more time at Adam. "And you are telling us that Malak was that man. That Malak paid Wilenek. To hide his past."

"His past is public information now, sir, you can read about it yourself in the files from the secret police," Adam pointed out. "I'm only saying what everyone will soon know."

"To kill a man — that is a big step, *Pan* Kaminski. If we start to investigate Malak's involvement, the people will rise up. They will not let us blacken his memory like that."

"Perhaps you will not need to dig too deeply," Sam suggested, looking at Adam. "Perhaps it will be enough to expose his past, his role as an informant. Let the people make their own decision."

Matuś stood and starting buttoning his coat. "We will find Wilenek. That, I promise you. We will find this killer, and we will deal with him as he deserves. And perhaps the truth will come out." He stopped and leaned over the table, looking Adam right in the eye.

"We will do what we have to do, sir, to bring this killer to justice. And the man who hired him. But make no mistake, this will not be easy. Malak did so much for Warsaw. For Poland. I am not happy about this, *Pan* Kaminski."

"When the truth comes out, sir, things will change. Łukasz has already published some of it, but more will come out. About the people he hurt, the people he turned on. Once that is out, the people will change their opinion. Public opinion is fickle, if nothing else."

Matuś glared at him one more time. Nodding to Sam Newman and Szczepański, he left the room.

CHAPTER FIFTY-FIVE

GOLDEN STONES, cold steel and warm red bricks caught the late afternoon light, a glowing panorama of historic buildings and modern structures arching into the distance. The view from the Łazienkowski Bridge was breathtaking. It was a place Adam wouldn't have come to without good reason and he was grateful for the opportunity to experience it.

This was a city of hope, a city looking toward the future. A city built by people bolstered by their past.

He expressed his appreciation for Warsaw's beauty to Łukasz, who nodded. "Basia felt the same way, you know?" He looked out over the city skyline from where they stood, halfway across the Wisła river. "She loved this country, but she also loved this city and everything it stands for."

Tears flowed freely down Łukasz's cheeks, and Adam turned away to give him some privacy. He looked down at the black waters swirling below them, tightening his grip on the railing as he did so.

Both men carried lilies, the flower of sadness, the flower of death. The scent Adam could never escape.

Adam waited quietly until his companion had composed himself. He spoke again. "Basia sounds like she was an exceptional young woman, Łukasz. I wish I could have met her."

"I, too, cousin." He smiled. "I think she would have

liked you. You have much in common. Your curiosity, your strength, your determination."

"She got those from you, I'm fairly certain." Adam put his arm around his cousin's shoulder. "And she lives on through you. Through your memory. And your actions."

Łukasz nodded again, then shut his eyes.

"To Basia," he said quietly, dropping the single flower toward the water.

Adam watched as it fluttered gently toward the tumultuous surface before he let go of his own. "To Basia."

The flowers landed on the water, twirled for a few moments, caught in the eddies that flowed along the surface of the water, then slowly sank, pulled down into the deeper currents.

"I have to leave tomorrow, cousin." Adam finally spoke. "I'm going home, back to Philadelphia."

Łukasz looked at him. "I am glad you were here, Adam. I thank you. And Basia thanks you, I know she does."

Adam smiled. "You'll be okay, cousin. I'm sure you will. You've made quite a name for yourself with this story — again. What will you do now?"

Łukasz shrugged. "Who knows? Keep writing, I assume. There are others, you know, like Malak. Others who have lied about their past, who have tried to profit off the suffering of others. I have been contacted by some publishers who would like me to write a book about Basia and her death."

"Would you do that? Would you want to revisit it?"

Łukasz looked out over the water, taking a deep breath of the crisp winter air, heavy with the sweet smell of the birch trees and winter grasses growing along the banks. He smiled. "You know, I think I would. I think I would relish the opportunity to help expose more men like Malak."

He turned to Adam. "And you, what does your future hold?"

Adam shrugged. "Back home. Back to work. And maybe..." Adam bit his lip. "Maybe I need to learn a little bit more about my own past. About my great-grandfather."

"Do not be upset over those letters, cousin. As *Pani* Stanko said, they are just one perspective. The perspective I have been told since I was young, that is true." He frowned and dipped his head. "But nothing about the past is certain. You have learned that while you were here, if nothing else."

Adam smiled. Patted Łukasz on the shoulder. "Thank you for that reminder, cousin. You're right, of course. I need to learn more before passing judgment. Before accepting anyone else's version of the past."

"Hmm..." Łukasz looked from Adam to the slowly darkening city, then back to Adam. "Then you have some more work ahead of you."

Adam looked down at the river, watching the water fighting against itself, currents circling currents, never ending. Never stopping. He looked back at Łukasz. "What we've done here, it will help me. It will make me stronger. Make me a better cop. I'm sure of that. I know I make some bad choices sometimes... but not this time." He looked at Łukasz. "I won't forget you, cousin. We'll stay in touch."

"Of course we will, of course. But now," he said, pulling his shoulders straighter, "now I am going to visit Basia. To tend to the flowers on her grave. Will you join me, cousin?" He turned to Adam.

"I'm afraid I can't, Łukasz. Please know I will be thinking about Basia. I won't forget her either. Will you forgive me for not joining you?"

Łukasz laughed. "Of course, cousin. I understand. I imagine you have plans tonight to see a different young woman?"

Adam smiled. "Good guess."

"And we shall see what your future really holds for

you." Łukasz smiled as the two men turned to walk back along the bridge toward the center of Warsaw.

BLUE VELVET curtains curled around a track on the ceiling, trailing down to the floor, closing off the front door from the rest of the restaurant and blocking out the cold night outside.

Inside, a bright fire danced in a brick alcove on the side. Well-worn wooden tables filled the space with quiet conversations and the scent of garlic and butter.

A candle flickered gently on the table between them as Adam and Sylvia leaned toward each other. They were tucked into a corner of the restaurant, each sitting with their back to a wall, their hands touching over the corner of the table between them. A carved wooden panel rose gracefully to Sylvia's left, cutting them off from the rest of the room, creating a private enclave for a quiet conversation.

Adam shifted to pick up his wine goblet, swirling the blood-red liquid and inhaling the bittersweet promises that rose as vapors from its surface. "I'm sorry that Malak hurt you, Sylvia, that he lied to you. I know how much you cared about him."

Sylvia nodded and raised her eyebrows as if to agree with Adam, but made no sound beyond a soft sigh.

The coming days and weeks, perhaps months and years, would be difficult for Sylvia. She had tied her future to Malak's, counting on him to lead the way. And now that career was lost to her.

She looked up at him over the tendrils of smoke rising from the candle. "I am sad for what Tomek did to me, but I am just as sad about what Poland has lost." She smiled and shrugged. "He was a great leader, Adam. I know you don't want to believe that, but he had good ideas. He had ways to make Warsaw richer, more successful, stronger. This would have been good for Warsaw and it would have been good for Poland.

Don't you see that?"

Adam shook his head. "All I see is that he was a thief, a liar and a killer, Sylvia."

She frowned and opened her mouth as if to speak, then closed her lips tightly. After a moment she asked, "Have you found your absolution, Adam? Does stopping Tomek help you fight your own demons?"

Adam didn't respond to her question. "How do you still see the good in him, Sylvia? I don't understand. He was a killer. An informant..." Adam's voice trailed off, his expression lost.

"Yes." Sylvia nodded. "I see that now, too. I didn't want to. I didn't want to believe it. Not about Tomek."

A waiter came to clear away their dinner plates, and they paused in their conversation. When they had both declined dessert or coffee, Sylvia turned back to Adam.

"It's not just the loss of this one man, though, you must understand." Sylvia spoke urgently. "It is the loss of trust. Who can we count on now, when even our great leaders cannot be trusted to have Poland's best interest at heart?"

"Malak was never a great leader, Sylvia." Adam took her hand again. "Just an actor. And he had us all fooled."

Sylvia frowned deeply, lines creasing her forehead and wrapping around her mouth. Adam knew she was fighting to keep the tears away and felt his heart breaking for her.

"He fooled me most of all." Her voice was harsh, accusatory. She closed her eyes while she spoke. "How could I not have seen this, Adam? How could I not have seen him for what he was?"

"You knew he was a criminal, Sylvia, you told me yourself."

She opened her eyes, the candlelight reflecting off the tears gathering in her perfect blue eyes. "Yes, a criminal, perhaps. But small crimes. Crimes that could hardly even count as corruption. And to what end? To bring lucrative business to Warsaw. To encourage new educational opportunities, new sources of renewable energy. These were not crimes. No, not what I knew." Sylvia shook her head.

"They were crimes, Sylvia. You thought you knew all his crimes, so when you saw him lie, or suspected he had a secret, you assumed you knew what that secret was. So you turned a blind eye to it. You assumed you knew him, but you didn't, did you?"

"I did not know him." Sylvia's voice was a whisper now. "You must believe me, Adam." She took his hand and squeezed it between both of hers. "You must believe me."

Adam looked at her and could see the worry in her eyes, her fears for the future and her need to have him believe her. "I do, Sylvia. I believe you."

She smiled then, and Adam's spirits lifted. It was as if their candle had grown brighter and the nearby fire merrier.

He put his other hand on top of hers, felt again the thrill of her touch. "I believe you."

THE PLANE'S engines roared, warming up as the crew prepared for takeoff. Adam leaned forward slightly in his seat, peering around the henna-red curls of the woman to his left. She turned to smile at him, but his attention was on the tarmac outside the plane. And the clouds looming above.

The cloud cover looked heavy but white, the fluffy appearance of snow-laden clouds that was becoming more familiar to Adam now. Weather forecasters had assured their audience that morning the snow would come later in the day. Adam felt a little nervous taking off into what could be a serious storm and tried to draw comfort from the fact they would be in the air, high above the clouds before the first snow came.

In eight hours, he would be back in Philly. Back at home.

Noticing the red-headed woman still smiling at him, Adam smiled and nodded. Then he turned to the aisle seat on his right.

Sylvia looked up at him, a smile in her pale blue eyes. "Don't be nervous," she said to Adam, seeing the worry in his expression. "We will be fine. We will make it to Philadelphia without problems."

He smiled back, drawing comfort from her confidence. What would his family say when he showed up back in Philly with Sylvia? His grandparents would be thrilled, he knew. They had told him enough times that he should find and marry a beautiful Polish girl.

And what would Pete think? Adam smiled to himself as he pictured Pete's expression.

He glanced back out the window. The sun was fully up now, though the colors of the morning light still lingered in the shimmering clouds. As he watched, the clouds seemed to float down toward them. He knew it was just the plane leaving Warsaw.

Author's Note

Thank you for reading *A Blind Eye*. I hope you enjoyed reading it as much as I enjoyed creating it. Of course, writing a book is never a solo effort. I am grateful for all the support I received from my early readers, mentors and friends who took the time to read, comment and critique. Lois Steinberg, Dave Pollan, Alan Ziskin and Doug Weiss for their work as writing group partners; Jack Engelhard for his patient instruction; Marci Spiegle, Ellen Herbert and Jacqueline Donaldson for their review and critiques. I also want to thank the Sisters in Crime and all the Guppies for sharing their wisdom, their experience and, when necessary, their commiserations. Most of all, I want to thank Chuck, for his unwavering belief in my writing.

Adam Kaminski lives on, in my mind and in the later books in this series. If you liked this book and want to read more, please visit my website to see the other books featuring Adam Kaminski as he steps up to the challenge of catching the killer, no matter where in the world he is.

www.janegorman.com

CPSIA information can be obtained at www.ICGtesting.com
Printed in the USA
LVOW07s1016041015

456838LV00006B/637/P